THE SOUND OF MURDER

I was feeling pretty good about my day, happy about the invitation order and my first actual sale, despite my general lack of customers. Then the telephone rang and I heard that desperate cry for help.

I stood staring at the telephone in my hand long after the woman on the other end had been cut off. I was pretty convinced that the call was no prank. Nobody could scream like that unless her life was in serious jeopardy.

Okay, I could stand there all evening in shock, or I could do something to help that poor woman on the other end of the line.

I dialed Bradford's private phone number, one of the perks of having the sheriff for a brother.

"Bradford, you've got to come to the shop."

"What's wrong?"

"I think I just heard someone get murdered."

Before I could explain what had happened, my brother hung up on me. Four minutes later I saw his patrol car rip up Oakmont, lights flashing and siren blaring. He slammed the cruiser into a parking spot in front of my shop, his gun drawn.

"Get back inside," he commanded in a gruff voice.

"The murder wasn't here, Bradford. It happened on the phone."

I explained about the telephone call and the bone-chilling scream I'd heard as the line had been cut off. . . .

INVITATION TO MURDER

A Card-Making Mystery

Elizabeth Bright

A SIGNET BOOK

SIGNET
Published by New American Library, a division of
Penguin Group (USA) Inc., 375 Hudson Street,
New York, New York 10014, USA
Penguin Group (Canada), 90 Eglinton Avenue East, Suite 700, Toronto,
Ontario M4P 2Y3, Canada (a division of Pearson Penguin Canada Inc.)
Penguin Books Ltd., 80 Strand, London WC2R 0RL, England
Penguin Ireland, 25 St. Stephen's Green, Dublin 2,
Ireland (a division of Penguin Books Ltd.)
Penguin Group (Australia), 250 Camberwell Road, Camberwell, Victoria 3124,
Australia (a division of Pearson Australia Group Pty. Ltd.)
Penguin Books India Pvt. Ltd., 11 Community Centre, Panchsheel Park,
New Delhi - 110 017, India
Penguin Group (NZ), cnr Airborne and Rosedale Roads, Albany,
Auckland 1310, New Zealand (a division of Pearson New Zealand Ltd.)
Penguin Books (South Africa) (Pty.) Ltd., 24 Sturdee Avenue,
Rosebank, Johannesburg 2196, South Africa

Penguin Books Ltd., Registered Offices:
80 Strand, London WC2R 0RL, England

First published by Signet, an imprint of New American Library,
a division of Penguin Group (USA) Inc.

First Printing, September 2005
10 9 8 7 6 5 4 3 2 1

To Serena Jones and Martha Bushko at NAL,
and to my agent, John Talbot:

Thank you all for believing.

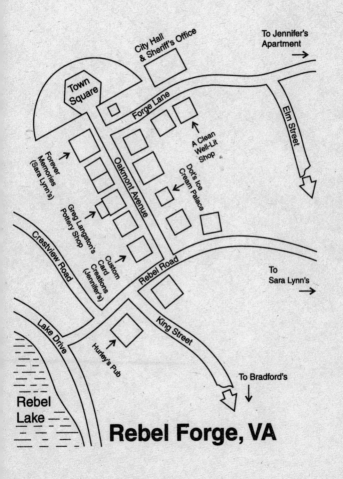

To Jennifer's Apartment →

City Hall & Sheriff's Office

Town Square

Forge Lane

Elm Street

Forever Memories (Sara Lynn's) →

A Clean Well-Lit Shop ↑

Oakmont Avenue

Dot's Ice Cream Palace ←

Greg Langston's Pottery Shop →

Custom Card Creations (Jennifer's) →

Crestview Road

Rebel Road

To Sara Lynn's →

Lake Drive

King Street

Hurley's Pub →

To Bradford's ↓

Rebel Lake

Rebel Forge, VA

Chapter 1

"You've got to tell her I won't stop it! She'll believe you. Please, you're the only one who can save me."

I frowned at the telephone, wondering if someone was having some fun at my expense. "Who is this?"

"Don't you know? Donna, you're my last chance. She's going to kill me if you don't tell her the truth."

"I'm sorry, but my name's not Donna. I'm Jennifer."

"Oh, no, she's here." There were a few choked sobs, and then she added in a whisper, "It's too late for me, isn't it?"

Just before the line went dead, I heard a scream that will haunt me till the day I die.

Earlier that Tuesday morning I'd been wondering if going into business for myself had been such a great idea after all. My name's Jennifer Shane, and I own and operate Custom Card Creations, my very own handcrafted-card shop. My specialized store was recently born from the need to get out on my own and away from my big sister Sara Lynn's scrapbooking store—aptly named Forever Memories—a place where I had worked after leaving my corporate sales job peddling pet food all over the Southeast. As much as I loved being around my sister, I knew I had to do something on my own when I'd tried to convince her that a handcrafted greeting card corner was a natural sideline for her business. Sara Lynn hadn't been interested. Not because it wasn't a good idea, mind you, but because her baby sister had come up with it and Sara Lynn hadn't thought of it herself first. So I took a deep breath, withdrew every dime of my savings and my inheritance from the bank and opened my shop on the opposite end of Oakmont Avenue. We were bookends on the town's main road where tourists browsed when they came to Rebel Forge, Virginia. Whether in the area for skiing in the winter or boating in the summer, there was a steady stream of shoppers most of the year. Scattered between our shops were old and charming buildings filled with crafters, antique dealers, an art gallery, a potter and a dozen other eclectic businesses that somehow felt just right to me.

The first real chance I had to make a sale for my shop was one I nearly turned down. I wasn't particularly interested in doing wedding invitations; that wasn't why I'd opened my handcrafted-card store, but the check Mrs. Albright waved under my nose convinced me otherwise.

She'd walked into my shop earlier that morning with her nose in the air and a look of complete and utter disdain plastered on her sharp ferret features. I couldn't see why her reaction had been so negative. The shop was in a quaint little tumbled-brick building with scarred hardwood floors and exposed oak beams in the ceiling. It had formerly housed a handbag boutique, but I hoped I had better luck than the last tenant. The poor woman had gone bankrupt, but before the bank could foreclose, she'd driven her car off the dam into Rebel Lake.

"I'd like to speak with the owner," my visitor said in a voice that dared me to comply. She had probably once been lovely, but the years hadn't been kind to her. Without even knowing her, I was certain that she was in a constant battle to lose that last thirty pounds—a battle I was pretty sure she was never going to win.

"You are," I said, offering my brightest smile. "How may I help you?" I gestured to the specialty areas I'd taken great pains to set up before I'd opened the shop for business. "I have handcrafted cards and stationery for sale up front, and if you're interested, I offer everything you need to make your own cards, as well. I have specialty scissors, rubber stamps, cutouts, stickers, stencils, pressed flowers and a dozen other different ways to enhance the cards you make. I offer a variety of paper and envelopes in several textures, thicknesses and colors, and if you want something totally unique, I can design and fabricate a custom batch of paper just for you. I've even got a computer, if you'd like to design something yourself that way. Oh, and I offer classes in card making in the evenings, but if you're already a card maker, we've got the Crafty Cut-Ups Club that meets here every Thursday night." Okay, the last bit was a stretch, but I honestly did plan to start the club just as soon as I found at least two people who liked making cards as much as I did. I'd memorized my sales pitch a few days before, and I promised myself to pause for a few more breaths the next time I had the chance to give it. I'd nearly passed out trying to get everything out in one breath.

The woman's disapproval was readily apparent. She studied me with her querulous gaze, and it was all I could do not to stoop down. I'm just a few inches short of six feet tall, and when my long brown hair's up in a knot like it was at the time, I knew I could be an imposing figure. Maybe if I was one of those rail-thin nymphs that weighed next to nothing I could still get away with my height, but I was solid—at least ten pounds overweight even for my frame—and that was saying a lot.

She sniffed the air, then said, "No, I'm afraid you won't be able to help me after all."

"Come on, it's way too soon for you to give up on me. If it involves cards, believe me, I can do it."

"I'm sorry, but I suppose I'll have to use a printing

business in a larger city. I had hoped to offer something at least a little above the ordinary to our guests and friends."

As she started for the door, I said, "Why don't you tell me what you want? Then I'll let you know if I can do it or not."

She paused, which was a good thing, because I was getting ready to tackle her before she could get out of my shop. I'd only been open two days, but in that time I'd had three people come in to ask me for directions to other businesses along Oakmont, and a spry little old man had wanted change for a single so he could buy a newspaper. I hadn't sold a card yet, not a single piece of card stock or stationery, or even a stamp for that matter, and my sister's prediction of doom kept echoing through my empty store.

"I need wedding invitations, but they have to be different: something bold, yet dignified; daring, yet classic."

I wanted a pony myself, or at least a way to make my first month's rent. "How many invitations are you going to need?"

"This is a very exclusive event," she said. "We're holding the guest list down to our four hundred closest friends." She looked around my small store, then said, "Perhaps I'd better see if someone in Charlottesville can help me. Thank you for your time."

As her hand touched the doorknob, I said, "Actually, that might be for the best. After all, I'm certain my designs would be too outré for you."

As I'd hoped, she looked intrigued for the first time since she'd walked into my shop. "What did you have in mind?"

"Let me get some samples for you." I raced to my workroom, a small space in back where I made the customized cards and papers I hoped to sell. I'd just finished a fresh batch of handmade paper, and I'd included some glitter and tinsel in the mix on a lark. I took a few sheets from the drying rack, grabbed a handful of my more experimental selections and hurried back before she could get away. If I'd been thinking straight, I would have dead bolted the front door to keep her there until I could make my pitch.

"Here are a few possibilities," I said as I laid the sheets out on the counter in front of her.

She studied the selection, paused over my latest effort and picked it up. "But it's still wet."

"Of course it is," I said as if it were the most common thing in the world to handle brand-new paper. "As I said, this is all cutting-edge. The textures are amazing, aren't they? I can create whatever paper we decide to use, based on your needs and tastes. There are lots of variations."

She looked around my shop again, then stared at me for a moment before speaking. "And you're certain you can handle this?"

"I can honestly say that I haven't had a single dissatisfied customer since I've been in business." Well, it was the truth. The man I'd made change for had been extremely grateful, and if there had been anything wrong with the directions I'd given, no one had come back to complain. That made it a perfect score, in my opinion.

"Then let's do this. I'll be in touch sometime in the next few days about the details." That's when she waved a check for the deposit under my nose. If I could pull it off, my business would be on its way. It surprised me that a woman who seemed to be such a control freak wouldn't want to settle the details on the spot, but Mrs. Albright seemed rushed, no doubt already late for her next appointment. After she was gone, I was still admiring the amount—afraid to put the check in my cash register lest it disappear—when my big brother, Bradford, walked in, decked out in his sheriff's uniform. He was two inches over six feet, and standing next to him, I somehow managed to feel svelte.

Before I could even say hello, he snapped, "When

are you going to get over your pigheaded stubbornness and start talking to Sara Lynn again?"

"Hello, brother dear, it's nice to see you, too. Did you come in to buy a card?"

He snorted. "Thanks, but I think I'll pass. Seriously, Jen, what's going on between the two of you?" Bradford was the middle child of our family, the consummate peacemaker when it came to his sisters' squabbles. I liked to think that all those years of maintaining harmony in our house had carried over into his career choice. Bradford was the sheriff for our resort community, keeping the peace now on an entirely different level. I just hoped he had more luck with the residents of Rebel Forge than he had with me and Sara Lynn.

"Talk to her if you don't like what's going on between us," I said. "I offered her a truce, and she blew me off."

"You did kind of step on her turf," Bradford said.

"You've got to be kidding me. Listen, if you're not going to buy anything, why don't you just go?" Then I realized that I was letting him off way too easy, especially since he'd just taken Sara Lynn's side instead of mine. "Hey Bradford, since you're here, you should buy something nice for your wife."

"If I walk in my door at home with a card for Cindy, she's going to think I'm up to something."

"If you don't, she's going to be even more suspicious, especially after I call and tell her you were in here shopping today and bought something romantic from my store." I scanned the room. "Let's see, what did you buy again? Oh, yes, that stationery and envelope set. You have excellent taste, Bradford. It's the very best I carry."

He knew when he was beaten—I had to give him that. "Give me a break, Jennifer. I've got two kids who will eat anything that's not nailed down. I'm having a tough time making it on a cop's salary, even with Cindy's income from the library."

I relented, as I almost always did when my big brother pleaded his case. "Okay, how about one of these, then? I just made them." I handed him one of my newest creations, a soft-violet-shaded card that sported pressed wildflowers embossed in the paper and the envelope. On the front of the card, it said in my best calligraphy, "Just Because . . . ," and inside, simply, "I Care."

"How much is this going to set me back?"

"You know," I said, snatching the card from his hand, "suddenly I'm not sure it's going to be enough. You didn't say a word about how pretty my new design is."

"It's gorgeous, an absolute work of art. Whatever it costs, I'm sure it's worth a lot more than you're charging me." He gave me his brightest grin, the same one I'm sure had won Cindy's heart. My brother, despite his Neanderthal leanings, could be quite charming when he put his mind to it.

"Okay, don't show too much enthusiasm. It's out of character." I rang the sale up, slid his card and envelope into a bag, then gave Bradford his change.

As he took the money, he said, "Now are you going to talk to Sara Lynn?"

"Hey, she knows where I am. It's completely up to her."

He shook his head. "You two are more alike than either one of you will ever admit."

I smiled at him. "That was smart of you."

"What, my powers of observation?"

"No, saving that crack until after I rang up your sale."

He tapped his temple. "Hey, nine years of police work pays off from time to time. Be good, Jen."

"You, too. Watch your back."

"Always."

After Bradford was gone, I realized I hadn't told him about the Albright wedding. But then again, he'd probably known about it before the bride. Our dear sheriff prided himself on being up-to-the-minute on the happenings and events in our town before they occurred.

I was feeling pretty good about my day, happy about the invitation order and my first actual sale, despite my general lack of customers. Then the telephone rang and I heard that desperate cry for help.

I stood there staring at the telephone in my hand long after the woman on the other end had been cut off. I was pretty convinced that the call was no prank. Nobody could scream like that unless her life was in serious jeopardy.

Okay, I could stand there all evening in shock, or I could do something to help that poor woman on the other end of the line.

I dialed Bradford's private cell phone number, one of the perks of having the sheriff for a brother.

"Bradford, you've got to come to the shop."

"Jen, I can't. I'm going to be late as it is. Besides, I'm not buying anything else, no matter how nice your cards and stuff are."

"This isn't some errant whim, you nitwit," I said, much shriller than I'd meant to. At least it got his attention.

"What's wrong?"

"I think I just heard someone get murdered."

"Are you in trouble? Jen, bolt your doors and hide in back. I'll be right there."

Before I could explain what had happened, my brother hung up on me. These abrupt disconnections were getting to be too much.

Four minutes later I saw his patrol car rip up Oakmont, lights flashing and siren blaring. He slammed the cruiser into a parking spot in front of my shop, his gun drawn and a look of intensity on his face that I hadn't seen since we were kids.

When I opened the door, I swear, he almost shot me.

"Get back inside," he commanded in a gruff voice.

"The murder wasn't here, Bradford. It happened over the telephone."

He stared at me a second, then frowned as he holstered his gun. "If this is some kind of gag, I'm going to lock you up."

"If you had given me the chance to explain before you came rushing over here, you wouldn't have made such a fool of yourself." Sure, it was a little harsh, but I couldn't help it. Hearing someone murdered kind of put a damper on my social skills.

"Okay, let's just both settle down," he said as he reached into his patrol car and shut his lights off. At least the siren had died when he'd stopped the cruiser, though we were getting enough attention along Oakmont as it was, thank you very much. An older couple had been walking toward my store's front door, but the second they spotted Bradford's car, they quickly veered off and went into Greg Langston's pottery shop. Greg and I had a history together longer than the Holy Roman Empire's, but I didn't care one whit about it at the moment. I had to get my brother off the street, and fast.

"Would you at least come inside so the tourists won't think I'm about to be arrested?"

"Sure, I can do that."

Once we were in the store, he asked, "So what's this all about?"

I explained to him about the telephone call, the errant search for a Donna who wasn't there, and the bone-chilling scream I'd heard as the line had been cut off.

He took it all in, then asked, "And you're sure it wasn't some kind of gag? No, forget I said that. I believe you think it was real, Jen. I'm just not sure what I can do about it."

"Somebody's in trouble, Bradford. You've got to help them. That's what you do."

He held out his hands. "I'd love to, Sis, but how?

That call could have come from anywhere in the country, or the world, for that matter, even if it was on the level. It's not much to go on."

"That woman had a Southern accent, and unless I'm way off, she grew up somewhere around here." A lot of folks think one accent from the South is pretty much like another, but I'd spent part of my life traveling in my region, and I'd gotten pretty good at telling Tennessee from North Carolina from Mississippi. I'd worked in corporate sales for several years for a pet food manufacturer, and while there were parts of the job I loved, the absolute worst was constantly being on the road away from home. It had seemed like a good idea to take the job right after college, especially since it was the only offer I'd received. I found it ironic that I couldn't have cats of my own until I quit my job selling pet food.

Bradford said, "I'm sorry, Jennifer, but it's too much to ask for what was most likely a prank."

"So you're not even going to try?" A part of me knew I was being unreasonable, but I couldn't help myself. Bradford was my big brother. It was his job to take care of things like this.

"Here's what I can do. I'll go back to the office and let Jody and Jim and Wayne know what's going on. They can keep their eyes open tonight, and if anything remotely comes in about this, I'll let you know. I'm sorry, Jennifer, but it's the best I can do."

I reached up and patted my brother's cheek. "I guess I'm the one who should be apologizing. I know I'm acting kind of flaky, but it really shook me up."

"I understand completely," he said.

"There's really nothing we can do, is there? I just feel so helpless."

"That's the story of my life, kiddo. I help when I can, and hope it's enough to make a difference."

After he was gone, I toyed with the idea of keeping the shop open past my posted business hours, but I'd learned from Sara Lynn that it would be a mistake. I was going to be at the Three Cs enough as it was without adding more time to my work schedule. I decided to straighten up and then leave for home. When the telephone rang again, I nearly dropped an expensive pair of specialty scissors I'd just gotten in. My hand hesitated before I picked it up, but I couldn't allow myself to cringe every time the telephone rang. Taking a deep breath, I answered, hoping it was someone ready to place a huge order for specialty card stock.

"Custom Card Creations, this is Jennifer speaking. How may I help you?"

The caller hung up before I could get the word "you" out of my mouth. I swear, people have gotten so rude lately. No one ever says "excuse me" after a wrong number anymore, clerks and cashiers say "no problem" instead of "thank you," and driving is getting riskier every day. I realized I was tired, and when I'm tired, I'm cranky. Throw in the fact that I was hungry, too, and I decided the only place I needed to be was home in my apartment. I had my key in the dead bolt outside when a familiar husky voice spoke my name behind me.

I'd been hoping to avoid dealing with Greg Langston, but that was one wish that wasn't going to come true.

Chapter 2

"What just happened, Jennifer?"

I ignored him while I finished securing my door, locking both dead bolts Bradford had insisted I install before I opened for business. I thought they made the place look like a prison, but I knew he was right. My brother saw a lot of break-ins in his job, and I couldn't afford to lose any of my stock, not if I was going to make my monthly payments on time.

"Bradford was just testing the equipment on his patrol car," I said as I tried to hurry past my ex-fiancé.

He wasn't buying it, though. "Was he testing his pistol out, too? I saw Bradford with his gun in his hand."

"Greg, I really don't want to go into this with you right now. I've had a long day."

He looked sheepish. "Yeah, I'm sorry I didn't come over to wish you well. Did you get the flowers I sent you?"

I had indeed, a lovely bouquet of yellow roses, which he knew were my favorite. "Thanks, but you really shouldn't be sending me flowers. I've been engaged to you twice. It's not going to happen again, I can promise you that."

Greg touched my arm lightly, and I felt a brush of static electricity from it. At least I hoped that was all it was. "Don't write me off yet," he said.

I rolled my eyes. "Oh, please, save it for someone who hasn't heard it before." I had a weakness for Greg like some women had for chocolate and others had for Ben & Jerry's, but it hadn't worked out the first two times we'd tried, and I would be dipped in honey and fire ants if I was going to give him a third chance at my heart. Maybe it was because all of my sense of reason seemed to vanish when it came to Greg Langston. A part of me was afraid that if I didn't hold him at arm's length, it would be too hard to say no to him again. The first time we'd been engaged I was fresh out of college, scared and on my own. Greg had offered me security and stability; at least I'd thought so at the time. The second time I'd said yes to his proposal had been right after my parents had died. By the time I'd come to grips with losing them in a car accident, I ended it again. I didn't need anybody to take care of me, and that seemed to be what Greg wanted most in the world. No, it would be better for both of us if I continued to keep some distance between us, if not physically, then certainly emotionally.

Now if I could only get Greg to agree to it. "At least let me buy you dinner. You have to eat, don't you?"

He really did mean well. I could see it in his eyes. "Greg, I'm fine, honest. It was all a misunderstanding. Listen, I do appreciate the flowers and the invitation, but I just want to go home, feed Oggie and Nash, then crawl into bed." My cats—a couple of strays I'd rescued from the animal shelter—were named in honor of my favorite poet. There was something about the way Ogden Nash wrote that appealed to my skewed sense of humor, so I'd named my two roommates for him, not that they cared what I called them. Neither cat would come if I spoke his name; the only thing that usually attracted their attention was the sound of an electric can opener.

"How are the two marauders doing?"

"They're both fine. I'll tell them you asked about them."

He grinned. "You do that." Greg's smile faded as he added, "Listen, you know I'm just a phone call away if you need me, right? No matter what's happened between us in the past, I still care about you, Jennifer."

This was getting way too serious for my tastes, especially out in the middle of Oakmont Avenue where all the world could see us. "Thanks, but I'm fine."

I got into my ancient Gremlin and headed home. After the day I'd had, it would be good to take a long, hot bath, eat some comfort food and hang out with my cats.

Unfortunately, life didn't always work out the way I planned it.

Sara Lynn—my big sister with an even bigger chip on her shoulder—was waiting by my apartment's front door when I got home.

Before she could say a thing, I decided to fire a preemptive strike. "Sis, I've had a really long day, and I'm not in the mood to deal with this feud right now."

My sister stood and, without a word, wrapped her arms around me. Suddenly the arguments, the conflict, the anger—all of it faded away as she held me close and stroked my hair. "Jen, I'm so sorry. Forgive me."

And then I remembered why I loved her so much.

In ten minutes, we were having coffee and watching Oggie and Nash eat their dinner. "Bradford called me, you know," Sara Lynn said.

"Of course he did. Can you imagine our dear sweet brother going a single minute without trying to fix something wrong between us?"

Sara Lynn laughed. "Well, that's what he's good at, isn't it?" While Bradford and I were both tall and dark like our mother, Sara Lynn resembled our father, right down to the wiry platinum blonde hair and petite stature. It had been hard for her to watch her little brother and sister shoot up past her, but Sara Lynn had made up for her height with an iron backbone and a will that was nearly impossible to bend. "Tell me about the phone call," she said.

I put my cup down. "Of course the sheriff felt the need to tell you about that, too."

"He cares about you, and he's worried. So am I. Listen, why don't you and your two comrades over there come stay at my place for a few days?"

"Yeah, I'm sure Bailey would just love that. He's still allergic to cats, isn't he?"

"My husband can take a pill if it bothers him." Bailey was known throughout the family for his myriad litany of mysterious pains and ailments, and we often wondered how Sara Lynn put up with him. She continued. "You're always welcome in our home. You know that."

"Thanks, but I'm happy right where I am." The only place I needed to be was exactly where I was: in my apartment. So what if the bathroom door stuck sometimes? It didn't even matter that there was a water spot growing on the ceiling that I hadn't been able to get the super to fix or that the kitchen floor sloped down in one corner. Regardless of its flaws, or maybe even because of them, it was home.

Sara Lynn frowned, then asked, "What if the person on the other end of the telephone tracks you down?"

"It's not going to happen," I said. "You know, the more I think about it, the more I'm starting to believe it was just a prank after all. Now can we please talk about something else?" I didn't believe it for one second, but I was willing to say just about anything to get my brother and sister off my back.

Sara Lynn took a sip of coffee, then said, "If that's what you want, we'll talk about something else. So how's business?"

I took a deep breath, then said, "Is there any chance we can go back to the telephone call?"

"Jennifer, you were still in college when I opened Forever Memories. The first three weeks I had a total of seven customers."

"At this point I'd gladly take that."

Sara Lynn patted my hand. "You'll do fine. Why don't I refer some of my regulars your way?"

"I can do this on my own. I don't need anybody's help. Are we clear on that?"

"That's my little sister, ready to tackle the world bare-handed."

I stifled a yawn, then said, "What I'm ready for right now is a bite to eat and my bed. Listen, I'm glad everything's good between us again, but truly and honestly, I'm beat."

She glanced at her watch. "And I'm late for dinner. Bailey's making his famous three-alarm chili tonight. I'm beginning to regret letting him take over my kitchen two nights a week. I'd rather cook myself than eat chili and eggs all the time on his dinner nights."

"So teach him to cook something else," I said as I followed her to the door.

"I'd have better luck teaching your cats to sing."

For some odd reason, Oggie decided to yowl at that exact moment. Sara Lynn said, "Sometimes those cats of yours are spooky."

"Didn't you know? All felines have ESP."

She rolled her eyes, but didn't comment. She knew better than to say anything about either one of my roommates. "I'd like to come by your shop tomorrow, if you don't mind."

"That depends on why you're interested. Do you want to check up on me, or are you sizing me up as your competition?"

"What if it's a little bit of both?"

I laughed. "Then I'd have to say you're welcome to visit. Make it early, though, could you? I'd hate to see you get trampled in the rush of customers."

"I'll be there bright and early," Sara Lynn said, and then she was gone.

Normally I would have called my best friend, Gail Lowry, before I ate, especially with what had happened earlier. But she was out of town for two weeks at a sales conference on the West Coast. Gail had been gone just two days, but I missed her already. We were two single ladies barely into our thirties, and while most of the other women we knew our age were either married or working on it, neither one of us was in any hurry to walk down the aisle.

I found myself humming softly to myself as I heated up some leftover lasagna from the night before. Even with everything that had happened, I still felt better than I had in weeks. Fighting with my sister had taken more out of me than I'd realized. I caught myself singing out loud when I noticed that Oggie and Nash were both staring at me like I'd grown a second head. "Come on, I put up with a lot of odd behavior from you two," I said. "You can just deal with it."

They were unimpressed with my argument and went back to their normal interests. Nash was playing with his catnip mouse, barely recognizable from wear and tear, while Oggie was staring out the window in earnest. I didn't realize why until a few minutes later when it started to rain. Blast it all, it was almost as if that crazy cat knew the storm was coming and was waiting for the first drops. I stuck my tongue out at him and went to bed. I had enough on my mind without worrying about a psychic cat.

The telephone rang at 2:47 A.M. "Hello? Hello."

"I'm drunk, Annie," the woman's voice said in a near whisper.

"I'm not Annie."

There was a pause, then she said, "Would you come get me anyway?"

"I think you need to call a taxi."

"Cabs cost money. Come on, be a sport."

"Good luck, and good night." I turned the ringer off before I cradled the telephone back in its base.

With the kind of calls I'd gotten in the past twelve hours, I was ready to throw every telephone I owned out into the street and go without.

Bradford was standing by my apartment door when I walked out to get my newspaper the next morning. It had taken half a dozen telephone calls and a monthly chocolate-chip-cookie bribe to convince the paperboy to deliver my edition upstairs on the second-floor landing outside my door every morning, but it was worth it not to have to trudge any farther than I had to before I was fully awake.

"Have you been out here all night?" I asked him.

"Relax. I just got here. So how did you sleep?"

"Fine." Then I remembered the drunken caller, and felt guilty about hanging up on her. "Were there any car accidents last night, by any chance?"

"Why, were you out joyriding in that rust bucket of yours?"

"Come on, Bradford, I need to know."

He scratched his chin a minute, then said, "No, it was a quiet night. As far as I've heard, there were no accidents, no break-ins, nothing out of the ordinary. Do you think your telephone call had anything to do with a car wreck?"

"What? How did you know about that? What did you do, tap my phone line?"

"Take it easy, Jen. You told me about the call yourself yesterday afternoon, remember?"

"Oh, you're talking about the call at the store."

He looked taken aback. "You mean there have been others?"

I told him about the drunk woman calling me in the middle of the night. He said, "It was probably just someone from one of the taverns."

"So why are you here?"

"I wanted to let you know that we haven't found anything that might relate to the call you got at the card shop. I don't know. I kind of thought it might ease your mind."

I kissed his cheek. "It helps, it really does. Thanks for coming by."

"You're most welcome."

"Listen, would you like to join me for breakfast? I'm just getting ready to eat." I'd been planning to have a yogurt for breakfast, but if my brother could come over and check on me, I could make him some eggs. I knew his wife had him on a strict new diet, but I figured a little real food wouldn't hurt him.

"That sounds great," he said as the radio on his belt suddenly squawked.

"Sheriff, are you there?"

He unclipped it. "Right here, Jody. What's up?"

His deputy said, "I need you at 136 Elm right away."

"What's going on?"

"We found a body, Bradford. She looks like she's barely out of her teens. It's pretty bad."

My brother said, "Don't touch anything. I'll be right there."

As he hurried to his squad car, he said, "Sorry, Sis, I've got to go."

I nodded and watched him drive away. There was a knotted fist in my gut as I found myself wondering if it was the woman I'd heard scream the day before.

Sara Lynn was waiting for me out front when I got to my card shop. "Wow, when you say early, you mean early," I said as I unlocked the door and let her in. The mail had already come—pushed through the slot in the door and scattered on the floor—and I gathered it up and laid it on the counter as I flipped on the lights.

"I didn't want to interrupt you during regular business hours," she said as she looked around. Most likely Sara Lynn didn't want to be away from her business if it was open. I'd been dreading the day my sister finally stepped into my shop; I knew that under her scrutiny all of its flaws would be exposed. I watched her walk around, studying everything, not giving away the slightest emotion as she did so.

"I love it," she finally said, and I felt the relief rush through me. "It's really quaint. Jennifer, you've done a wonderful job."

"Let's hope my customers think so," I said.

"They'll come; don't you worry about that. Have you planned any grand-opening sales events or advertising? I can help there, you know."

"I thought I'd take a few days to work out the bugs before I made any formal announcement to the world."

"Don't wait too long. Now is the time to strike, while your store is brand-new. I've got some wonderful ideas on how to promote your shop."

I could see the wheels turning in her head. I wasn't about to let my sister take over my card shop, as much as I loved her. "Don't, Sara Lynn."

"What? I can't help my baby sister?"

"I can handle it myself." I glanced at the clock. "Shouldn't you be getting ready to open your own shop?"

"Goodness, look at the time." As she started for the door, she turned back to me and said, "This discussion isn't over, young lady. I can be a valuable resource for you, and I'm not going to let you squander it."

"Bye," I said, not trusting myself to say anything else. There were some great things about being the baby of the family, but sometimes they were all outweighed by my siblings' desire to run my life for me. I was going to have to stand firm and keep saying no until it got through to Bradford and Sara Lynn that I was going to do this on my own, whether it meant roaring success or dismal failure.

After Sara Lynn was gone, I was officially open for

business, but customers hadn't been waiting in line to get inside. The stack of mail was still sitting on the counter, but I couldn't imagine that there was anything but bills and unwanted solicitations in the pile. If the past few days had been any indication, I wouldn't have much to do all day, so I decided to save the mail for later. I couldn't start working on the Albright wedding invitations until I spoke with the mother of the bride again. She'd made a deposit, but I still had no idea what she wanted. That didn't mean I couldn't make a few cards of my own. I browsed through the shop with a basket, pretending for a moment that I was a customer instead of the proprietor. I decided to make a card without any intention of selling it, just for the joy of the creation. I chose a burgundy paper I'd made myself, and grabbed another sheet of shimmering silver I'd bought, a gel pen, some scissors, a couple of punches and a nice selection of star stickers. I lingered over the selection of pressed flowers and thought about adding a violet. I was really interested in botanicals at the moment, even pressing my own flowers when I had the chance, but I decided this card would be flowerless.

I'd positioned a small table near the front window where I'd laid out a selection of cards as a display. Since it didn't seem to be drawing anybody in, I gathered everything together and put it all on the checkout counter. What a perfect work space the table made! I could look out along Oakmont once I moved my chair there, and I found that the height was just right for working. I folded the two sheets in half after marking them, then trimmed both pieces with stirrup pattern scissors, making the burgundy sheet an inch smaller all around than the silver. Using one of the punchouts, I made a few balloon-shaped holes in the burgundy paper; then the paper was ready to glue to the backing. Silver balloons seemed to float in the burgundy field. How lovely! I still wasn't sure what the theme of the card was going to be—something I usually made certain I knew before I even chose my paper—but I could always come up with something. I was still considering the possibilities when the front door of my shop opened.

"May I help you?" I asked.

An elegantly dressed young woman in her thirties came inside. She studied my card and then said with a Boston accent, "That looks lovely. I was walking by your shop and saw you working through the window. Tell me, is it difficult to do?"

"It's the easiest thing in the world," I assured her. "Here, sit down and I'll show you."

"I'm sure I couldn't," she said, but from the way she was looking at my card in progress, I knew she wanted to.

"You're in luck; I'm giving free lessons today. Now, what kind of card would you like to make?"

"Well, my mother's birthday is coming up soon, and I'd hoped to find something special for her."

"You came to the right place." I offered my hand. "I'm Jennifer."

"I'm Leslie," she said.

"It's nice to meet you, Leslie. Tell me a little about your mother so we can make this the best card she's ever gotten in her life."

We spent a pleasant half hour making her card, and by the time Leslie was finished, she'd told me more about herself than she had probably ever mentioned to her hairdresser or her priest. Crafts were funny that way. People really opened up when they were happy and busy doing something productive. Leslie left the shop with a great deal more than her mother's complimentary birthday card. She'd chosen a wonderful selection of products and supplies from the shop, and I decided after she was gone to make up a few more kits just like it.

When I'd opened the Three Cs, I'd had folks exactly like Leslie in mind. Sharing my love of cards was what it was all about for me. I was still feeling the joy from her visit when I decided it was time to tackle the mail.

One letter stood out from the rest. There was no stamp, no postmark, not even an address on it. "JENNIFER" was the only thing printed on the front in large block letters.

Inside, it said, "Forget what you heard or you'll be next."

Chapter 3

At first I thought it had to be a mistake. There was only one thing I'd heard in the last twenty-four hours that the note could possibly apply to, but what was I supposed to forget about that haunting phone call I'd received? I replayed the young woman's words in my mind before her scream. I didn't have any trouble coming up with the exchange; I doubted I'd ever forget it. She had said I had to tell the other woman the truth, that she would believe me. When the young woman realized I wasn't Donna, there had been an air of resignation in her voice just before her final scream. I couldn't think of anything I'd heard that would be a threat to anybody. But then I remembered that the killer had walked in during the middle of our conversation. She wouldn't know what I'd been told, would she? The killer, whoever she was, probably thought I knew more than I did. And then I thought of something that chilled my heart. The note had been dropped off at my card shop. That meant that the killer knew who I was! She must have hit the redial button after the earlier call. That's when I remembered the hang-up right after I'd identified myself and my shop's name. At the time I'd written it off as another rude sign of the times, but now I was firmly convinced that a murderer had been on the other end of the line, and worse, she was looking for me. I started to punch Bradford's cell number on my phone

when I saw his squad car pull up in front of the store.
For once I was glad to have him checking up on me.

The second he walked in the door and spotted me,
he said, "Jennifer, what's wrong?"

I handed him the note. "This came with my mail
this morning."

Instead of taking the letter from me, he said, "Just
put it down on the counter."

I did as I was told, and he put on a pair of rubber
gloves he had stashed in his pocket. "Where's the
envelope?"

I gestured to it on the floor where I'd dropped it after
reading what was inside. "It didn't go through the mail.
Somebody put it in my slot. Bradford, my fingerprints
are all over that letter and the envelope, too. I probably
ruined whatever evidence there was on them."

As he carefully collected both pieces of paper, he
said, "I'll make a deal with you. You don't tell me
how to run the sheriff's office and I won't teach you
how to make cards."

"This is tied in with that telephone call—it has to
be. What did you find out about that girl? Is she mixed
up in this?"

"I'm not ready to say anything about that just yet."

"At least tell me who she was."

He shook his head. "I can't do that, Jen. I'm sorry."

I frowned. "Why not? Is it part of your precious
police procedure? Are you going by the book when
you should be easing my mind about all of this?"

"Jennifer, the reason I won't tell you who she was
is because we haven't been able to notify her parents
yet. Is that all right with you?"

"I'm so sorry," I said. "Of course you're right. But
Bradford, I'm not exactly an uninterested party here.
That note proves it."

"Believe me, I'm not happy about it, either. Why
don't you move into our guest bedroom for the next
few days? Cindy would love to have you, and the kids
would be bouncing off the walls with joy."

"Thanks, but I can't. Sara Lynn made the same offer, cats included, but I'm not going to run and hide. Besides, if this mad-dog woman wants me, she can always find me here at my shop."

"Jennifer, I can't afford round-the-clock protection for you if you don't cooperate. This is serious."

"Do you think I don't know that? I'll be careful, Bradford, but I'm not crawling into a hole. Don't worry. I'll take precautions."

He rolled his eyes. "What are you going to do, bring your two furry bodyguards with you to work?"

"With all this paper just waiting to be shredded? You're out of your mind. I've got your old baseball bat by my bed. I can bring it to work with me, then take it home at night." I bit my lip, then said, "I can't stop thinking about that poor girl. Was it bad?"

"It was pretty tough to see."

I felt a shiver run through me. "I'll be careful. I promise." I knew my brother was always overprotective of me, but at that moment, I was kind of glad to have him looking out for me. It wasn't that I couldn't take care of myself—I could—but sometimes having him watch my back was good, too.

He sighed, then said, "I'm sorry, but carrying a baseball bat's not good enough. I'm going to keep an eye on you for the next few days whether you like it or not."

"Bradford, be reasonable," I said as I gestured outside. "Nobody's going to come into a card shop with the sheriff on duty at the counter and his patrol car parked out front. You'll destroy my business before it even has a chance to get started."

"And which do you prefer, being ruined or being dead?"

"I'd like to avoid both of them if I can."

He thought about it for a few seconds, then said, "How about if I stay in the back? Would that suit you?"

"And what is Rebel Forge supposed to do while its sheriff is babysitting his little sister?"

"Jennifer, I'm not leaving you here alone."

I thought about it, then came up with the answer. "I've got it. I'll call Aunt Lillian. She's been complaining that she's bored with her life right now. She can help out here at the card shop and keep an eye on me at the same time."

Bradford said, "You're kidding, right? Do you honestly think you're going to be safe because you'll be under the protection of our crazy old aunt? Sis, you've lost your mind."

"Hey, Lillian has had seven ex-husbands; she knows how to handle herself. One of them was a karate instructor, remember? We'll be fine."

"Please tell me you don't honestly believe that. She'll be so busy looking for husband number eight, she won't have time to watch out for you. Karate or not, I still don't like it."

"Well, it's the most I'm willing to do." I grabbed the telephone, and Bradford said, "You mean to tell me you're calling her now?"

"There's no time like the present." I dialed our aunt's phone number as my brother shook his head in utter disbelief. He always underestimated Lillian, something a lot of folks did. She was the original source of Sara Lynn's strong will, and I would rather have my aunt watching out for me than the entire Rebel Forge police department.

After I got her on the phone, I said, "Lillian, are you still bored with your life?"

"To tears, my dear," she said. "Save me from this desolate existence."

"Come work for me at my card shop. I can't afford to pay you anything, but on the plus side, I think somebody's trying to kill me."

There was a whoop of laughter on the other end. "I knew I could count on you. I'll be right there."

"She's coming," I told Bradford as I hung up the telephone. "Problem solved."

"So why don't I feel any better? You don't mind if I check this note for prints, do you?"

"Go right ahead," I said. As Bradford started to leave, I asked, "You're not hanging around? She'll be here in ten minutes."

"That's why I'm leaving now. Don't worry. I'll stay outside until she gets here, but then I'm taking off. Those screeching tires you hear will be me."

"Sissy," I said as he left.

Just knowing Lillian was on her way made me feel better. Since our folks had died, she had been a constant source of amusement and support for the three of us. It would be wonderful having her at the shop with me. My aunt prided herself on marrying well and divorcing even better. She'd dyed her hair red ever since I could remember, claiming that with her temper, it was too good an opportunity to pass up. There wasn't anything in the world we couldn't handle together, even a killer on the loose in Rebel Forge.

As I peeked out the window waiting for Lillian to arrive, I saw my brother in earnest conversation with Jody Jeffords, one of his deputies. Jody was in blue jeans and a T-shirt, and judging from his tousled hair and the way he kept rubbing his eyes, I was willing to bet that my brother had summoned him from a dead sleep. They both turned in my direction, so I ducked back behind the edge of the curtain and watched them. Jody studied the shop for a few seconds, bought a newspaper from one of the vendors across the way, then wandered off down the street. He finally settled on a bench in front of Dot's Ice Cream Palace, a name much grander than the tiny shop merited. As Jody opened his paper, I noticed that it was upside down. That was some crack surveillance team watching over me. A part of me wanted to protest my overprotective brother's action, but another part was glad he was the sheriff. That note had bothered me more than I'd been willing to admit to him. It wasn't exactly a death threat, but it was close enough for my tastes. True to his word, Bradford got into his patrol car and left thirty seconds before Lillian pulled up in front of my shop in her vintage candy-apple-red Mustang convertible.

I held the door for her as she approached, and Lillian ducked into my arms and gave me a bear hug squeeze. "It's been forever since I've seen you, Jennifer. Let me look at you." She grabbed my cheek. "You need more exercise; you're getting plump, girl."

"So we're playing that game today, are we? Now is it my turn to tell you what you need?"

She frowned for a second, then burst out laughing. "It will be good for me to spend some time with you here. So what's this about someone wanting to kill you?" With just a little too much excitement in her voice, she added, "Do you think I'm in danger, too?"

"This is serious," I said. After I told Lillian about the telephone call and the note, she grew somber.

"Don't worry about this, Jennifer. We'll keep an eye out for each other."

"We have help, too." I pointed to Jody sitting on the bench, his newspaper still upside down. "That's our police protection." As I said it, the paper drooped in his hands, and I could see that Jody had fallen asleep.

Lillian said, "Oooh, I feel so safe. Should one of us go wake him?"

"Let him sleep," I said. "In his defense, he probably worked all night."

Lillian dusted her hands. "Fine. Now enough of this chatter. Teach me to make cards."

As I led her to the table that had become my demonstration area by serendipity, I said, "You know, I've been expecting you to show up ever since I opened."

"I've been busy with a new suitor. Besides, after the riot act you read me about wanting to do this on your own, I didn't dare come by unannounced. Young lady, the only way I was ever visiting this shop was by your personal invitation."

"Sorry if I came on a little strong," I said. "I guess I've been a little overprotective about my shop."

She squeezed me with one arm. "Jennifer, I simply can't imagine where you inherited a quality like that. Now let's make some cards. Remember, you need to start with the basics for me. I've never done more than address a card and mail it before."

"It's really loads of fun," I said.

Lillian picked up an ornate three-dimensional anniversary card with an intricate bouquet of paper flowers nestled in a woven basket; the card was watercolor-washed, embossed and hand-stitched. "Let's start with one of these."

I gently took the card away from her. "That might be a little advanced for you just yet."

I handed her a sheet of regular white card stock, already cut to its basic size of five inches by ten inches.

Lillian asked, "What am I supposed to do with this?"

"Patience, dear Aunt. It's the first card you're going to make."

"With this?" she asked as she held up the blank white card stock.

"Believe it or not, this is the best first step. We can create two basic cards with this size stock. I've already cut it to the right size. The easiest card to make is to just fold it in half, and then it's ready to adorn."

She started to fold the sheet when I handed her a metal ruler. "I like to make the fold with this so you get a nice crisp edge. Put a light pencil mark at five inches on each side; then fold the paper over the ruler until you have a sharp crease."

"Jennifer Shane, I can certainly fold a piece of paper in half without your detailed instruction."

I shrugged. "Go ahead, then."

She bent the paper in half, matched up the edges, then folded the stock. "See? It's not that difficult."

I took another sheet, did as I'd instructed her, and handed her my fold. "Now compare our results."

She studied both cards, then acknowledged, "Okay,

your edge is crisper; I'll grant you that. But is it really that important?"

"Lillian, in handcrafting cards, everything is in the details. If you can't understand that, then I'm sorry I bothered you, but I won't be able to use you here."

That got her attention. I hadn't meant to spank her so harshly, but I was serious about cards, and if she couldn't match my commitment and dedication, I didn't want her working in my shop.

Lillian said, "Okay, you're the teacher. I'll do better, I promise." She grabbed another sheet, folded it as I'd suggested, then asked, "What's next?"

"The other card we can do with this size folds together in the middle like a pair of doors. We do the same thing as before, only we space the folds to give us three sections. The two creases on the outside should be two and a half inches from either edge. Then fold them with the ruler again."

"That looks nice," she said as she handed me her newly folded card. I noticed she'd done exactly as I'd taught her this time. "What do you think?"

I examined it, then said, "Good job."

"That's really all there is to it?" she asked. "No offense, Jennifer, but that was easy."

"The basic steps are simple to perform; that's why card making is such a good craft for anybody to try. Now comes the fun part."

I grabbed a clear plastic template and said, "You can make your own guide out of plain paper or even graph paper, but I had some of these made up for the shop." The thin template was a five-by-five-inch piece of Plexiglas with a square cut inside it that measured three inches by three. That gave me two pieces when they were separated: a two-inch framed border and a square that fitted exactly within it. "First we lay the outer frame on the front of our single-fold card. Then we put a little transparent tape on the inside square and secure it to the paper."

"So that automatically centers it," Lillian said. "I get it."

"Very good." After she'd done as I'd told her, I said, "Now lift the border off and your square is exactly where it needs to be."

"What comes next?" The enthusiasm in my aunt's voice was readily apparent. I was beginning to believe she might work out after all.

"Now we can get started on adornment."

I flipped the card open as I turned it over so the square was now on the bottom, attached to the lower half of the stock. After that, I grabbed the smooth wooden stick that resembled a letter opener, then said, "Now we press the creases where the square is. By the way, this is called a boning tool."

"Is it really made of bone?"

"Some are, but this one's made of polished maple. Would you like to try it?" I asked as I rubbed an edge of the paper.

"Certainly," she said as she took the tool from me and rubbed the paper. "Is that enough?"

I looked at the card. "It's perfect. Now flip it back over and gently peel off the tape. Then you can remove the square."

She did as instructed, then examined the results. "My goodness, it looks so professional."

"It is," I said. "You did a very nice job."

"So what are we going to put inside it?"

"Why don't you set that aside and we'll work on some more basic shapes and cutouts first." The look of disappointment on her face was obvious, so I added, "Don't worry; we'll make lots of cards before we're through. We don't seem to have to be concerned about customers interrupting us."

"Jennifer, they'll come. In the meantime, this is fascinating. What are we going to do next?"

"Let's see. I think we should make a simple cutout." As we cleared off the table, I saw a few folks glancing in through the window as we worked. Maybe Lillian's public lesson would serve as free advertising for the shop. I could certainly use all that I could get.

I laid out a cutting mat with the grid already printed on it, put a thin piece of corkboard over that, then said, "Get another piece of the white stock and fold it once." After she'd done as she was told, I said, "Now take the template for the outer frame and lay it on the front of the card. Then take this awl and push it gently through the card stock in each corner of the frame."

"Why, it's nothing but a needle on a stick," she said.

"I never claimed the tools were complex. It's a very user-friendly craft."

Once she'd punched the four holes, I said, "Now pull off the template. Take this metal ruler and the craft knife and cut the paper, connecting the dots until you've got a square. Careful, that blade is sharp."

Lillian made the cuts, then lifted the card up, with the square left neatly behind. "How lovely," she said.

"You're a natural. Are you ready to embellish it even more?"

"I'd love to," she said just as the bell over the door chimed. It looked like we were going to get our first honest-to-goodness customer for the day.

"We'll continue this later," I said softly. As I approached the young woman with lustrous red hair pleated in long braids, I asked, "May I help you?"

"I need a birthday present for my grandmother. Do you have anything here I can give her? She loves to work with her hands."

"Absolutely. I've got lots of supplies for the amateur, and instruction books, as well."

"You don't happen to have any kits for sale with all that stuff already in it, do you? I'm kind of in a hurry."

It was all I could do to hide my grin. "I think we can find something you'll be happy with," I said as I led her to the proper section. When I glanced back at Lillian, I saw that she'd taken another piece of stock

and was folding it. It appeared that my aunt and un-
paid assistant had been bitten by the card-making bug,
as well, and I couldn't be happier about it.

By the end of the business day, we'd had several
actual customers, and we'd even made enough in sales
to justify opening our door. Lillian had left promptly
at five to meet her new beau and I was getting ready
to lock up. I was feeling pretty good about the situation when Bradford walked in. From the dour look
on his face, I could tell that he was about to ruin the
rest of my day.

HANDCRAFTED CARD-MAKING TIP

I like to personalize my cards whenever possible.
For example, a discarded set of Scrabble tiles deliv-
ers a wonderful message to an aficionado of the
game. Letters cut out to resemble crossword puzzle
blanks also make a neat way of letting the receiver
know you care.

Chapter 4

"What is it, Bradford? Has something else happened?"

"Not that I know of. It's a good thing, too; I've got enough to deal with as it is. You wanted to know more about that girl who was murdered last night. I finally got in touch with her parents, so I feel a little better talking to you about it now." I could tell it must have killed him telling them that their little girl was gone. It had to be one of the worst parts of my brother's job, and I didn't know how he found the strength to do it.

"So who was she?" I asked, not sure I really wanted to know.

He flipped open a notebook stored in his front pocket. "Her name was Tina Mast, and she was just barely twenty years old. I didn't know her, but one of my deputies went to school with her older sister. Wayne Davidson said she was a pretty little thing, but you couldn't prove it by me from the way I found her inside that house. She was a senior at Tech, but she came home this weekend to help one of her friends out, according to her folks. They were pretty torn up about it when I talked to them in Florida. They were on vacation, if you can imagine that," he said as his voice started to get deeper. When my brother got upset, his voice went down an octave, and he was talking so low at the moment I could barely believe it was him.

"I'm going to hate myself for asking you this, but how did she die?"

Bradford hesitated, then said, "Somebody worked her over pretty good with a chunk of wood. It was bad, Sis. I won't lie to you."

He hesitated so long that I knew there was something my brother wasn't telling me. "Why are you giving me all this information?"

"Hey, you said you wanted to know." He sounded petulant, and I knew there was more of a reason than that.

"I ask you about a lot of things, but I rarely get any answers that satisfy me. So I'm going to ask you again. Why are you giving me so much information about your investigation?"

"Blast it, Jennifer, the truth is, she had a telephone clutched in her hand when we found her. The cord was still connected to the base, and somebody had smashed the daylights out of it. I'm guessing that's what killed your connection yesterday."

My heart started pounding so hard I thought it was going to jump right out of my chest. Suspecting something and knowing it were two different things. I'd guessed that something bad had happened to the girl on the other end of the phone, but hearing my brother confirm my suspicions was just about more than I could take.

"Hey, are you all right?"

I leaned against the counter, thankful for the support, as my legs fought to hold me up. "I'm not, but I will be. I knew that girl on the phone was from around here, Bradford. I just knew it."

"Well, I wish that was one hunch of yours that hadn't paid off. Now that we know you heard a murder over the telephone, I'm not asking you to move in with Sara Lynn or me; I'm ordering you to."

"Bradford, you're going to have to lock me up in

handcuffs to get me to leave my apartment. This doesn't change anything. Tina Mast was dead yesterday, and the killer didn't come after me then. What makes you think she's going to do it now?"

"Are you forgetting about that note you got in the mail this morning?"

"I doubt I ever will, but I'm not a threat to anyone right now. I wouldn't even know where to start digging into this. The killer will see that I'm harmless and she'll have to leave me alone."

It might have been wishful thinking on my part, but really, it made more sense my way. If the woman who'd killed Tina Mast wanted me dead, I had been unguarded at my apartment the night before and this morning, and then again at the store before Lillian came. I had to admit that if I'd had more of an idea about who the killer could have been, I might have nosed around more. After all, Bradford wasn't the only kid in our family who could think logically and rationally. Growing up, I'd won more games playing the Clue board game than he'd ever dreamed of. Why was it so hard for him to imagine that I couldn't do the same thing now?

"I've seen that look in your eyes before, baby sister. You think you can solve this yourself, don't you? Jennifer, I'm warning you, you're in way over your head here."

I wouldn't have been so aggravated with him if he weren't right. "You don't know everything just because you're sheriff here. I've got a good head on my shoulders when it comes to things like this, and you know it."

He shook his head. "We're not kids anymore, and this isn't make-believe. That girl's really dead, and she's not coming back."

"That's why we need to make sure her killer doesn't go free, don't you think?" Honestly, sometimes my brother could be so thick. "We can figure this out together, Bradford."

"Even discounting you including yourself in my investigation, there are two guys from the state police over there right now. Do you honestly think that we can come up with something that they might miss?"

"We'll never know unless we try. Come on, what's it going to hurt if you take me to the crime scene so I can look around for myself?"

"You are absolutely out of your mind. There's no way I'm letting you get within two miles of that house."

"Afraid of a little competition from your baby sister?"

He shook his head. "What I'm afraid of is that the killer is still keeping an eye on the place. How's she going to react if she sees you snooping around after she warned you to butt out? Kid, do you have a death wish or something?"

"I'm not a kid," I snapped automatically, but maybe my brother had a point. He'd discussed a few cases in the past with me, and I'd even given him a nudge in the right direction on occasion, but I was directly involved in this one, and it could have dire consequences for me if the killer found out what I was up to. "You say the killer shouldn't see me going to the murder scene. Fine then, I'll wear a disguise and you can take me by after the state cops leave."

"How do you plan to disguise yourself? Are you going to wear a mask or something? Yeah, you're right. That wouldn't look too suspicious."

"Be serious, Bradford. I'll borrow one of Lillian's wigs—goodness knows she has enough of those—and I'll wear high heels and put on some of those big sunglasses. Sara Lynn won't even recognize me by the time I'm finished."

"Why the sudden desire to dig into this, Jennifer? You've never shown this active an interest in any of my cases before. All your help has been from the sidelines in the past."

"I never heard anyone get murdered while I was talking to them on the phone, either. Come on, Bradford, this is important to me. If my life's at risk, which you seem to think it is, shouldn't I have the right to investigate the crime scene myself?" I knew I was on shaky ground as far as logic went, but it made a lot more sense to me to actively go after the killer than to wait around for her to decide to knock me off. I always favored action over delay, sometimes even when I would be better served by having a little patience. I was willing to admit that about myself.

He scratched his left ear, walked over to the window and stared outside. "I was right; you have lost your mind."

"So you'll take me?" I asked.

"I'll never hear the end of it if I don't, will I? I suppose you want me to sneak you into the morgue so you can see the body, too, huh?"

"Don't be gross, Bradford. I've got no desire to see that poor girl laid out on a cold steel table." I grabbed my purse. "Let's go."

"You mean right now? I thought you had to get your disguise together."

"I do, but I'm finished here, and the quicker we do this, the sooner I find out what really happened to Tina Mast. The state police should be gone by the time we get there, shouldn't they?" I held the door open for him, but he didn't budge. "Are you coming, or do I have to go without you?"

My brother frowned as he walked out the door I held for him. "Sometimes I honestly wish I were an only child."

"Well, life's full of disappointment sometimes, isn't it? Meet me at Lillian's. I need half an hour to get ready."

"Yes, Ma'am."

As I drove my Gremlin to my aunt's house, I felt my pulse speed up. Odds were that I wouldn't be able to find a clue that everyone else had missed, but I owed the attempt to that girl who had been on the other end of the line.

It was a good thing Lillian never threw anything away. I slipped through her back door using my key, then made my way to her dressing room. Most people had a closet or two where they stored their clothes and accessories, but not my aunt. Lillian had taken an entire bedroom of her old house and had converted it into one huge closet. My aunt loved her Victorian place, and each new groom had been required to move his belongings in immediately following the nuptials. How she got them to agree to that was beyond me. I was certain that one of the reasons she refused to leave was the room I was standing in. It was like walking through a time capsule as I browsed through her clothes trying to find something that would distract anyone watching from my face. I knew it would be a lot harder to be recognized if I was in clothing I would never wear ordinarily. After all, how many people would recognize their pharmacist if he was dressed as a priest or a police officer? I found just what I was looking for after twenty minutes of digging around through paisleys, polka dots and leopard prints. There was a duster jacket that brushed the ground, made of a material that defied description, in a color combination only for those with strong stomachs. Lillian must have wallowed in the jacket, but it was a snug fit for me. A cross between tie-dye and paisley, it had more colors than a psychedelic rainbow. Content that no one would recognize that coat as anything I could possibly wear, I found one of Lillian's wigs—red, of course—that reached halfway down my back. I couldn't resist grabbing a pair of her rhinestone sunglasses off the stand, and I tried the entire ensemble on in front of her three-way mirror. I didn't even know the stranger looking back at me. I could only

look for a few seconds—the coat was that blinding—
but what I saw would do perfectly.

That's when I heard giggling coming from the master bedroom. Oh, no. I had forgotten all about my
aunt's rendezvous with her latest suitor. There was no
way I wanted to catch them canoodling, so I tiptoed to
the back door so I could make my escape unnoticed.

My hand was on the door when I heard my aunt's
stern voice behind me. "Stop right where you are. I've
got a gun."

I started to turn around when she said, "I mean it.
I'd rather face a jury for shooting you than wait for
you to come back here some night and try to kill me."

"Lillian, it's me." I turned around slowly until she
could see my face.

"Jennifer? What in the world are you doing? You
look positively ghastly."

"In my defense, I'm wearing your things." Lillian
did indeed have a gun trained on me, a rather large
one at that. "Would you mind pointing that thing
somewhere else? Where did you get it, anyway?"

As she lowered the barrel, she said, "You know
how Percy loved to hunt. He left this behind so I
could protect myself. Girl, I'd like an explanation for
that outfit. I haven't seen that duster since the sixties."
She frowned, then said, "It had to have looked better
on me than it does on you now."

"It's a long story, but I didn't think you'd mind if
I borrowed a few of your things."

Lillian scowled. "Jennifer Shane, you know that
whatever I have is yours. Not without an explanation, though."

I wasn't about to tell her what I was up to, at least
not until I had something more concrete to reveal than
I had so far. "How about your beau? Should you
really keep him waiting?"

"You heard him?" There was no humor in her voice
when she asked me the question.

"All I heard was a giggle. Good for you."

That appeased her. In a low voice, Lillian said, "He's got potential, but I'm not at all certain he'll make the final cut."

"I would think not. After all, he let you come out here by yourself to confront an intruder."

Lillian shook her head. "Jennifer, my dear sweet child, not every man is built for battle. It's my shotgun, and I know how to use it. If he tried to scare somebody off with it, most likely he'd end up shooting himself in the foot. No, I'm using a different litmus test to see if he'll do. I sincerely doubt he'll pass, but in the meantime, he's an interesting diversion." She paused, then called out over her shoulder. "It's fine; it's just my niece. I'll be in shortly." Lillian turned back to me, then said, "Now I must know what you're up to, young lady. Does your brother know you're planning to parade around Rebel Forge dressed like that?"

I knew then there was no use trying to stonewall Lillian anymore. "Bradford's taking me to the crime scene."

"What are you talking about, Jennifer? Has something else happened?"

That's when I remembered that Lillian had already left for the day when Bradford had come by to update me on what had happened to Tina Mast. After I explained how I'd coaxed my brother into letting me help him investigate, Lillian said, "Give me five minutes and I'll go with you."

"It was all I could do to convince him to let me go. If I show up with you, I won't get to step inside the front door. I know how far I can push him, Lillian, and bringing you with me is about four steps farther than he'd be willing to go." What I didn't say was that she had to know how my brother felt about her. Some people in this world, whether they're related by blood or not, were never meant to get along, and my brother and my aunt were two of them. Throwing them together for anything short of a wedding or a funeral was asking for trouble, and I had enough of that to deal with already without worrying about them. To appease her, I said, "As soon as I finish, I'll come back over here and return your things. That way I can bring you up-to-date on what happened without anyone being the wiser." I gestured to the bedroom, then added, "That is if you think you'll be finished up here by then."

"Jennifer, I believe you've entirely killed the mood for any romance this evening."

"I'm so sorry. I didn't mean to."

She hugged me, then said, "To be honest with you, it's time I moved on, but I've been reluctant to do so. This gives me the perfect opportunity to let him down easy and see what else is out there waiting for me."

"Now I feel really terrible," I said. "Are you sure you want to do that?"

"There's no doubt in my mind. Now if you'll excuse me, I have a heart to break." She must have seen the sadness in my eyes, because she quickly added, "I'll be gentle with him, I promise. You always were a sensitive child."

I surely didn't want to stand there discussing that with her. Bradford was probably beginning to think that I'd been abducted; I'd taken so long to put my disguise together. We were meeting at the fire station—neutral ground—and when I glanced at my watch I saw that I was going to be late. "I've got to run," I said as I hurried out the back door. I'd thought about adding high heels to make me taller, but I didn't have the time, and in all honesty, I doubted I'd need to hide my appearance any more than I already had. After parking a block from the station, I walked the rest of the way so no one would associate my outfit with the Gremlin. Only part of that had to do with my safety. I honestly didn't want anyone in Rebel Forge to think that I'd chosen that particular outfit myself.

I pulled the duster tight, cinched the belt and patted my wig before I went inside. The sunglasses were a little dark for my taste, but at least they managed to cover more of my face than one of the masks Bradford had mentioned. He was standing near the town's only fire truck as two of our volunteers polished a bumper. I thought I'd fooled him when he said, "Are you ready?"

I just nodded, disappointed that he'd seen right through my disguise. Once we were in his patrol car, I said, "I can't believe you knew it was me."

"Jennifer, I'm a trained police officer. I'm paid to be observant." He added with a grin, "Besides, I remember when Lillian wore that jacket to a Halloween party one year. It triggered a migraine headache that I'll never forget. There's one more thing, too. You still have on the same shoes you did when I saw you earlier."

"Should I change?" The last thing in the world I wanted was to be recognized, especially in that outfit.

"You did a good job, Sis. Nobody's going to know that's you dressed like that. You fooled Darrel and Lee, didn't you? Can you honestly believe one of them wouldn't have said something to you if they'd recognized you? Oh, man, I'd better call Cindy and tell her what I'm up to before the town gossips call her and tell her I'm stepping out on her." He dialed his cell, and had a brief conversation with his wife. Small towns are big on talk, and I was certain he was right in calling Cindy before somebody else did, just trying to be "helpful." After he hung up, Bradford looked a little miffed.

"What's wrong? Didn't she believe you?"

He said, "No, she didn't have any trouble accepting it. That's what's bugging me. I'm still a good-looking guy, right?"

I had to laugh, which was exactly the wrong thing to do at that particular moment.

"You mind telling me what's so funny? I'm going

out on a limb here, Jennifer. Is it too much to ask that you show me a little respect?"

"I wasn't laughing at you, Bradford. It just struck me as funny that you're concerned your wife doesn't think you're capable of having an affair. Come on, Cindy trusts you, and I've never known anybody more in love than your wife is with you—though only the Good Lord knows why. You've got something half the world is searching for. Be happy for that."

He took my appeasement as more than it really was. "Don't worry, Jen. You'll find someone."

"I might if I were looking, but the last thing in the world I need right now is a man getting in my way. I honestly don't know when I'd have the time for him. Trust me, I'm happy with things just the way they are right now." It was true. I was long past waiting for the man of my dreams to come along. It wasn't that I was closing myself off to the possibility of love sometime in the future, but I had a business to build, and now a murder to solve before the killer decided to come after me. That didn't leave much time for moonlit strolls or breakfast picnics by the lake.

I was saved from further comment when Bradford pulled the patrol car up in front of a small house down by the railroad tracks. It had one story, sided in vinyl, and a roof that needed replacing, if the missing shingles meant anything. There was a FOR SALE sign in the front yard peeking through the high grass growing there. The state police had come and gone, but there were ribbons of that bright yellow crime scene tape wrapped around the steps of the front stoop.

Bradford cut off the engine, but before he made a move to get out, he asked, "Jennifer, are you sure you want to do this?"

I thought about the violence that had happened inside there a little over twenty-four hours before, about how a young woman had lost her life in a violent, horrific way. But I never hesitated. "Bradford, I don't have a choice. Let's go in before I lose my nerve."

He shrugged. "I'm ready if you are."

As we walked up the sidewalk, I asked, "Is this where she lived?"

"No, Tina and her family lived all the way over on Hughes Drive. We haven't figured out how she ended up here. The state police think it had something to do with drugs, but we both know better, don't we?"

"Do you have any idea who owns this house?"

"I was able to backtrack and find out that it used to belong to the family of a boy she went to school with, but nobody's lived here for months."

Another thought suddenly occurred to me. "Bradford, did you tell the state cops about the telephone call?"

"I tried to, but they blew me off before I could go into much detail. They were both kind of skeptical that the phone call and the murder were related."

"But you think they are, don't you?"

He hesitated as he removed some of the tape. "We're here, aren't we? I've got to warn you, the body may be gone, but there's no doubt what happened inside."

"I'll be okay," I said as I followed him to the door. Before he'd let me in Bradford handed me a pair of latex gloves. "Here, put these on."

"I thought you-all were through here."

"Jennifer, this is still an active crime scene. I don't want the state cops to come back and find my little sister's fingerprints all over the house."

The gloves were clammy, but I put them on anyway. It was time to face something that scared the daylights out of me. Hopefully, it would help answer some of my questions.

Chapter 5

The smell was the first thing that hit me when I stepped across the threshold directly into the living room. There's something about a house where no one is living; it takes on smells and odors of its own accord, but there was more than that there. I didn't know if it was just my imagination kicking into high gear, but I could swear I smelled death inside.

Bradford must have noticed the expression on my face. "You picked up on that, too, huh? We found a couple of sprung mousetraps in the kitchen. This place would have been tough to sell before the murder. It's like I told you: there's not much to see here, is there?"

"Give me a minute, will you?" I pulled off my disguise and laid the coat, the wig and the sunglasses on a table near the door. As I walked around the room, I saw a couple of shattered pieces of plastic on the floor that must have been from the battered phone. That's when I noticed dark brown stains on the worn shag carpet. A patch had been cut out of the rug, exposing the concrete underneath, and I wondered what the evidence would yield. I didn't spend too much time worrying about that, though. It was up to the state police labs to find any clues hiding there.

As I walked through the small house, I kept wondering what had brought Tina there in her last hours. Had she been running, looking for refuge at an old boyfriend's house, or had she been lured there to her death? The first scenario would mean she was being chased, while the second was much darker. If the woman who had killed her had tricked Tina into coming to such a far-off place, then that meant the murderer had known her, and fairly well, to know of her connection to the empty house. I gave the bathroom a perfunctory look, but something caught my eye as I turned to tell my brother that I wasn't going to be much help. Kicked behind the toilet, I found a teardrop earring with its back missing. It was small enough for a man or a woman to wear, though I'd never been all that comfortable with men wearing earrings of any size or shape. When I started to retrieve it, Bradford said behind me, "Hold on; what did you find?"

"There's an earring back there. Any chance Tina lost one in the struggle?"

"I'm not sure." He carefully picked it up, sealed it in a tiny evidence bag, then said, "Let me check the report." Bradford scanned a sheaf of documents. "Sorry, she didn't have pierced ears. It's probably been here awhile."

He started to hand me the earring when I asked, "If it wasn't Tina's, could it belong to the killer?"

"Come on, Jennifer, that thing's probably been here since the Claytons moved. Do you honestly think the killer left it behind?"

"Bradford, the back's missing. I'm betting she didn't even realize she lost it until she got home."

"So what was she doing in the bathroom?" my brother asked.

"Maybe she was cleaning up. You said yourself it was pretty bloody." I leaned over and tried the faucet, but no water came out.

He shrugged. "Sorry, Sis. It was a nice theory, but it doesn't hold water." If Bradford knew he'd just made a pun, he didn't show any awareness of it.

I had a sudden thought. "There's more than one way to get water in a bathroom." I grabbed the toilet reservoir lid, thankful that I had gloves on for a reason that had nothing to do with fingerprints. As I pulled the lid off, I saw that there was still water inside and worst of all, there were splatters of blood on the sides of the tank. "I was right. She washed up in here after all."

Bradford leaned over and looked down at the reddish pink water. "Well I'll be dipped in Tabasco. I don't know how we missed this."

"It proves my point, doesn't it? There's more reason than ever to believe that the earring belongs to the killer."

My brother looked at me with new respect in his eyes. "I'm impressed, Jennifer." He looked sheepish, and I asked him what was wrong. "I'm not sure how I'm going to tell the state police that my sister found this."

"That's easy; you don't. Tell them you came back to have another look around, which is true, and you found this, which might be stretching the truth just a little, but who cares?"

He rubbed his chin. "Jennifer, that last part's not even close to what happened. I don't know if I can do it."

I swear, men can be so anal sometimes. My brother was more concerned with propriety and society's rules than I'd ever been. I was more of a results-oriented kind of gal myself. "Tell them what you want to, but if you mention my name, you're crazy. Just imagine what kind of paperwork you'd have to fill out for letting a civilian into a crime scene. Isn't it just easier my way?"

"You don't get it, do you? It might be less of a hassle in the short run, but what happens when I have to testify in court that I'm the one who found this earring? There's something called the chain of evidence, and I'm not about to lie under oath just to keep from getting a little heat. No, we're doing this by the book." He thought about it thirty seconds, then reached into his wallet, pulled out a one-dollar bill and handed it to me.

"What's this, a finder's fee?" I asked as I took the buck.

"No, that's your retainer. I just hired you as a consultant to help me investigate the crime scene. I'm doing it because I'm after a woman's perspective. Do you get what I mean?"

"Hey, I've never been a cop before. Do I get a badge and a gun and everything?"

My brother was not amused by my grin. "Jennifer, this is serious. It's one thing to let a civilian in here, but if you're on my payroll, I've got a way out of this without taking a real hit."

I folded the dollar bill and slid it into my pocket. "Sorry, I know this is important. So what do we do now?"

"I want you to finish looking around, and then I'm going to call the cops who missed this."

I finished exploring the place, but if there was anything else there, I couldn't see it. "Bradford, I just had a thought. Is there any way we could go look around Tina's room in her parents' house? There might be something there that could help us."

He seemed reluctant to agree, so I added, "Hey, I'm on the payroll now, remember? If I'm going to be a consultant, I need to see everything."

"Maybe hiring you wasn't such a great idea after all."

I smiled. "Maybe not, but you're stuck with me now. So what do you say?"

"Why not? I'm already in it this deep. What's a few more feet over my head?"

"That's the spirit," I said as I opened the front door, ready to step outside.

He pulled me back in abruptly. I said, "Hey, what are you doing, Bradford?"

"Aren't you forgetting something?" He gestured to

the table and I saw my disguise still sitting there. Okay, that was a boneheaded mistake, but I was new at all this subterfuge stuff. "Thanks," I said as I snugged the wig in place and belted the jacket up. Once we were outside, I felt really conspicuous in my Halloween outfit, but Bradford was right. If the killer was watching the house, I didn't want her to know that I was snooping around. I wondered if she realized she'd lost that earring yet. When she did, I had a feeling that there was going to be another break-in at that house. "Bradford, shouldn't you assign somebody to watch the house in case she comes back?" I explained my reasoning to him.

"I wish I could afford to do it, but I'm shorthanded as it is, and there's no way I've got the manpower to do any surveillance."

"You could always ask the state police for help," I said.

"Tell you what, why don't you let me handle that end of it, okay? You don't want to lose that dollar, do you?"

I covered my pocket with my hand. "You'll have to arrest me to get it back. I think it's the first buck you ever gave me in your life."

"I didn't give you anything; you earned it." As he held the door to the squad car open for me, he said, "Now let's see what you can turn up at the Mast house."

We were halfway there when the radio in Bradford's cruiser squawked. "Chief, are you out there?"

"Right here, Jody. What's up?"

"There's a wreck on Third and Milton. The caller was pretty hysterical. It sounds like there might be a fatality or two."

"I'm on my way," he said as he pulled over to the curb. "Sorry, Jen, but the Mast house is going to have to wait. I don't know how long I'll be, so we'll check out Tina's house another time."

"Her parents are coming back tomorrow, right?"

"First thing in the morning. Listen, I don't have time to debate this. Hop out."

As I jumped out of the car, I said, "Come by my apartment as soon as you're finished. We need to look around before her parents get home."

"We'll see," Bradford said as he sped away. I knew he had to respond to the accident, but it was frustrating not being able to go to Tina's and see what I could find there. Maybe I could drive over and check it out myself. I didn't have a key, but neither did Bradford. I was willing to bet one of the neighbors did, though, and with my new official status, it shouldn't be too tough getting them to let me in. Okay, maybe I was reaching, but it was still worth a shot.

I was about half a mile from my car, and as I walked down the road I was suddenly very glad I'd decided against the high heels I'd planned for my disguise. The shoulder, what there was of it, was filled with debris and castoffs that tend to collect at the side of large roads everywhere. It was dark out, and though a few cars passed right by me, no one offered to give me a ride. To my surprise, I saw Sara Lynn's car approach, and before I could stop myself, I started to wave her down. She raced past me like she owed me money, and only then did I remember that I still had on my disguise. I must have done a pretty good job at that if my own sister couldn't recognize me.

A few minutes later, a convertible with four teenage boys drove by—hooting and whistling at me as they passed—but I didn't let it go to my head. They were out doing some young-male bonding, no doubt on a hormone rage that would have spurred them on to give my aunt Lillian the same reaction. I'd dismissed them from my thoughts when I saw a car coming back from the other direction, and wondered if they were looking for a little more sport than just harassing me from the road. I watched as the car approached, but I was relieved to see that it was a different make. That was about all I could say for sure, since I've never been someone who cared about the difference between a Chrysler and a Chevrolet, if there was one. I'd always driven cars with character, like my sweet little Gremlin.

I was still watching the headlights when I saw the driver suddenly jerk the wheel and send the car careening right at me. I couldn't tell if the driver was on a cell phone or reaching for a dropped doughnut, but I was about to get run over if I didn't do something fast. I jumped off the road into a tangle of briars, and the car still barely missed me as it raced past. As I pulled myself out of the brush, I looked down the road to see if the driver was at least going to come back to see if I was all right. The car just kept going, though. He probably didn't even realize he nearly killed me. Except for a few scrapes on one hand and a scratch on my right cheek, I was no worse for the encounter, though my legs did shake a bit as I started walking again. I was a fair distance from the Gremlin when a car's headlights picked me up and the vehicle slowed down. Oh, no, whoever had run me off the road was coming back to take another stab at it. Without waiting this time, I jumped off the pavement to get clear when I heard a voice I knew. "Where are you going, Girl? Have you lost your mind?"

With a sigh of relief, I turned back toward the car and greeted my aunt Lillian.

"What happened to your big investigation?"

"Bradford had to answer an emergency call," I said, not wanting to go into too many details.

"So you decided to keep the disguise on and go for a midnight stroll along the highway? I would have spotted that coat anywhere. There's not another one like it in all of Virginia."

For good reason, I thought, but kept it to myself. "Thanks for giving me a ride. Bradford had to drop me off kind of fast."

She snorted once. "That figures. Would it have killed your brother to at least drive you back to your car?"

"There was an accident out on the highway, Lillian. They needed him out there."

Lillian caught a glimpse of my face. "What happened to you? You look like you just wrestled an alligator and lost."

I explained about being forced to jump off the road to keep from being hit.

Lillian paused, then asked, "Jennifer, how can you be so sure it was an accident?"

"What, you think someone just felt like committing a little homicide and chose me?"

"Remember why you're wearing my outfit? You wanted to disguise yourself. Well, have you considered the possibility that you failed, and that the killer was trying to tie up one more loose end?"

The idea chilled me to my soul. "I liked it a lot better when it was just a random act of violence."

"No one wants to be targeted, my dear. You really should take some precautions."

Before she could say another word, I snapped, "If you invite me to stay with you tonight, I swear, I'll get out of the car this instant and take my chances with another drive-by."

Lillian looked absolutely startled as she pulled in behind my Gremlin. "Honestly, I didn't mean anything by it. I was just trying to help."

I seemed to be alienating everyone who loved me. I put a hand on hers and said, "Listen, I'm sorry. I shouldn't have overreacted. It's just that no one thinks I can take care of myself, and it's starting to get to me."

"Jennifer, my dear, we all realize you're quite capable of dealing with adulthood, but none of us want to see you in danger. You're our family, and we love you."

"I love you, too," I said.

"We've discussed everything but what I'm dying to know. Did you have a chance to go to the crime scene?"

I thought about refusing to answer, since Bradford had gone out on a limb to get me into the murder scene, but I knew my aunt well enough to know that she wasn't about to be thwarted, so I took the path that was easiest. "I found an earring on the scene that had to be the killer's."

"So it was the woman from the phone after all."

"It looks more and more like it. There were pieces of a battered telephone there, and I don't even want to talk about the blood." It was odd, but the scene I'd explored hadn't bothered me nearly as much when I'd been there as the memory was doing at the moment. Somehow it was just sinking in that a young woman had lost her life right where I'd stood. Hearing it on the telephone was bad enough; seeing it was pretty horrible, too; but putting the two together was beginning to scare the wits out of me. Maybe I should stop being so pigheaded and take one of my relatives up on their offer to relocate for a while. But if I did that, I was admitting that I couldn't handle the situation on my own, and I wasn't about to concede anything like that.

Lillian patted my shoulder. "It must have been difficult seeing it like that."

"It wasn't a treat, but I'll manage," I said.

"If you don't mind my asking, where are you off to now? I trust you're going home."

I had a decision to make, and I didn't hesitate for a second. "Actually, I'm going over to Tina Mast's house to see if I can learn anything about the girl from her room."

"That sounds like a solid plan. I don't suppose you have a key, do you?"

"No," I said, "I planned to wing it once I got there."

Lillian laughed. "I just love a little breaking and entering. Count me in."

"Who said you were invited?" I wasn't at all sure I wanted to put my aunt in jeopardy. After all, I'd been drawn into it when Tina had dialed my number by mistake, but it wasn't fair to put Lillian's life in danger just because I wanted some company.

Lillian said, "My dear, try to stop me. My life has been so stale lately. Thank you for livening it up."

"Let's hope it doesn't get too lively," I said. Leaving my car behind, Lillian pulled out and started driving toward the outskirts of town. "How do you know where she lived?" I asked.

"Child, I had a feeling you'd be going there next, so I looked the address up in the phone book. We make quite a team, wouldn't you agree?"

All I could do was laugh. My aunt was many things, but predictable wasn't one of them.

I was excited about the prospects of searching Tina's room, but as we approached her house, I saw a patrol car sitting in the driveway. Wayne Davidson, one of my brother's deputies, was leaning against the side of his squad car as we parked behind it. Before we could even get out, he approached us. "Nice night for a drive, isn't it?"

"Let me guess. Your boss sent you over here to keep us out of the house."

He smiled and took the toothpick out of his mouth. "Don't think you know everything about the sheriff just because he's your brother. As a matter of fact, he had me get a key from the neighbor so you could look around." He gestured to my aunt. "Bradford didn't say anything about her, though."

"We come as a package deal, young man," Lillian said.

"I still have to get his approval before I let you both inside."

As Wayne got into his patrol car to call Bradford, I said to my aunt, "He'll never let you in; you know that, don't you?"

"Just because your brother and I don't get along doesn't mean he won't do the right thing. He knows I could be of some help to you, and as sheriff he can't afford to thwart me on this."

I looked at her to see if she was kidding, but from the stern line of Lillian's lips, I knew she believed every word of it. Personally, I didn't see any possible way my brother was about to let her inside. In all honesty, I was kind of surprised he was letting me go in without him.

Wayne came back a minute later and handed Lillian a dollar. "You can go in, too. He said Jennifer would know what the dollar meant. Only thing is, I have to be right with you both the entire time we're inside, so you two have to stick together."

"Of course, Officer," Lillian said, giving me a smug look as she did so.

"Okay, you were right and I was wrong," I said as I started toward the house.

"Nonsense, I've just seen your brother's sense of fairness at work more than you probably have."

We went into the Mast house—both wearing the gloves that Wayne had urged on us—and flipped on the lights as we walked through the place. I found Tina's bedroom on the third try. Inside, there were posters of rock stars on the walls, beads where a closet door should have been and a lava lamp on the dresser. The walls and ceiling were painted midnight blue, and one wall sported a hand-drawn mural of a coconut tree, a setting sun, and a bird painted over the top of the window molding. The room looked like a cave even with the light on.

Lillian asked, "What exactly are we looking for?"

"Anything that doesn't belong."

"Where should I start the list?" Lillian asked.

I ignored her comment and looked at the open suitcase on the bed. Being careful not to disturb anything, I searched through Tina's things with a feeling of violation. This poor girl had no idea she was going to die so soon, and here we were pawing through her belongings barely a day later. I couldn't find anything that looked out of place, and Lillian wasn't having much luck, either. I'd expected Wayne to search with us, but he spent most of his time just watching the two of us.

"Could this mean anything?" Lillian asked as she held up a newspaper clipping.

One side was from a tire ad, and the other was a. listing of movie times for our duplex theater. "I'll ask Bradford if she had a ticket stub on her when they found her," I said. "Lillian, I'm stumped. If there's anything important here, I don't have a single idea what it could be."

"I confess I'm at a loss, too. Does that mean I have to give the dollar back?"

I tried to smile, but there was too much sadness in that room. "I'd keep it. We tried, didn't we?"

She took my hands in hers. "Jennifer, we did our best, but we're not trained at this sort of thing."

Wayne said, "It's not as easy as it looks, is it?"

I rolled my eyes. "And how would you know? All you've done is stand there."

His cheeks reddened, and I felt bad about the jab, but I hated failing at anything, especially this, since there was more at stake than bragging rights with my brother. "Let's go, Lillian."

As we walked back to her car, my aunt said, "You were a little rough on him, weren't you?"

"I know, but blast it all, I was hoping to find something."

"Perhaps the movie ad will turn something up."

"Maybe." I started to get in the passenger door of Lillian's car, then knew what I had to do first. As Wayne was locking the front door of the house, I said, "Listen, I'm sorry about that crack. I'm just aggravated, but I had no right to take it out on you." I was a master at apologizing; I'd had enough practice at it over the years.

Wayne smiled briefly. "That's okay. You did your best."

"Yeah, that's what bothers me so much about it. I

just hate it when my best isn't good enough. Now I have to call Bradford and tell him I couldn't do it."

"If you'd like me to, I can tell him about the clipping. You know I'll give you both credit for it, but it might be easier for you that way."

"Thanks, I appreciate that."

"Listen," Wayne said softly, "you want to go get something to eat or something?"

"Are you asking me out?"

His cheeks immediately reddened. "It's not a real date. You know, we could just grab a bite or something. Forget it. It was a lousy idea."

"The idea is fine; the timing's just off."

He shrugged. "Yeah, that's the story of my life."

I tried to ease the rejection. "It's got nothing to do with you, and I'm flattered that you'd ask, really. But with the shop just opening up and everything involved with that, I don't have much time for anything else. Is that okay with you?"

"I don't have much choice, do I?" he asked. Then, adding a slight smile, he said, "Don't sweat it, Jennifer. It was just an idea."

When I got back to the car, Lillian asked, "What was that all about?"

"You're not going to believe this, but Wayne Davidson just asked me out."

"So when are you going?"

"Lillian, I've got too many complications in my life without adding a man to them."

My aunt laughed dryly. "My dear, there's always room for that particular complication."

By the time I was back home with my car parked in front of my apartment building, I began to wonder if Lillian was right. I knew there was more to life than work, but did I really want to go out with one of my brother's deputies? I'd known Wayne casually for years, and in all honesty, I wasn't exactly attracted to him that way. It was hard for me to make the transition from a man who was a friend to someone who could be more. When I fell, and it had happened a few times in my life, it was usually for a man I didn't already know, a mystery to be unveiled, not a guy I'd seen play junior varsity basketball or eat watermelon on my back porch with my older brother. No, Wayne was just going to have to go in the file of "Might Have Been but Never Would," a folder that seemed to grow thicker with each year.

There was a sound behind me of scuffling shoes as I approached my front door. It was all I could do not to run when I heard someone behind me say, "It's okay, Jennifer. It's just me."

"Why did you follow me home, Wayne? Wait, let me guess. It was my dear brother's idea, wasn't it?"

"I won't deny it or confirm it," he said. "I'm just glad you're home safe." He lingered near me, and for the oddest reason, I thought he was about to try to kiss me. That was the last thing on earth I wanted him to do, and I knew in an instant that I'd made the right decision earlier about turning him down.

"If that's all, I need to get inside so I can feed my cats."

"Good night," he said, showing no signs of moving on.

I unbolted my door and rushed inside, suddenly glad to have a lock between us. As I turned around, Oggie stood there staring at me, and Nash ran and hid under the sofa. I couldn't figure out what had gotten into my weird cats when I suddenly realized that I was still in disguise. As I pulled off the wig and tossed the coat on the sofa, I could swear Oggie nodded in approval.

I wanted to tell someone about it, but there was no one I could call. I knew I'd done the right thing turning down Wayne's invitation, but it still would have been nice to have someone there.

Chapter 6

When I got to the card shop the next morning, I half expected Lillian to be waiting for me on the front stoop, but there was no sign of my aunt as I unlocked the door and prepared to get ready for a new day. I thought about calling her at home, but with Lillian, the only thing that was predictable was her eccentric behavior.

I was pleasantly surprised when a woman came in precisely at ten o'clock. She had the most lustrous natural red hair—nothing like the sharp henna of my aunt's dye job—and a figure that made me wish for just a second that I'd skipped dessert for the last six or seven years.

"May I help you?"

"Oh, I'm just looking around," she said in a soft and wispy voice. "I absolutely adore your store, but I don't recall ever seeing it here before. How long have you been open?"

"We've been in business about a week," I said.

"Well, that explains that. So tell me, what's the easiest card there is to make?"

I grabbed a piece of scrap stock six inches square and handed it to her. "There you go. I've got envelopes that match it, too." Well, they were close enough.

She laughed. "My, aren't you the underachiever?

Darlin', if you're going to stay open another week, you're going to have to push a little harder than that."

I couldn't help myself; my returning smile came on without warning. "You're right, aren't you?" I fetched a gift box with linen paper and heavily lined envelopes that were a perfect match. "These are nice."

She took them from me, flipped the box over and saw the price, then smiled in earnest. "Now that's more like it." She waved a hand at the selection of cards up front. "Do you actually make these yourself?"

"Absolutely, and you can, too. It's really quite easy. Would you like to see how?"

She looked tempted; then she glanced at her watch. "How about a rain check? I promised my husband I'd be back in time to go on a hike. I just love this area; it's so charming."

"On behalf of the chamber of commerce and the town of Rebel Forge, I thank you."

I rang up the card set and was walking my customer out the door when a stern woman wearing an over-sized black coat walked in. From the way her gaze darted around my shop, I suspected she was about to rob me. "Are you sure you can't stay for that free lesson?" I asked the redhead.

"Sorry, but I will be back. I promise."

And then I was alone in my shop with a woman who looked like she was up to no good.

"May I help you with anything?" I asked, half expecting her to pull a shotgun out of her jacket and start shooting.

"No, I'm perfectly capable of helping myself."

As she browsed through the shop, picking up an item occasionally as she went along, I kept hoping that Lillian would show up. At that moment, I would have welcomed Bradford or even Sara Lynn; any warm body to act as a backup or a witness would do. The woman kept glancing toward the front door as if she was waiting for someone else to show up. After a few minutes, she walked toward me with a determined look in her eyes. This was it. I was about to experience my first robbery.

I was bracing myself for the assault when she asked, "Do you have any baskets? There's quite a bit I need."

I couldn't hide my relief. "Absolutely. They're right here. Let me grab you one."

She took it from me, then said, "You should move these over by the door so people can get them when they come in." The woman moved to the scissors and picked up one of my most expensive pairs. "These are nice. I've only seen them in catalogs before."

"Are you a card maker?" I asked.

"I used to be a scrapbooker, but I ran out of scrap." She chuckled at her own joke, a sound that resembled a serrated knife cutting through a rusty nail.

"You'd be surprised how many people do both," I said.

"Wouldn't surprise me a bit. Got to do something with all that stuff left over. Why not make cards?"

"I couldn't agree with you more."

She made her way to my paper selection. She picked up one of my newest creations. "Some of this is custom, isn't it?"

"I make it myself," I said proudly.

"You use too much glitter. Paper's to use, not to show off."

I picked up a piece of drab gray. "You can always use this, if you'd prefer."

She shook her head. "If I want stock made from newspaper, I'll make my own. This is nice, though." She picked up a sample of a maroon paper I'd been playing with. I'd pressed it on a different rack to yield an unusual texture. It was tough to write on—I'd learned that early on—but it was wonderful for pasting and cutouts. As she added a nice selection to her basket, the front door chimed and another woman walked in. In her late fifties, she wore a crisp linen suit and had a dragonfly pin on her lapel with what looked suspiciously like real diamonds for eyes. Her silver hair was long and carefully layered, and I knew the cut had cost more than the dress I was wearing. I couldn't believe it; I had two customers in my store at the same time, a record for me. If she'd just come in to use the telephone, I was going to cry. I wouldn't survive if my customers kept coming in single file.

I was torn between helping the woman who was buying lots of stock or the new customer when my original shopper said, "Go on, I'm fine right here."

I nodded, then approached the new customer. "May I help you?"

"Are you the owner?"

"I am," I admitted. "My name is Jennifer."

"I'm Melinda Spencer. I was hoping to get a private lesson on card making from you. You do that sort of thing, don't you?"

"Of course," I said, willing to do just about anything to make another sale at that point. "What kind of card would you like to make?"

"Oh, I don't mean right now. I would like to set up an appointment after hours when I can have your undivided attention. Are you free tonight?"

"Absolutely. Why don't we make it seven o'clock?"

"That would be perfect." Melinda looked at the woman in the black coat for a moment, then said, "I'll see you at seven, then."

After she was gone, my first customer said, "The world's full of dilettantes, isn't it?"

"Hey, I'm happy for all the customers I can get."

The woman looked around some more, then said, "Okay, that should do it for now."

As I followed her to the register and started ringing up her purchases, she said, "Now that's interesting."

I followed her glance to the poster I'd put up for the Crafty Cut-Ups Club I'd been hoping to sponsor. "When does it meet?"

"It's going to be every Thursday, but I need three members before I can start."

The woman nodded. "That sounds great. I'll bring Betty and Dot with me. They're old scrapbookers, too. Not that they're old, though they are, but they've both been doing it a long time. I'm Hilda, by the way."

I took her extended hand, not surprised at all by the strong grip. "I'm Jennifer," I said. Here I thought this woman had shown up to rob me and she might just turn out to be the best thing that had happened to me since I'd opened my doors.

After she paid for her purchases, Hilda said, "I'll call them as soon as I get home. We'll see you tonight."

"Wait a second," I said. "I won't be able to start until next Thursday."

She nodded. "That's probably better, anyway. Knowing those two, they're probably already booked for tonight. We'll clear our schedules for next week, though."

"I'm looking forward to it," I said as I handed her the bag and her change. As she was walking out, Lillian came in.

Before I could say a word, my aunt said, "Jennifer, I'm so sorry I'm late. I see we had a customer already."

"We've had three," I said a little too stiffly.

"Dear, I said I was sorry. I was up late talking with Hiram. That was the gentleman with me when you visited yesterday."

"Please, spare me the details of your love life, Lillian," I said gently. That was the last thing I wanted to hear, especially since I didn't have one at the moment. I had to admit, I'd spent more than a little time struggling to get to sleep regretting the abrupt no I'd given Wayne. I knew I was still right in theory, but a principle was tough to snuggle up to at night.

"I told you it wasn't like that at all," Lillian said. "We've decided to move on and see other people."

"And you both decided that?" I asked her pointedly.

"Well, I admit the idea was mine at first, but eventually he came around to my point of view. It did take quite a bit longer than I expected it to, though. That's why I'm so late." She hugged me, then said, "Two single women searching for romance, that's us."

"That's you," I corrected her gently. "I'm just looking for more customers."

"Then perhaps we'll both find what we're looking for."

I was getting hungry and starting to think about taking my lunch break when the front door opened. Mrs. Albright—the woman who had commissioned the wedding announcements for her daughter—came into the shop. She looked flustered and harried, and I couldn't imagine what was wrong this time.

"Mrs. Albright, are you ready to make some decisions about the wedding invitations?"

"I'm not at all certain there's even going to be a wedding at this point," she said, surprising us both with her candor. "That's why I came to see you."

"Hold on one second." I turned to my aunt. "Lillian, why don't you go ahead and take your lunch break."

"I'm not all that hungry," she said, watching the mother of the bride with a gleam in her eye.

"Still, I think that this would be a good time for you to take your break."

Lillian reluctantly agreed, though she frowned at me with great displeasure as she nodded her acceptance. "I'll be back in ten minutes," she said, daring me to try to keep her away any longer than that.

After my aunt was gone, I asked Mrs. Albright, "Have they decided not to marry after all?"

"Oh, they're getting married." She looked around the deserted shop and asked, "Ms. Sheen, may I speak candidly with you?"

"Of course," I said, ignoring the fact that she'd butchered my last name. "And it's Jennifer. I assure you, I'm very discreet." It was true, too. I'd always taken secrets shared with me very seriously ever since Vinola Ridge had blabbed about my crush on Kyle Day to him when we'd all been in the seventh grade. Kyle had laughed in her face and then he'd done the same thing to me. I still felt a twinge whenever I thought about that particular Day. Since then, I'd been careful about who I shared secrets with, and promised myself to keep any confidences entrusted to me.

"Jennifer, my daughter is under a bit of a deadline to hold the wedding in a timely fashion. After all, a gown can only cover so much." She hesitated, then added, "There are other considerations, as well."

So Anne Albright was going to be a grandmother, and from the expression on her face, it was coming a lot sooner than she'd hoped. "You can count on me. I can have the invitations done in a week. In fact, I'll work all weekend to make sure you have them as soon as humanly possible."

"My dear, I wasn't goading you into action. At least neither one of them has cold feet, though I'd have been wearing thermal socks if I were in their situation. No, I'm afraid it's more complicated than that."

"Is there anything I can do to help, anything at all?"

"I don't see how. I'm afraid Donna's maid of honor has met with an unfortunate accident. Jennifer, are you all right?"

I was many things at the moment, but "all right" was not anywhere on the list. I felt my stomach lurch, and I was glad I hadn't had a chance to eat anything yet. A great many things were falling into place, and none of them were good.

"You're talking about Tina Mast, aren't you?"

Mrs. Albright looked at me as if I'd slapped her. "How in the world did you ever know that?"

"My brother's the sheriff in Rebel Forge." I debated telling her that Tina had called me just before she'd died, but it was something I decided to keep to myself. "I'm curious. Did your daughter plan to come with you to the shop originally when you visited me the first time?"

"My dear, you must be absolutely psychic." She frowned, then added, "Donna was going to accompany me, but she changed her mind at the last minute. To be honest with you, we had a bit of a tiff, and she canceled in a huff. Something was going on between my daughter and Tina, and Donna was going to try to patch things up with her. She feels horrible about what happened, losing her best friend before they had a chance to make up. It's dreadful, really. But how could you possibly know about that?"

I couldn't lie to the woman outright, but I could shade the truth a little. "I just can't imagine a woman not choosing her own wedding invitations."

The explanation appeared to appease her. "Of course, that makes perfect sense. I'm doing my utmost to persuade Donna to go ahead with the wedding as quickly as possible, but I'm afraid she's fighting me on it. I understand her reluctance to celebrate a marriage with her friend dying so tragically, but as I keep telling her, we'll be celebrating another blessed event if we don't move quickly on this. Jennifer, how much time do you need to make up the invitations? Can you really do it in a week?"

"Do you still need four hundred?"

"No, I'm afraid we're going to have to pare that list considerably. I believe one hundred will be more than enough."

I tried not to let my disappointment show, since I'd been counting on a much larger check than I was going to get, but at least I was starting to get some walk-in business to supplement my income. "I can have them ready for you in four days," I said, hoping I wasn't stretching myself too thin. I'd never made cards in such massive quantities before, just doing a few now and then as the mood moved me. But this was my business now, my livelihood, so fun wasn't the primary consideration.

"That would work nicely." She pulled a piece of paper out of her purse. "Here, I've drawn up what I'm looking for. We can use the paper you showed me earlier, or anything you believe will look nice. You know my tastes. Can you really have these ready by next Monday?"

"I can, but I thought Donna wasn't sure about going ahead with it," I said as I took the notepaper from her. The first thing that caught my attention was that the wedding date was just eighteen days away. That didn't leave anybody involved in the festivities much time.

"She's not now, but she will be. I'll see to that."

I had visions of being left with a hundred handmade invitations that I couldn't use. "I'll need the balance before I begin," I said, trying to keep my voice level. "It's store policy." Well, it was now.

Mrs. Albright didn't even bat an eyelash. "Of course. Let me write you a check. Since I will be requiring fewer cards, I expect a discount."

"Of course," I said. "But you have to remember, the supplies are just a fraction of the total expense. You're paying for a creative design, and that's true whether you order a single card or a thousand."

"Yes, I understand that," she said.

"I can take ten percent off the total," I said, holding my breath, hoping she'd go for it.

As Mrs. Albright paid the balance, she asked, "Can you think of a unique place that would be suitable for the wedding? We're going to present this as a spur-of-the-moment lark to our friends. The real reason is that by the time we set something up formally, I'm afraid my grandchild would be able to be a guest at her parents' own wedding, and I will not allow that to happen."

I didn't doubt that for one instant. Mrs. Albright

was a force to be reckoned with, and I said a silent prayer for the groom. It would be bad enough to be raised under the woman's iron fist, but marrying into that family might be even worse. I had a feeling he was going to have the prototype for the original mother-in-law who had inspired all those jokes and terror.

She pressed me. "Do you know of such a place?"

"Are you looking for a church?"

Mrs. Albright scoffed. "There will be no church wedding, not under these circumstances. That's where I draw the line. Besides, they've been done to death. Never mind, I shouldn't have bothered asking you."

Probably not, I thought as I jotted a few ideas down on the back of a flier for the shop. I named a jutting point of land that overlooked the lake, in case the couple wanted an outdoor ceremony, and a topiary garden that I always thought would be perfect for weddings. I briefly considered adding the Putt Putt Palace to the list, but I knew better than to turn her scorn onto me. "You could always try these two places," I said as I handed her my thoughts.

"I appreciate your help, Jennifer. I'm counting on you to get those invitations done in time."

I glanced at the date she'd selected, and wondered how on earth she expected people to respond in time. A thought suddenly occurred to me. "We need to do RSVP cards, too. Do you have any ideas about that?"

"My dear, they can come or not; it's entirely up to them. Trust me, this will be fine."

I wondered if she had any intention of anyone showing up for her daughter's proud moment, but then I realized that could be the point. The invitations would announce the wedding to her friends without requiring them to attend. I had a hunch they were being issued for the presents that would surely follow as much as for legitimizing the ceremony and explaining the happy, healthy, "premature" baby that was sure to arrive in six or seven months.

"I'll get right on them," I said. "When would you like to see the first card so I can get your approval?"

"I don't have time for that," Mrs. Albright said. "I trust you'll do a good job."

After she was gone, Lillian came back into the shop. "I waited outside for her to leave so you wouldn't fuss at me. What was so confidential, Jennifer?"

Ignoring her question, I said, "I've got to have a hundred invitations ready in four days. Are you willing to help?"

"You know I am, but I'm the first one to admit that I'm not all that competent a card maker."

"Think of it as on-the-job training, then," I said, promising myself to make ten extra invitations so we could select the best hundred from the batch. I was trying to figure out the most efficient way to meet my deadline when the front door chimed again. I'd put the electric signal in to announce customers, but it was becoming a harbinger of trouble for me.

My visitor matched that description perfectly when I saw that Greg Langston had decided to visit my shop in person after all. Perfect, that was just what I needed—another complication in my life.

Chapter 7

"Greg, I'm really busy at the moment," I said, trying to convey the message that I didn't have time to deal with him.

"Yeah, I can see you're overwhelmed with customers."

I wanted to dispute his impression, but I couldn't do a thing about it. "Just because no one is here doesn't mean I'm not busy."

"You always were so good at expressing your opinions clearly and succinctly. Hey, Lillian."

"Hello, Greg. I can see you two would like some privacy, so I'll get out of your way." With that, she moved two steps back, still within easy eavesdropping range. For some odd reason, my silly aunt was grinning broadly. Oh, well, there was nothing I couldn't say to Greg in front of her.

I turned back to him and said, "I mean it. I really am busy."

His eyebrows arched, but he didn't comment again. "I won't keep you, then. I just wanted to know how long you've been dating Deputy Wayne behind my back."

"What? Have you lost your mind?"

"Don't deny it, Jennifer. I saw the two of you on your front porch last night. I don't know what kind of silly fantasy you were acting out in that ridiculous coat and wig, but I knew it was you."

I was speechless. There were so many things I wanted

to address I literally couldn't figure out where to start. "Greg Langston, have you been stalking me?"

"No, of course not." He looked sheepish about something. "I just happened to be passing by."

"Of course, I'm just seven miles out of the way between your pottery shop and your apartment, but you 'just happened' to be in my neighborhood."

"Don't avoid the question," he said sternly.

"Which one? None of them are true." I ticked them off on my fingers, which were perilously close to his nose. "I am not dating Wayne. Even if I were having the affair of the century with him, it wouldn't be any of your business. I wasn't acting out anything." I thought about explaining to him that I'd been hiding my identity from a killer, but I was too mad to go into it. Then suddenly it dawned on me. "Bradford put you up to it, didn't he?"

"I don't know what you're talking about." He broke eye contact with me, a sure sign that he was lying.

"Don't bother denying it. My brother thinks that I'm in need of protection. Why he called you I'll never know."

"I'll tell you why he asked me to watch out for you. He knows that I still care about you, Jennifer, and I don't want to see you throwing your life away on somebody like Deputy Wayne."

"You mean instead of somebody like you?" I snapped, being a little snippier than I'd meant to sound.

"You could do a lot worse," he said, then threw his hands up. "Forget it—this isn't worth it."

"I couldn't agree with you more." As he stormed out, Greg did his level best to slam my front door, but the shock absorber on it was brand-new, and it merely whispered shut. Loaded for bear and ready for a fight, I glanced over at Lillian. "Is there something you'd like to add to the conversation?" I asked her.

"Me? I sincerely doubt it," she said.

"Good. Now let's get started making some wedding invitations."

"She's certainly given you a lot of leeway, hasn't she?" Lillian said as I went through my stock searching for a paper that would please Anne Albright. I chose a white paper I'd made myself with flecks of gold glitter in it; different enough for her tastes but traditional enough for a wedding announcement. I handed the stock to Lillian and said, "We need these cut into sheets that are five and a half inches by eleven. Can you handle that while I gather the rest of the supplies together?"

"Certainly," Lillian said. "Should I use regular scissors or that craft knife I used before? Or do you have a special tool for me?"

I grabbed a stationery paper cutter and handed it to her. "Use this." I took one of the full sheets, carefully marked the different cut lines for her, then said, "Use this as a template. You'll be able to get the most invitations per page this way. Don't throw the excess away. We'll use that later."

"Yes, Ma'am. And what happens if a customer happens to wander into the shop?"

I thought about shutting down so I could meet my deadline, but I really couldn't afford to turn any potential customers away. "I'll handle the foot traffic. You just focus on making those cuts."

Lillian nodded, then took the cutter and sheets to the table we'd worked at before. I said, "Would you mind working in the back on my bench? I need to be up front where I can wait on customers."

"Do you think it is wise for you to work in the window like that? You're awfully exposed."

"Lillian, if the killer wants to get me, there's not much I can do about it, but I won't let myself be driven into a hole to avoid her."

She nodded. "I knew what your answer would be, but I still felt obligated to ask. If you need me, just call."

With Lillian in back cutting the blanks, I started playing with design ideas based on what I knew of the mother of the bride. It wasn't the ideal situation for me, but I didn't have much choice, and there was no way I was returning the full fee just because my guidelines were looser than I'd hoped. I grabbed a few of my nicest pencils and some plain typing paper, then sat down at my table with Mrs. Albright's crib sheet and got started. I didn't know whether to be happy about it or not, but not a single customer interrupted my work. I played with a dozen different designs. Paper flowers always enhanced a formal card, and I often used a technique called quilling for wrapping spirals out of strips of paper to create teardrop petals, but I needed something different, something with real snap. I played with the idea of bells, tuxedos and wedding gowns on the front, then searched through my collection of stamps and even looked at the manufactured accessories I used on some of my cards, but nothing grabbed me. I wasn't beat yet, though.

"Lillian, I'm going out for a few minutes. Could you watch the front?"

She came out with a partially cut sheet in one hand. "Should you go anywhere alone? I'd be happy to accompany you."

"Then who's going to wait on our customers?" Before she could make a crack about that, I added, "If we should get any?"

"Honestly, Jennifer, do you actually think I'd be able to help anyone if they did come in? I know next to nothing about making cards."

"I'm not asking you to give private lessons. You can run a cash register, and the prices are marked on everything. If you get something you can't handle, tell them to hang around or come back later."

I left before she could raise any more objections. It was a short walk to the place I used as a secret storehouse for my card supplies. Farrar Hardware had the neatest selection of doodads in town, and I wasn't above using something I found there in one of my own designs.

"Hey, Grady," I said as I walked into the ancient building with its scarred hardwood floors. The light fixtures hanging from the ceiling had been there since before I'd been born. The owner, Mr. Grady Farrar, was an older man with a full head of silver hair and a quick comment on just about everything.

"Jennifer Shane, you didn't close your business already, did you?"

"Thanks for that vote of confidence," I said as I smiled. "My aunt's watching the store for me."

"And what does Miss Lillian know about card making?"

"She's learning," I said.

Grady laughed. "So the saying about teaching an old dog must be wrong."

"I'm going to tell her you said that."

Grady blanched slightly. "Now you know I was just teasing you. You wouldn't say anything to her, would you?"

"Of course not." I knew firsthand how acidic my aunt's tongue could be, and Grady was too nice a man to be on the receiving end of it.

"Bless your heart. So what can I help you with this fine day?"

"I'm not really sure," I said as I rummaged through some of the drawers near the register. Grady's place had been in the family for over a hundred years, and I doubted the man himself had any idea about what all he had in stock. "I'm doing wedding invitations for a customer."

He held up a shotgun shell. "How about using one of these on every card?"

He was smiling about it, but it was a little too close to the real situation for me. "No, I need something unexpected."

"Well, help yourself. If you need a hand, just ask, and if you need a price, I'll make one up right on the spot for you."

I kept browsing, searching for something that would give the cards an edge. After twenty minutes I was about to give up when I passed the aisle stocked with screws, nuts and bolts. On one of the bottom shelves, I found a box of brass fittings no bigger than a quarter that looked like gold wedding bands. "Do you have any thin brass wire?" I asked him.

"Got all kinds," Grady said as he led me to an area with picture-framing supplies on it.

I grabbed a roll of wire and put it on the counter next to the brass fittings. "What do I owe you?" I asked.

"Let's see," Grady said as he made a few of his chicken scratches on the back of a brown paper bag. "I think five bucks should do it."

"Are you sure? I don't want to cheat you."

Grady said, "Young lady, don't ever doubt I'll charge you all the market will allow."

I laughed and grabbed the bag as I threw a five on the counter. "I need a receipt, please."

He turned another bag over and jotted down my receipt. "Don't you have something a little less casual?" I asked.

"That blamed cash register is busted again, so that will have to do. Government doesn't mind, just as long as it's signed and dated, and I took care of that already."

"That's great, thanks."

As I raced for the door, Grady said, "Come back soon."

"You know it."

Lillian was waiting in the doorway when I got back to the Three Cs. "What is it?" I asked her as I brushed past. "Is something wrong?"

"You took an awfully long time, Jennifer. I was just about to call your brother."

That was all I needed, another episode with Bradford attracting all of the wrong kind of attention to my shop. "I'm glad you didn't. It took me longer than I thought to find what I was looking for."

She gestured to the small bag in my hand. "And you believe you found it?"

"There's only one way to find out." I went back to the table, moved my drawings out of the way, then retrieved a pair of small pliers and a hole punch. Folding a piece of card stock into thirds, I attached sections of wire to each of the front doors of the card, threading a brass fitting as I worked. A touch of hot glue to keep the pieces firmly in place, and I had a card I could work with. "So what do you think?" I asked Lillian as I handed the card to her.

"But it's blank inside," she said as she opened the doors of the card.

"Of course it's blank. I'm fast, but I'm not that fast. Besides, I'm not sure what kind of card I want it to be yet. I'm talking about the design on front."

"That? Why, it's lovely. A little modern, though, isn't it? It looks a little industrial to me."

"Good, that's exactly what I was going for. Now, what color pen should I use for the calligraphy? Would gold be too common?"

Lillian tapped the card with her fingers. "Don't you think a fancy script inside would be a bit jarring with this exterior? I should think you'd want something a little starker, don't you?"

I hugged my aunt, and she asked, "What was that for?"

"For having a great idea. Why don't you search through the fonts we have on the computer, and when you find something close to what you have in mind, I'll use it for the cards."

"You mean you're going to print the invitations out on your computer?"

"Well, I could hand-letter all one hundred, but she needs them in four days, and my arm would fall off before I could manage that. Don't worry; I have a good idea about what I'm going to do."

"You're the one in charge," she said. "I finished cutting the stock just before you got back. I thought she wanted a hundred even. Why are we making more?"

"There's always a chance we won't like our first

few," I said. "And besides, I want to be able to pick our best efforts for her. I'm a little nervous about my first paying job here."

"You'll do fine," Lillian said. "After all, you've got the best assistant in town. Now I'll just go find that font."

I started marking and folding the cards, happy with my choices. I just hoped Mrs. Albright would be satisfied. While I wanted Donna to be pleased, it was just as important to me that the bride's mother was happy with the results, too. One bad bit of word-of-mouth could probably kill my shop so soon after opening.

Lillian found a font we both agreed on, and we were busy tweaking the design when my aunt said, "Look at the time. We should have locked up an hour ago. I just realized something. You worked straight through your lunch, Jennifer."

My stomach rumbled at the mention of lunch, and I realized she was right. That happened sometimes when I was absorbed in a new project. "I'll grab something later. We're making real progress here."

Lillian said, "Still, you have to eat something. What time is your class tonight?"

"What class?" I asked absently as I played with the wording inside the invitation.

"The class you're teaching, young lady."

I'd forgotten all about my private lesson scheduled for later that evening. "I don't have time to eat," I yelped as I started gathering the materials together to clear the worktable in front of the shop.

"Nonsense, there's always time for that," she said as she helped me. "Here's what we'll do. You have forty-five minutes before your new pupil is due to arrive. You set up for your class, and I'll pick up something for you to eat. What would you like?"

"A burger would be fine," I said absently as I kept cleaning the table.

"You need more than that. How about a salad to go along with it?"

"Fine, whatever. I have to get this ready."

As Lillian started to go, she said, "Now don't forget, you need to lock the door behind me."

"I won't forget," I said as I dragged a rag across the table to shove any leftover remnants into the trash can.

"Lock it now, Jennifer," she said, "or I'm not going."

"Fine, I'll do it. Just go."

She walked out the door, then lingered on the steps until I locked the door as instructed. I stuck my tongue out at her, which she returned; then she finally walked down Oakmont, no doubt going to HamSmith's. Hamilton Smith ran a boutique grill on our block, offering everything from salmon to my favorite hamburgers in the world. By the time Lillian got back with the food, I had the supplies laid out for my first lesson with ten minutes to spare.

I peeked in the bag. "Hey, there's way too much food in here."

"I thought I'd join you. I skipped lunch, too, remember? You don't mind, do you?"

"I'd be delighted," I said. "Get enough out of the cash drawer to pay yourself back, okay?"

She waved a hand in the air, dismissing me. "It's not important."

As hungry as I was and as great as that hamburger smelled, I pushed it away from me on the counter.

Lillian asked, "Is there something wrong with the food?"

"There surely is."

"What is it?" she asked. "I ordered your usual."

"I'm sure the food's fine. The problem is that I didn't pay for it. It's bad enough that I can't afford to pay you for your work here, but I draw the line at accepting your handouts."

Lillian's eyes sparked. "For heaven's sakes, don't be so pigheaded. I want to do this. Let me treat you to lunch or dinner, or whatever this is."

I had to wonder if I was just being stubborn, if I could afford to stand on principle when I didn't have the money to back it up. "I'll make you a deal," I said as my mouth started to water. "I'll let you pay for this if you let me buy lunch tomorrow." I'd have a check from my student tonight to cover lunch the next day.

"That sounds lovely. Now eat your food before it gets cold."

"Yes, Ma'am," I said as I bit into the hamburger. I surprised myself by finishing my salad, too, though I normally wasn't big on leafy greens. It was amazing how hunger could make just about anything taste good. I shoved the wrappers and containers into my bag and threw it into the big trash can. "That was great. Thanks."

"You're most welcome." Lillian had skipped ordering a burger and was still pecking away at her salad. That woman made an event out of every meal, making it stretch as long as possible. I was more of a grab-and-go kind of gal myself.

There was a tap on the front door, and I fully expected to see Melinda standing there.

Instead, it was Greg, and from the sour look on his face, it appeared that he was back for round two.

HANDCRAFTED CARD-MAKING TIP

Charms can be successfully used on handcrafted cards to make them really stand out. Not only do they give each card a personal touch, but the recipient can add your contribution to her bracelet after she's enjoyed your card, and think of you every time she looks at it.

Chapter·8

"What are you, some kind of glutton for punishment?" I asked as I unlocked the door.

Greg brought one of his hands out from behind his back. He offered the roses to me with a contrite look on his face. "I'm sorry."

I just couldn't blast him again, not with that hurt-puppy look in his eyes. But I wasn't about to let him off the hook that easy, either. "What are you sorry about?" I asked, not taking the flowers from him.

"Let's see, let's start with my attitude earlier, and the way I jumped to the wrong conclusions. How's that?"

"Surely you can think of more to add to that list, can't you?"

Lillian spoke up behind me. "Don't be so hard on him, Jennifer. He's offering to make peace."

Without turning, I said, "Don't you have something you need to be doing right now?"

"Oh nonsense," she said, but I could hear her move away.

"Go on," I said to Greg. "I'm still listening."

"What else do you want me to apologize for? I said I was sorry."

I frowned at him. "How about for spying on me?"

He lowered the flowers. "That's one thing I'm not sorry about at all. I agree with Bradford. As long as a killer is on the loose in Rebel Forge and you could be the next target, I'm going to do everything in my power to keep you safe, and if that includes lurking outside your apartment at night, then so be it."

"When is everyone going to get it? I don't need any help."

"You don't know what you need," he said as he thrust the flowers into my chest. "Here, take them."

Before I could say another word, he was gone. I knew I'd been a little too hard on him, but I hadn't been able to help myself. Greg had a tough time apologizing about anything, and I'd ground him down pretty good, but it was the only way I could be sure he got the message. Once upon a time I would have meekly accepted his offering without hesitation, but I'd lived and learned since then. If he was truly sorry, he was going to have to do better than he had so far. I considered throwing the flowers away, but they were too pretty to just toss into the trash can, and besides, I loved roses. It wasn't fair to them. I grabbed a vase, arranged the flowers, then put them by the cash register. Lillian came out of the back just as I finished.

"So you came to your senses and accepted them," she said, smiling.

"I took the flowers, but not the apology."

Lillian started to say something, but from the look on her face, it was pretty obvious she changed her mind at the last second. Once I was sure she was content to leave it alone, I said, "You can go home now. There's no reason to hang around, because I don't know how long the lesson's going to last."

"And leave you here alone with a stranger?" she said. "Your brother would have my hide. I think I'll stay in back until you're ready to go home."

I felt my blood pressure spiking. "Now don't you start with me. I won't have it!"

"Jennifer, I have an idea. What if I stay, but for a completely different reason? I need to learn to make cards as quickly as possible if I'm going to be of any use to you at all. May I audit your lesson tonight?"

I frowned and considered it. "If it weren't such a good idea, I'd refuse on general principles. Tell me something, Lillian. I know I drafted you into doing this, but do you really want to help me here at the shop? It's not that I don't love your company, but I feel guilty forcing you to work with me here, especially since I can't even afford to pay you."

"Dear, sweet Jennifer, there is nowhere I'd rather be. If we're being honest with each other, I'm not certain I have your passion for handcrafted cards, but I do feel it's possible I'll develop it. What we've done so far has been fun, but I need more experience before I can decide if this is how I want to spend my time. Is that a fair answer to your question?"

I hugged her, then said, "It's the best one you could give. In that case, I'd be delighted to have you join us here tonight."

There was a knock on the front door, and I saw that my student had finally arrived. I said, "I'll let Melinda in, and you gather up more supplies from the back so you can join us."

After I let Melinda in, I was going to tell her about Lillian joining us when I noticed her eyes were red. "Is everything all right?"

"I'm sorry I'm late, Jennifer," she said.

"I don't give a flip about that, but I can see that you've been crying."

She dabbed at her eyes. "I thought I would be all right, but I'm not all that certain this is a good idea."

"Tell me what's wrong. I'm a good listener." The woman was obviously distraught about something, and if I could help her, I would. I hated seeing anyone in pain.

"A young woman I was very fond of is dead." She blurted it out, then covered her face with her hands.

"Are you talking about Tina Mast?" I asked as I patted her shoulder.

She jerked her hands from her face. "How did you know that?"

"My brother's the sheriff," I said, trotting out the

same tired old excuse I'd used before. It was a nice little generalization that didn't come close to explaining the entire truth about my involvement in the situation, but it seemed to satisfy everyone I gave it to, so who was I to mess with perfection? "So how did you know Tina?"

"She was a friend of my son's. Tina was set to be the maid of honor at Larry's wedding. Now I'm not even certain there's going to be one."

"He's the young man marrying Donna Albright. I didn't know you were the groom's mother."

Melinda said, "Now you're scaring me."

"I'm doing the wedding invitations. I just never put you together with the groom, that's all. As far as the wedding going forward, Anne Albright was here this afternoon, and she ordered a hundred invitations. I'm working on them right now."

Melinda shook her head. "That woman is determined that this wedding is going to occur, but I'm not so sure it's the best idea for everyone involved."

"Have you talked to your son about it?" I asked. Out of the corner of my eye, I saw that Lillian was listening to every word from the back room.

"He swears he wants to go through with it, but I honestly believe that if he had the opportunity to back out, he would in a heartbeat."

"I understand there's a time constraint involved," I said. Boy, that was a euphemism if ever there was one.

Melinda nodded. "You'd think that Anne would want to keep that news to herself. Yes, there's a pregnancy rushing matters, but we're in the twenty-first century. I don't necessarily approve of having children without the benefit of marriage, but a forced union can be worse than none at all. At least that's what I keep trying to tell everyone. No one's listening, though." That brought another trickle of tears, which were banished immediately. "I'm sorry. I really would love a lesson, but I'm afraid I'd be useless tonight. May we do it another time?"

"Of course. Just let me know and I'll be happy to reschedule."

After she was gone, Lillian came out of the store-room. "Well, imagine that."

"It does seem we're involved in this up to our eye-brows, doesn't it?"

Lillian said, "I just can't help wondering if Anne Albright and her daughter are the only ones who are pushing for this wedding to go on."

"I'm not even certain the bride wants it. She's never even bothered to come by to check on the invitations to her own wedding. That's rather telling, isn't it?"

"Perhaps she's too busy picking out her nursery fur-niture," Lillian said. "So, should we have our lesson anyway?"

I stifled a yawn. "Sure. Just give me a minute to regroup."

"Nonsense, you're exhausted. Why don't we save it for later? I know enough right now to help you with the invitations, and I can pick up the rest as we go along. Besides, there's no need for you to have to teach the same class twice in a row."

"Are you sure? It's true that I am worn-out, but I promised you."

"And I'm relieving you of that promise. Honestly, there's plenty I can do instead. I have an idea. Why don't we go out and see what mischief two single women in Rebel Forge can get themselves into? It might be nice to put our troubles behind us."

I considered going out carousing with my aunt, but we'd spent the entire day together, and as much as I loved her company, I was badly in need of some soli-tary time. "Could I take a rain check? I'm beat, and there's some paperwork here that I really need to catch up on before I go home."

"I can stay with you until you finish it," she said.

"Come on, go have some fun. I'll be fine here. I promise, I'll be careful going home. Besides, do you think for one second that my self-appointed body-guards are going to leave me alone? Go, you deserve a night out on the town."

Was that a glimmer of relief in her eyes? It looked like her offer to stay had been out of politeness more than a desire for my company, but I wasn't about to say anything. She said, "Jennifer, you may cash your rain check at any time. Good night, then."

When I let her out, I half expected to find my brother or Greg waiting outside the door, but Oakmont was deserted. I wasn't sure if I was relieved by the discovery, or uneasy. I'd been proclaiming my self-sufficiency to everyone in sight, but now that I was alone, I was having second thoughts. I hated the feeling of vulnerability, that I couldn't handle everything myself, and I resented the fact that the killer had stolen my confidence from me. I was going to have to buck up and handle it if I was the grown woman I kept telling everyone I was. I worked through the bills, sadly gazing at the dwindling balance in my card shop's checkbook. Business was slow—I'd known it would be—but seeing the steady decline on paper was more than I could bear. I decided to get out of there and forget about the Three Cs for a while. As I locked my front door, I saw someone standing in the shadows across from my shop. There was no streetlight close by, so I couldn't even tell if it was a man or a woman. I couldn't help wondering whether it was someone watching over me or someone meaning me harm. I clutched my purse to my chest as I hurried off to my car, hoping that the watcher wouldn't follow me. As I walked fast to the Gremlin, I swore if I ever got out of this I'd get some Mace or something to defend myself with. A gun was out of the question; I hated the things, and was never really comfortable with my brother's carrying one around all the time. But I didn't have any problems spraying chemicals into someone's eyes if he was coming after me.

I was ten feet from the Gremlin, my keys in my hand, when I felt an arm grab me from behind. "Suzanne, where are you going?"

I whirled around to face a homeless man, his clothes dirty and his face smudged. He was huge, over six and a half feet tall, and he must have weighed three hundred pounds. I tried to break free of his grip, but it was like steel.

"I'm not Suzanne," I said, fighting to keep my voice calm.

The pressure on my arm was suddenly harder. "Don't lie to me, Suzanne. You know I won't take that from you."

"Will you let go of me if I admit that I am Suzanne?" I thought about hitting him with my purse, but I wasn't sure what kind of damage I could do to him.

His grip didn't ease. "What kind of a game are you playing? You're going to see him, aren't you?"

I could smell the liquor on his breath, overpowering even the stench from his clothing. "I don't know what you're talking about," I said.

"You're lying." He pulled back his free hand, forming it into a fist.

That was all I could take. "Let go of my arm, you jerk." I shouted it in his face, close enough to blow his straggly hair. My words snapped his neck back like a blow.

"You're not Suzanne, are you?" he asked, his voice clearly mystified.

"That's what I've been trying to tell you." My temper was out in full force. "Now let go of my arm before I make you sorry you ever tangled with me."

He pulled his hand away and I was free. Without hesitating an instant, I jammed my key into the Gremlin's lock and jumped inside. When I was safely away, I pulled over to the side of the road until my nerves settled down. Then I dialed Bradford's cell number.

He answered on the second ring. I said, "So much

for your watchdog patrols on me. Somebody just came after me."

"What happened? Are you all right?"

"I'm fine," I said, suddenly very sorry I'd called him. Here I'd been complaining about too much surveillance, and now I was whining because nobody had been there when I'd needed them. Nice consistent behavior there, Jennifer. "It was just some homeless guy. He shook me up."

"So Frank's still around."

"You know him?" I asked.

"Was it a big man, maybe six six? He weighs a ton, too."

"That was him. What's his story?"

Bradford hesitated, then said, "I probably shouldn't tell you this, but he was dumped out of a mental hospital in Richmond and he somehow made his way to Rebel Forge. You know, when we found Tina Mast's body, I had a thought that Frank might have done it, but he was in the shelter at the Presbyterian church all night. He's an ex-marine, and he knows how to kill in more ways than I can even imagine."

"You mean he's capable of murder?" That was great. My safe little mountain town was suddenly turning out to be a dangerous place to live.

"That's what he was in the hospital for. I heard he was committed for killing his wife after he found out she was having an affair with his best friend."

I nearly dropped the phone. "Let me guess. His wife's name was Suzanne, wasn't it?"

Bradford hesitated, then said, "Yeah, I think that's right. What happened?"

"He grabbed me before I could get to my car, and he kept calling me Suzanne."

"What did you do? Why didn't Wayne step in?"

"So it was his night to watch me? Well, your deputy dropped the ball; he was nowhere in sight." Wayne had probably been too embarrassed to face me after I'd blown off his request for a date.

"I'll have his badge for that," Bradford said.

"Was he on the town clock, or was he doing you a favor?" I asked.

"He was off duty, but that doesn't matter. A promise is a promise."

"Bradford, you can't fire him for that, and you know it. Besides, I handled it fine myself."

"What did you do?"

"I screamed at him," I reluctantly admitted.

"And that worked? You were lucky, Jennifer."

I swear, my brother never would learn, but I decided to let that one slide. After all, he was probably right. "So what are you going to do about him?"

"Well, I guess I should hear what he has to say for himself. You're right, I can't fire him. But I can surely make him wish he was working for somebody else."

"I'm not talking about Wayne, you nitwit. I'm talking about Frank."

I could hear the weight in Bradford's voice. "He threatened you, so I've got to take action. I was kind of hoping he'd move along, but I've got to step in now."

"What are you going to do to him?" As frightened as I'd been in the middle of the confrontation, I wasn't sure I wanted some stranger locked up because of me, even if he was delusional.

"I've got to arrest him. Then I'll let the courts decide what to do with him."

"What if I don't press charges?"

Bradford snapped, "You're willing to take that kind of chance with the next woman he goes after? Do you really want that on your head? Besides, if he's in the system again, maybe they'll be able to do him some good this time."

"Do what you have to, but I don't necessarily have to like it," I said.

"Little Sister, you'd be amazed at how many times I don't like parts of my job description. Listen, I've got to take care of this right now. Are you going to be okay?"

"I'm fine. Sorry to have bothered you, Bradford."

"Hey, I'm here to protect everybody I can, including my baby sister."

I drove home, unsettled by what had happened. I hated the idea of anybody's being locked up in a cell, but I knew in my heart that that was exactly where some people belonged. I wouldn't hesitate to throw Tina Mast's murderer in prison, so why should I draw the line there? The world was a strangely complex place, and the more time I spent in it, the more confusing it became. It amazed me how the black-and-white distinctions of my teens and early twenties were getting grayer by the minute. Maybe it was a good thing that it wasn't all left up to me.

By the time I got home, I found Wayne sitting on the staircase outside my apartment.

"Listen," he said before I could say a word, "I dropped the ball tonight, and I'm sorry. It won't happen again. I promise."

"You don't owe me any explanations," I said.

"According to my boss, I do. I was gone maybe three minutes, but when I got back the lights were off and you weren't around. I didn't know what else to do, so I drove over here to wait for you."

I felt sorry for him, knowing how my brother must have chewed him out. "Don't sweat it. I'm fine."

He grinned slightly. "From the way I heard it, you did more than fine. I wouldn't be eager to tackle Frank with a stun gun and a net."

Suddenly I was tired, of Wayne and the rest of the world. "Good night."

Without even looking back, I stepped inside my apartment and locked the door behind me. I hated that my entrance to my apartment was outside. Oggie was waiting for me by the door—at least it looked that way—but the second I put my keys on the table, he turned his tail up and stalked off. It was almost as if it were his birthday and I'd shown up without a gift. That cat was nuts—there was no doubt about it—but that didn't stop me from loving him. Nash came in and rubbed against my legs. I picked him up, and a few minutes of stroking his fur did more for my nerves than two drinks and a hot bath. I released my grip on him and he dropped to the floor like he was on strings. Oggie popped his head around the corner and mewed, announcing that he was ready to eat, no doubt.

After I fed my roommates, I tried to decide what to do next. There were a thousand things on my mind, but I couldn't come up with a single action I could take to help with any of them, so I popped in *While You Were Sleeping*—my all-time favorite movie—made some popcorn and settled in for the night.

At least that had been my plan.

Chapter 9

I almost didn't answer my door when I heard the pounding knock a few hours later. My movie had just ended, and what I wanted more than anything in the world was to put the day behind me and just relax before I went to bed. I knew if it was my brother out there and I didn't answer his summons in about twenty seconds, he'd have the SWAT team there before I could say "Boo." I turned the outside light on and looked through my peephole out onto the landing. When I saw who was standing there, I decided the full police force of Rebel Forge would have been more welcome than this particular guest.

"What is that?" I said to Sara Lynn as I opened the door.

"It's my suitcase," she said as she brushed past me and walked into my apartment uninvited.

"I hope that means you're collecting old clothes for the Salvation Army."

Sara Lynn sniffed the air. "If you won't come stay with me, I'm going to move in here with you."

"You've been sniffing too much spray adhesive at your shop. There is no way I need another roommate." Another thought occurred to me. "What's your husband think about all of this?"

"Bailey didn't get a voice in the matter," Sara Lynn said as she moved toward my smaller second bedroom. I knew I should have gotten a studio apartment. The best way to be sure I didn't have houseguests, welcome or not, was to make sure there was nowhere for them to sleep.

"He might not get a say, but I do," I said, grabbing the edge of her suitcase before she could unpack.

Sara Lynn tried to tug it out of my grip, but I was holding on for all I was worth. I added, "Listen, Sis, it's not that I don't appreciate the gesture, but this place is kind of small for one person. Throw in two cats and with one more body here, we'll be stepping all over each other."

"Nonsense," Sara Lynn said. "I think it will be cozy." She tugged her suitcase again and it slipped out of my hands. With a look of smug satisfaction she went into the spare bedroom and laid it on the dresser. Oggie and Nash were both on the guest bed, staking out their territory. At least they were on my side.

Sara Lynn looked at them, raised one eyebrow and scowled. The cowards both leaped off the bed and scampered out the door, no doubt taking up residence on my bed in the other room. Sara Lynn smoothed the comforter with her hand, then sat on the edge of the bed. "This will be perfect."

"Come on, I'm a grown woman. I don't need a babysitter."

"Bradford and I disagree." Her features softened for a moment. "Jennifer, you shouldn't be alone until our brother catches this killer. There's strength in numbers."

"What are you going to do if somebody breaks in? I'm bigger than you are," I said flatly. It was ludicrous that my sister, nearly a foot shorter and sixty pounds lighter, would be able to spring to my defense.

"Size isn't everything, Jennifer." She unzipped her bag, and I wondered if there was any room left for her clothes after I spied the arsenal inside. Sara Lynn rummaged through her collection and handed me a canister on a key chain. "That's Mace. You should keep that with you at all times."

"Is that a stun gun?" I asked, peering into her bag.

"It is," she said proudly. "I make the bank deposits for my store every night. You'd better believe that I'm fully prepared for anything that might come my way. I've got passive defenses in here, and some more aggressive ones, too." She pulled out a doorstop and something the size of a tennis ball on a looped wire.

"I'm not even sure I want to know what you're going to do with those."

Sara Lynn walked out past me, and I was tempted to stay behind to check out the rest of her arsenal, but I had to see what she was up to. As she nudged the wedge under the front door, she said, "This is the cheapest and easiest way to keep someone from coming in through the door." She hung the ball on the inside doorknob and explained, "If they happen to get through it, though, this ball senses vibrations, and if the door moves a fraction of an inch, it lets off the most awful shrieking you've ever heard in your life. Now let's have a look at your windows."

After Sara Lynn made her security sweep of my apartment, she said, "There, now don't you feel better?"

I wasn't about to admit that it would be nice having her there with me. "I feel like I'm in jail," I said.

"Better there than in the ground. Do you need the bathroom, or can I grab a quick shower?"

"Be my guest," I said. After I got her a fresh towel and washcloth, she started for the bathroom, then hesitated at the door. "Oh, and don't go snooping into my bag while I'm gone. There are things in there that bite."

"Please, that thought never crossed my mind." Blast it, she'd known exactly what I was going to do before I did. That was the trouble with being around someone who had known me my entire life.

I walked back into my bedroom and saw both cats curled up on my pillows. "A fat lot of help you two were. You caved the second she looked at you."

Both of them continued to ignore me, a condition that was more status quo than anything. They'd taken the forced relocation without the slightest protest, and I wondered if Oggie and Nash were trying to tell me something. No, most likely they were just responding to Sara Lynn's forceful personality. Sometimes I gave my cats too much credit for their behavior. As I sat down on the edge of my bed, both of them came over to me and nestled into my lap. As I stroked them, I heard the dual humming of their purrs, and despite my agitated mood, I had to admit that I did feel better having them there with me. By the time Sara Lynn got out of the shower, I'd resigned myself to having my sister as a temporary roommate. She was blow-drying her hair when I walked to the bathroom door. I started to say something, but she held up one hand, signaling for me to wait until she was finished. I reached over and pulled the plug out of the outlet, and her dryer died instantly.

"What's so urgent?" Sara Lynn said, watching the plug, which was still in my hand.

"We need to get a few things straight. As much as I love you, you are an uninvited guest, so I expect you to do things my way or you can go home to your husband. I'm not sure how long you can stay, but when I say it's time for you to go home, you go, no arguments and no fights. Okay?"

"You won't even know I'm here," Sara Lynn said as she pulled the plug out of my hands. I wasn't sure how it would be having my sister staying with me, but it didn't look like I was going to have much choice in the matter. Later, with all the lights out and my bedroom door shut, I could still feel her presence with me. If I was being honest with myself, I had to admit that it was a nice feeling. I just hoped she didn't have to stay long. I valued my privacy above most things in my life, and I'd grown used to living on my own.

*   *   *

The next morning, I woke up to the smell of waffles wafting into my bedroom from the kitchen. Grabbing a robe, I walked out, rubbing the sleep from my eyes.

"Morning," I mumbled. "That smells great."

"Sit down and have one while it's hot," Sara Lynn said. She was already dressed for work and was bustling around in my kitchen like it was hers.

"Was that in your suitcase, too?" I asked as I pointed to the waffle maker.

"Bailey and I bought it for you as a housewarming present when you first moved in here," she said. "I found it in your hall closet, still in its box."

"So that's where it was," I said. Sara Lynn had even heated the syrup on the stove top, just like Mom had always done. I took one bite, then decided that having a roommate might not be such a bad thing after all. "You're up pretty early," I said.

"After we finish breakfast, I'm going by the house before I open the shop. I have a few more things to get that I didn't bring with me last night."

"That doesn't sound good," I said, despite the golden treat I was eating. "You're not moving in to stay."

"Jennifer, it hardly makes sense for me to scramble back and forth every time I need something."

"Look at it this way," I said after swallowing another bite. "It will give you and your husband a chance to see each other every morning. I'm sure he misses you already."

"You're kidding, right? If I know Bailey, he's already been to the doughnut shop, no doubt coming home with a dozen different treats. That man would wallow in sugar and lard if I let him."

"So you should be there with him to protect his health," I said. I took another bite, and my argument for my sister's eviction was growing weaker by the moment. I'd forgotten what a good cook she'd become, and if Sara Lynn stayed too long, I'd have to start jogging again so I could fit into my clothes.

"He'll be fine on his own for a while," she said. "In fact, it might do him some good to realize how much I do for him."

I didn't want to go there, not for a second. Both my siblings had married spouses that I got along with, but if the positions were reversed and I'd been forced to stay with one of them, I think I would have checked in at the Rebel's Call Motel downtown.

Sara Lynn grabbed a plate, popped a freshly made waffle on it, then sat down beside me. "I cooked, so you get to do dishes."

"I knew there was a catch," I said, though honestly I didn't mind doing them, not if I was going to feast like this.

"So what would you like tonight?" she asked.

"I thought I'd grab something on the way home," I said. "What do you feel like, Chinese or Italian?"

"I feel like a home-cooked meal, Jennifer. Don't concern yourself; I'll pick up some groceries on the way back here after work. Isn't it convenient that you already gave me a key to your apartment?"

I'd done it so she could take care of Oggie and Nash on the few occasions I left town, but I'd never meant for it to be a permanent thing. "Just don't get too used to it. Like I said, this is just temporary."

She waved a hand in the air, dismissing my comment like she was shooing away a gnat. After we finished eating, Sara Lynn said, "I'm going to go, but I'll see you this evening. If you need anything in the meantime, let me know."

"I will," I said as I watched my sister disarm her apartment defenses.

Once she was gone, I stretched and decided to do the dishes before I took my shower. It was quick work, and before long I was ready to start my day. Going to my car, I saw a figure standing across the way watching me. My heart stuttered until I recognized Wayne's pickup truck parked at the end of the lot. I wondered if he'd been out there all night doing penance for losing me the night before.

Bradford was at the shop waiting for me. I pointedly ignored him as I brushed past him on the sidewalk and unlocked my front door. He said, "Hey, why the cold shoulder?"

"How would you like it if Sara Lynn came to your house to stay, unannounced and uninvited?" I said.

"If she cooked for me, I could probably learn to live with it."

"That's not funny, Bradford. Between the two of you, I don't have a minute to myself. Oh, and stop punishing Wayne. He was still outside my door this morning keeping a lookout."

"Are you sure about that?"

"I saw his truck, and he was in the bushes right across from my apartment. You should teach your deputies how to stake someone out better, Bradford."

My brother shook his head. "Maybe I did come down on him a little harder than I should have. I told him to go home last night at midnight."

"Great, so now he's stalking me."

Bradford said, "I sincerely doubt that. Don't worry; I'll have a talk with him."

"I think you've done entirely too much talking, big brother. Did you arrest Frank last night?"

Bradford scratched his chin. "I would have if I could have found him. He wasn't in any of his normal hangouts, and they hadn't seen him at the shelter, either."

I remembered the icy steel grip of his hand on my arm. "Do you think he's after me, too?"

"No, chances are, he hitched a ride and left town before I could get him. Frank's a little off, but he's not stupid. I bet the second he realized what he'd done, he hit the road. I'm pretty sure you won't have to worry about him anymore."

I wasn't at all certain my brother was right, but I didn't want to give him the slightest reason to increase his security around me any more than he already had. "Was there a particular reason you came by this morning?" I asked him as I got ready for my day.

"Can't I come by to say hi to my little sister without having a reason?" he asked.

"No, sorry, that's not one of your choices today. So why are you here?"

Bradford shrugged. "I just wanted to make sure you were okay this morning. That's it, I swear."

He could be sweet when he wanted to. I kissed my brother on the cheek, then said, "I'm fine, I promise. Now get out there and make Rebel Forge safe for the world."

"Yes, Ma'am," he said as he offered me a two-fingered salute.

Lillian came in two minutes before it was time to open. Though she was skilled at applying her make-up, I could see the bags under both eyes.

"How much sleep did you get last night?" I asked as I watched her drain a cup of coffee.

She laughed. "There will be plenty of time for sleep once I'm older. You missed a delightful time last night."

"I can't imagine having more fun than I had. Sara Lynn moved in with me."

I searched my aunt's face for a clue as to whether she knew about the new arrangement or not, but if she did, she was too good at hiding it. "Is that so?" she said. "Are she and Bailey having trouble?"

"She's there watching out for me," I said. "Was that your idea, or Bradford's?"

"I don't have a clue what you're talking about. Now, are we going to make some cards and invitations today, or are we going to just stand around and chat all morning?"

If there was anything that would make me feel better, it would have to be creating some new cards. "Let's get started," I said, suddenly very glad I had a shop of my very own, even though everything I owned in the world was committed to its success.

I played with the scripted-type font Lillian had found until I had a design and layout I was happy with. Lillian, watching over my shoulder the entire time, said, "You're not going to print that out and paste it to the card, are you?"

"Actually, I have a couple of ideas." I ran one copy on gold paper using my color printer, then trimmed it with some specialty scissors and laid it inside the prototype card I'd made. Before my aunt could say a word, I said, "I'm not finished yet." I grabbed a sheet of transparency with adhesive on one side and ran it through the printer; then I cut around the announcement and laid it in place of the other one.

"So which one do you like better?" I asked.

"Let's make another prototype so we can see them side by side."

I grabbed my pliers and wire. Lillian asked, "Do you mind if I try it myself?"

"Be my guest." After carefully folding one of her blanks into thirds, she snipped the wire and attached it to the front parts of the card. "There, how is that?"

I didn't say a word, but I handed her the two brass fittings we were using to represent rings. She'd forgotten to thread them before she'd attached the wires to the stock.

Lillian frowned, took the fittings from me, then made another card. It was a much better job, all the way from the fold to the wire attachment. She handed it to me, and I said, "That's quite good."

"You mean with the rings?"

"I mean all of it. You're going to be a pro at this in no time."

Lillian took the card back, careful not to show that she was so pleased with the effort. "I'll get better," she said. "Now let's see that insert."

She took the transparency and removed its back,

placing it inside the card. While she did that, I grabbed a glue stick and fastened the other one in place. We put both cards on the counter, standing up so that their sides made them stable, then stood back and examined the results.

"So what do you think now?" Lillian asked when the front door opened.

"I think they're both atrocious," a voice I knew said behind me.

Evidently Anne Albright had decided to take a more active role in the wedding invitations after all.

Chapter 10

"Excuse me," I said. "I thought you were leaving the invitations up to me."

Mrs. Albright snorted. "I had second thoughts. Obviously it was a good thing I trusted my instincts." She was back to her old self, and I wondered where the sweet, concerned woman had gone.

"I think they're just what you need," I said. I was in a stronger bargaining position than I'd been in before. After all, I'd already deposited her check. If she thought she could bully me now, she was mistaken. "I've already bought supplies to make the announcements this way," I said. "It would be awfully expensive to change the design at this stage, since I can't return my purchases." That was true, at any rate. It took an act of Congress to get Grady to take anything back once it was purchased. Maybe I stretched things on the claim that the supplies had been expensive, but I was counting more than the five-dollar bill Grady had charged me. I'd also put in quite a bit of my time designing the cards and finding just the right tone.

"I can write you a check to cover those . . . things," she said, and she whipped out her checkbook. "Name a figure."

"These really are quite lovely," I said, having no desire to start over. "I don't know why you don't like them."

"They're stark instead of elegant. We're not announcing the opening of a discotheque; this is a wedding." She scribbled furiously in her checkbook, and before I could protest, Mrs. Albright shoved the check under my nose. I was about to shove it right back when I saw the figure she'd hastily scrawled. The amount was for considerably more than my time and materials had cost.

She said, "I trust that will be sufficient. Now I suggest you go back to your sketchbook and present something to me that's acceptable by tonight."

"I've got store customers, too, you know," I said. "I can't just drop everything to make more invitations."

"For what I'm paying you, you certainly can." She gestured to Lillian. "I'm sure your assistant will be able to handle the foot traffic in your shop. I'll be back at five p.m., ready to see two design choices other than those things." She swept the invitations off the counter as she gestured, and before Lillian or I could protest, the mother of the bride was gone.

Lillian and I stared at each other ten seconds; then we both burst out laughing. My aunt said, "I thought you were going to explode at any moment, but you kept your cool. Jennifer, I believe you're more mature than I am myself."

"You didn't say anything, either," I said in my defense.

"No, I didn't think it was my place. After all, you own Custom Card Creations; I'm just here doing volunteer work. Now show me that check. I'm dying to see the amount it took to keep you quiet."

I handed it to her, and Lillian's smile faded quickly. "My word, she's certainly paying for the privilege, isn't she?"

"I never told her how much it would cost to start the process all over again," I said. "It surely would have been less than that."

Lillian said, "Don't misunderstand me; I think you were right to take it."

"Even though I've got five bucks in materials invested in my design?"

"Come now, Jennifer, you have more than that, and you know it. Your professional design services shouldn't be free, and besides, I think Anne Albright just assessed herself a rudeness penalty fee."

"You're right there. Well, I guess I'd better get back to work. Do you mind handling the customers while I do a little more brainstorming?"

"Not at all. I may need some help, though. Remember, I'm not a professional."

"No, but you are an eager apprentice. Now let me see what I can come up with." I grabbed a dozen books from the rack on basic and advanced card-making techniques, hoping that something in one of the books would spark an idea. I didn't mind taking another card maker's concept and making it my own. I thought of it as inspiration rather than theft. I certainly wouldn't mind if someone took one of my ideas and did the same thing. I glanced through the sections on wedding invitations, but they were all too safe, too conservative for Mrs. Albright. Then I spotted a card for a July Fourth party and started wondering if that was what she might approve of. Instead of the colored streamers used on the card's design in the book, I decided to use a fireworks burst of silver and gold. After drawing the bursts and cutting them out, I went to my papers to see what color would reflect them best. The wedding was at seven, and while it would be light at the beginning of the ceremony, it would be dark by the end of it. I placed the fire bursts on a black background, then tried a midnight blue. Much better. I wouldn't have to make the paper myself; that was a big plus given my deadline. I still liked the tri-fold invitation, so I made the creases, then laid the bursts on one side of the front doors. With the card closed and the two faces folded to meet in the middle, it appeared that the fireworks were exploding in the sky. I got a piece of foam tape, applied it to one side of the matched bursts, then pressed them into place. That was much better. The fireworks explosion appeared to float above the card, and it was easy to open the two doors of the front to reveal the message inside. After I had my front piece set, I went to my computer and started playing with fonts until I found something I liked. Using a golden script, I printed it out on a transparency sheet and my first mock-up was ready. The upside of this card was that I was using stock I had on hand. The downside would be cutting out all of those bursts under deadline.

Now it was time to come up with something so hideous that Mrs. Albright would be forced to choose the first design. I briefly considered using a Halloween theme, but I knew it had to be at least slightly credible. Instead, I finally decided to aggressively cut a piece of red stock with jagged edges; then I pasted it onto silver background paper. Another run through the printer for the announcement itself—this time using black letters on the transparency—and I had a card that was so outré it should have been outré with the trash.

I held the red, silver and black abomination up to Lillian, but she was nose deep in one of the books I'd just gone through. "So what do you think of my design?"

She looked up, then stared at the card for a few moments before trusting herself to speak. "It's certainly unique, isn't it?"

I couldn't hold my smile in any longer. "Relax. This is the bad choice to make sure she picks the one I like." I put the jagged invitation down and grabbed the fireworks display. "I'm just afraid this might be a little too much for her, too."

"I think it's perfect," Lillian said as she took the card from me. "She'd have trumpets announcing the wedding if she could. Are you telling me that you just came up with this?"

"Well, I borrowed the basic idea from one of the books centered on an Independence Day celebration, but I doubt it's ever been used for a wedding invitation before."

"I feel you're pretty safe saying that."

I frowned at the card I favored. "Do you think I should come up with something else?"

"Heavens, no. If she doesn't like either of these, she can go back to your original design or take her business somewhere else. If she threatens to do that, though, remember, we keep all of the checks."

"I'm tempted to run down to the bank and cash this one before she can change her mind," I said with a laugh.

"You're just joking, but I'd do exactly that. You don't want to give her time to stop payment on it if she changes her mind yet again. Go on; I can handle things here."

That was pretty obvious, since we hadn't had a customer all morning. "You know, I think I'll do it. Can I get you anything while I'm out?"

"No, I'm going to study a little more. Cards really are fascinating, aren't they?"

"I think so," I said, happy that Lillian was getting into the spirit of card making.

I felt a little guilty walking down Oakmont Avenue toward the bank. After all, if Mrs. Albright wanted her money back, was I really in any position to say no? I didn't want to give any of my customers bad service, no matter how truculent they might be. But then again, I couldn't afford to be a pushover, either. If I was going to succeed in running my own business, then I was going to have to toughen up and hold people to their commitments. That didn't mean I wouldn't give a refund if someone was unhappy with a purchase, but special orders were going to have to be something else entirely, especially when I felt I'd already met the spirit of the agreement I'd had with Mrs. Albright in the first place.

Corrine Knotts was waiting in line ahead of me at the bank. I'd been her babysitter a dozen years ago, and she'd blossomed into a lovely young woman. "Hey, Corrine, how are you?"

"I'm fine, Miss Jennifer. I heard you opened your own shop."

"I sure did. It's called Custom Card Creations. You should come by and see it. Hey, why aren't you in school?" Corrine was a junior at Tech, and I'd heard she'd gotten a full scholarship for mathematics. It always amazed me when people were good at something I was dreadful at. I could barely balance my checkbook.

"We're on break, so I thought I'd come home." She frowned a second, then said, "Do you mind if I ask you something?"

"Go right ahead."

She bit her lower lip, then asked, "How well do you know Wayne Davidson? He's been working for your brother for years, hasn't he?"

"I know him a little. Why do you ask?"

Corrine frowned, then said, "We've been going out lately, and I thought things were going pretty well, but he just broke up with me. He said he was suddenly interested in an older woman."

Oh, no. I hoped I wasn't the older woman he was talking about. I was a good six years older than Wayne was, but I resented the term if he was using it about me.

"I'm so sorry," I said. Knowing Corrine like I did, I thought Wayne was out of his mind if he'd dumped her to ask me out. She was as pretty on the inside as she was on the outside.

"You know, I'm just puzzled by the whole thing." She lowered her voice. "If you want to know the truth, in a way I'm kind of relieved."

"Why's that?" I asked as our line moved forward.

"He's been getting pretty possessive lately, showing up on campus and following me around in the shadows. Truthfully, it was starting to creep me out a little."

"You mean he was stalking you?"

She started to say something when it was her turn at the teller's cage. I could barely contain myself wanting more information as she made her withdrawal. When it was my turn, I said, "Wait one second. I'd like to talk to you more."

She glanced at her watch. "I'm so late as it is. We'll talk later, I promise. It was good seeing you."

"You, too," I said as the man behind me coughed to show his impatience. "You should get that throat looked at," I said as I smiled at him sweetly.

I cashed the check, not even feeling guilty as I stuffed the bills into my pocket. At least now I could afford to buy lunch. I went over to Hirasi's, a place that had Mediterranean food, something I knew Lillian loved and that I was acquiring a taste for. I just hoped the owner made a go of it. Restaurants on Oakmont were either there forever or disappeared overnight, and Earl and his family were too nice to just vanish.

Lillian looked pleased by my choice for lunch. I said, "It's my treat, remember?"

"I trust we're dining on Anne Albright's check."

"Absolutely," I said. "I might not even bother putting this in the register." Before she could protest, I said, "Hey, I'm kidding. I worked for Sara Lynn long enough to know that everything has to go on the books. You know, having her in my apartment isn't as annoying as I thought it might be."

"You sound surprised."

"To be honest with you, I am," I said as I took a bite of food. "I couldn't believe it when she just showed up on my doorstep."

"I'm glad she did," Lillian said. "I was wondering when one of your siblings was going to step up and be counted."

"I'm not sure how long she's staying," I said. "We're doing this on a day-by-day basis."

"Jennifer, you need someone there with you besides those cats of yours."

Okay, it was time to get the lunch topic off me. "I heard the oddest thing at the bank when I was cashing that check." I told Lillian about my conversation with Corrine.

She didn't look all that surprised by the news. "It seems that Wayne is a little too dedicated to his relationships. This just proves it."

"How come I haven't heard anything about it?"

"My dear, people seem to just open up around me. It must be something about my sympathetic nature."

A thought occurred to me. "If you knew about Wayne, why did you urge me to go out with him when he asked me?"

Lillian looked sheepish. "I hadn't heard anything at that point, but when you told me he'd expressed interest in dating you, I started asking around. I wonder if we should say something to Bradford about him?"

"I'm not sure. I've already gotten him into trouble this week with my brother. I think I'll wait a bit and see if he does anything else. It's not fair to smear him if I don't have anything specific to back it up."

"I suppose that's for the best, but I would watch my step around him if I were you."

I pushed my plate away. I'd had enough, and though it was good, I was more of a burgers-and-shakes kind of gal. "Believe me, I'm watching everybody around me right now, including you." I gave her my best stare; then we both cracked up laughing.

After we cleaned up, Lillian said, "So, more of the same this afternoon?"

"No, I'm happy with those cards, and if I keep messing with them, I'll overdo the designs. Why don't we have another lesson while things are quiet?"

"That sounds lovely," she said. "There's something I'm dying to try."

Before we could get our supplies out, though, the front door chimed and another customer walked in.

There was a steady stream of people in and out after that, making purchases of everything from premade cards to the nicest kits I offered. It appeared that my little card shop was meeting a need that no one else in town had seen but me. I was just totaling out the register for the day when the door chimed again. "Sorry, we're just closing," I said without looking up.

"I'm here to see your samples," Mrs. Albright said.

"Absolutely," I replied as I met her near the door.

Lillian said, "Jennifer, if you don't need me, I'll be going now."

"Of course," I said, shooting her a dirty look for leaving me alone with that woman. "I'll see you tomorrow, bright and early."

Lillian waved a hand in the air. Then I locked the door behind her.

"So what do you have for me?" Mrs. Albright asked.

"Let me just get them. I made two samples, so you've got a choice."

"My dear woman, you'll do more than two if I don't find one I like."

It was all I could do not to roll my eyes at her. I retrieved both card choices; and, without a word, I handed them to her. She studied both carefully, then said, "You've captured the spirit of what I was after. Well-done." She paused, and added, "Jennifer, I know I've been short with you, and I'm sorry, truly I am. You can't imagine the pressure I've been under lately."

She was right. I hadn't even tried putting myself in her place, with a pregnant daughter she was eager to marry off.

"That's okay. I'm glad you approve of the prototype."

She flung the fireworks card down on the table and handed me the garish nightmare I'd created. "This will do nicely. I like the bold color choice, and the design is perfect."

For a rave party maybe, I thought as I tried to hide my surprise. "So you're happy with this?"

"Absolutely. You have my approval to start production."

A joke was one thing, but this was going too far. "Don't you want to ask your daughter and her groom what they think?" Surely saner minds would prevail if she took a poll among the people concerned. Melinda would never speak to me again if I went ahead with the order.

"My daughter mentioned wanting to be consulted, but really, she's just a child. What does she know?"

"That may be so," I said, not believing it for a second. "But it is her wedding."

Mrs. Albright frowned, then grabbed the card back from me. "I suppose it couldn't hurt. I'll be in touch."

I let her out of the store, then wondered if I'd been too quick to muddy the waters, especially after she'd finally approved of my design. No, the expedient way was not necessarily the best way here. I'd never be able to forgive myself if I had a part in ruining a wedding. Better I should jump through more hoops than let my passion be smeared by what was turning out to be a very bad joke. I'd had fun making up the dummy, but I didn't know if I could face doing a hundred of those atrocities.

I balanced the register report, then tucked the deposit into my handbag before heading out the door. Getting out of the shop, making the deposit and driving home were all uneventful activities, something I was extremely grateful for.

I couldn't wait to get inside my apartment and close the world behind me, even with my sister staying there.

Something was strange about my door as I approached it, but it wasn't until I was ten feet away that I saw what it was.

Someone had taken a wig, much like the one I'd

worn investigating Tina Mast's murder scene and house, and nailed it to my front door.

Written above it in something that looked like blood were the words "I WARNED YOU."

Chapter 11

I stared at the wig for a minute before I could move. After fumbling around in my pocket for my cell phone, I dialed my brother's number. "Bradford, I need you over at my apartment as soon as you can get here."

"I'm kind of covered up right now in paperwork, Sis. Can it wait?"

"Listen," I said, trying to keep my voice calm. "I don't want to alarm you, but something's happened."

"Okay, before I rush over there with my siren blaring and my gun drawn, tell me about it."

I took a deep breath, let it out slowly, then said, "I just got home, and I found a red wig nailed to my front door. It's just like the one I wore when we went to the house where Tina Mast was killed."

Bradford paused a moment, then said, "It couldn't just be some kind of prank, could it? I normally don't like coincidences, but is there any chance it might be?"

"Maybe if that's all there was, but there's one other thing I haven't told you yet. Over the wig, somebody wrote 'I warned you' in something that looks like blood."

"Okay, here's what I want you to do. Do not go into that apartment, do you understand me? I want you to go back to your Gremlin, get inside and lock the doors. Don't move after that until I get there. Do you understand?"

"Bradford, if they could get into my apartment, they wouldn't leave the warning on the front door. I'm safer inside than I am in my car."

"Blast it, Jennifer, listen to me. That door could be booby-trapped. Now do what I'm asking."

"Fine, I'll be in my car when you get here."

After we hung up, I stared at the wig a few more seconds, then hurried downstairs to the parking lot. If the killer had meant to put me on edge, then she'd done a marvelous job of it. I rushed back to my car, got in and locked the doors. Suddenly I found myself wishing for a bigger automobile, some kind of monster SUV that might give me more protection. But the Gremlin was all I had, and it would have to do.

I kept watching my apartment door, half expecting the killer to come out at any minute after Bradford's alarming comments, so I nearly missed it when Sara Lynn showed up with a bagful of groceries in her arms. Rolling down my window, I called out, "Sis. Over here."

"What is it, Jennifer? This bag is heavy."

"We can't go inside right now," I said as I unlocked the passenger door and popped it open.

"What is it, some kind of gas leak or something?" she asked as she hurried over to me.

"It's something else," I said.

After she was safely inside the Gremlin, I locked the doors. She looked at me a second, then said, "Would you mind telling me what this is all about?"

"Somebody left me a message on my door. I called Bradford, and he told me not to do anything until he got here."

"What kind of message was it, Jennifer?"

I repeated it, mentioning the wig, too. Sara Lynn whistled under her breath, something she always did when she was nervous or unsettled about something.

"Yes, calling Bradford was the right thing to do. Do you have the slightest idea about who's doing this?"

I was about to answer when our brother pulled up in his cruiser, slamming the car into place as he jumped out. I started to get out to join him when he said, "You two stay right there."

Bradford pulled out his gun and started toward my apartment, then hesitated and came back.

"Do you want me with you after all?" I asked.

"I need your key," he said.

I started to protest when Sara Lynn said, "For heaven's sake, take mine." She thrust her keys out the window to him, and he nodded his thanks.

"Why did you do that?" I asked. "If we'd held out a little longer, he might have let us come in with him."

"Jennifer, sometimes you are reckless beyond belief. Our brother's a trained police officer, he's got a gun and he knows how to use it, and you want to tag along to see what he's doing. This isn't a scavenger hunt or a church picnic; someone means you harm."

I hated it when my sister lectured me, especially when I deserved it. "It's my life that's being threatened, not his or yours, either, for that matter. I have a right to be in on this. I know Bradford's a good sheriff, but he's not infallible. There might be something he misses."

"Then you'll see it and point it out to him. I'm positive of that. In the meantime, let's allow him to assess the situation and determine if there's a threat or not."

"Sara Lynn, you've been watching crime shows on television again, haven't you?"

My sister, an avid reader who vehemently denied ever watching television on general principle, nodded. "I'm addicted to *Law and Order,* I confess, but that's beside the point." She looked up toward my apartment and said, "It appears that Bradford is signaling for us to come upstairs."

We met him at the door. "Ladies, don't touch anything. I want Jim to come over and get some photographs for the record."

"You mean they got inside?" I asked, suddenly feeling hollow. I couldn't stand the thought of someone violating my space. Well, anyone but my family.

"No, your apartment hasn't been touched. I was talking about the front door."

Sara Lynn said, "I've got to get some of these groceries in the freezer before they melt. That's all right, isn't it?"

Bradford said, "Go right ahead."

After Sara Lynn was gone, I took a step closer to the door and studied the wig for a few moments. "That's not the wig I borrowed from Lillian."

"I didn't think it was," Bradford said. "But it still shows that the killer saw through your disguise when we went inside the crime scene. She knows who you are, Jennifer."

"Yes, but she doesn't know that Lillian played a part in it. I'm guessing that whoever saw me didn't see our aunt, so that must mean that whoever was at the house where the murder took place wasn't at Tina's home."

Bradford grabbed his cell phone, and I didn't even have to ask who he was calling. After a minute, I heard him leave a message. "Lillian, call me on my cell phone as soon as you get this. Don't worry about the time, okay?"

"You think she might be in trouble, too?" I asked. "I'll never forgive myself if something I've done puts her in danger."

"Take it easy, Jen. I'm just touching all the bases right now. I'm sure she's fine."

"So what do we do now?" I asked.

"Like I said, Jim's coming by with his camera so we can get some good shots of this door. Then we'll bag the wig and save it for evidence."

"That's it?" I asked.

"What else do you suggest I do, Jennifer? I can't

afford to guard you around the clock, and you won't leave your apartment or your store. I'm doing the best I can."

"I know you are," I said, ashamed at my outburst. "I'm sorry I overreacted. It's just so frustrating."

"Welcome to my world," Bradford said.

Sara Lynn rejoined us. "Bradford, why don't you stay and have dinner with us? It will be just like old times."

He looked like he was tempted by the offer. "I'd love to, but Cindy will have my hide if I skip out on her. This diet she's got me on is killing me." He frowned a second, then asked, "What are you having?"

"Oh, nothing special. I'm throwing together some meat loaf, scalloped potatoes and green beans. We're having a special treat for dessert. There's going to be plenty for you, too, if you'd like to stay."

He looked at me. "Jennifer, would you feel better if I hung around here awhile?"

The pleading in his gaze was obvious. "It would help," I said.

"That's all I need, then. Cindy will have to understand that. After all, it's family."

He turned his back to us and called home on his cell phone. Sara Lynn smiled brightly when I said, "That was cruel. You know he's on a diet."

"Nonsense, he doesn't need to lose weight. He's just big-boned. Now I'd better get started on dinner. It will be wonderful being together again."

"Sara Lynn, we're together all the time," I protested.

"Not like this, without work or our spouses or the errant murderer thrown into the mix. It will just be the three of us."

I could swear I heard her humming as she went back inside the apartment. My sister was big on our family, but it was an odd thing. While our parents had been alive, she'd been just as reluctant to spend her free time with us. But as soon as she was the oldest member of our immediate family, Sara Lynn became a demon for get-togethers and family time. Lillian wasn't always invited to our little mini reunions, and I understood why. As much as I loved our aunt, she wasn't a part of our core, the three of us. Sara Lynn, Bradford and I had gone through quite a lot together, both good and bad, and somehow I always felt better knowing that they were close by.

Bradford hung up and looked at me. "I guess you heard all of that, huh?"

"To be honest with you, I was thinking about something else. Did she give you a hard time?"

"She actually accused me of making excuses so I wouldn't have to eat at home. Imagine me turning down a tofu burger so I could get meat loaf." His grin was so big he could barely contain it.

"I, for one, do find it hard to believe."

"Listen, do you mind staying out here and watching the door until Jim shows up? I need to talk to Sara Lynn about something. I'll be here in a second if you need me."

"Go ahead," I said. "I'm fine."

He patted my shoulder. "I know you will be. Besides, you've just gotten the warning; I can't imagine you being in any real danger yet."

"Thanks, you're all heart," I said as I sat down on the top step and looked out into the growing night, amazed that Rebel Forge could look so calm and peaceful from a distance. There was a killer loose somewhere out there, and I wondered if she was watching me now. What did that warning mean? I hadn't done anything productive to help my brother in his investigation. So why had the killer chosen this particular method of communication? If I could unmask her, I would do it without fear or hesitation, but in all honesty, I didn't have a clue who might have killed Tina. A thought suddenly struck me. Could the murder be tied in to the upcoming wedding somehow? If the killer was watching my shop, seeing the mothers of both bride and groom visit me might give her the impression that I was looking into the murder more actively than I was actually doing. What was I supposed to do, though, bar anyone from coming in who had the slightest connection to the happy couple? That gave me an idea. If the killer thought I was getting closer, then I had to be on the right track. Chances were, Tina's murder had to be tied in to the wedding. But could I go to Bradford with that suspicion, and more importantly, would he take it seriously? I kind of doubted it. No, if that connection was right, I was the one in the best position to use it and find the murderer. I'd never been discouraged by threats. If anything, they would just make me dig my heels in more.

I was still thinking about the possibilities when I saw someone coming up the steps toward me. Instead of Jim, Wayne Davidson was there, a camera slung around his neck, ready to take pictures of my front door.

"I thought Jim was coming," I said, not at all happy to see Wayne coming to my apartment again for any reason.

"Nice to see you, too, Jennifer. Jim was buried in paperwork, so I volunteered to come by." He looked around, then asked, "Where's the sheriff?"

"He's inside. Would you like me to get him for you?"

"No, that's fine. I know the drill." As he got ready to take the photographs, my first instinct was to go inside where my family was. Then I thought about what Corrine had told me, and I realized this could be the perfect time to reconcile the two versions of Wayne I'd been hearing about lately.

As he lined up a shot, I said, "I ran into an old girlfriend of yours this week."

"Yeah? It wouldn't take much around here. Rebel Forge isn't all that big, and the dating pool is kind of shallow."

I waited until he snapped his first picture, then said,

"Actually, she hasn't lived in town for a while. She's been away at college."

Wayne had been ready to take another photograph, but he lowered the camera and stared at me with a glare that chilled me. "What did she say?"

I was getting nervous being with him. "Nothing important," I said as I eased toward my door. My apartment had been built like a bomb shelter, and while I usually relished the sound protection offered inside it, I was wishing for paper-thin walls so my brother could hear me if I got in trouble.

Wayne stepped forward, cutting off my way inside. "I asked you a question, Jennifer. What did she tell you?"

He was so close I could smell the slightest trace of liquor on his breath. It appeared that Wayne was the kind of man who got mean when he started drinking, and I didn't want to do anything to set him off. "She told me you just broke up with her. Corrine seemed surprised by your excuse."

For some reason Wayne looked relieved by the admission. "Yeah, well, it was a long time coming." He backed off and started to shoot again.

"Why were you so upset about her saying anything to me?"

"I don't like people talking about me behind my back, that's all," he said nonchalantly.

"Aren't you a little old to be dating college girls?" I asked him, wondering why he'd reacted so strongly to my earlier statement.

"In case you hadn't noticed, there aren't a lot of women my age in town. Why, are you interested after all? If you changed your mind, I'd still like to take you out."

Great. It looked like if I gave him the slightest encouragement, I was going to get a stalker of my very own. "Thanks, but no thanks. The reasons I told you before still hold. I don't have the time or the interest to date right now."

He shook his head slightly, whispered something under his breath, then went back to taking photographs. I was just about to push him a little more when my door opened and Bradford walked out. "What are you doing here?" he rumbled at Wayne. "You're off duty."

"I was hanging around the station when you called, and Jim was loaded down with paperwork. No big deal, I was happy to come."

Bradford took the camera from him and said, "Go home, Wayne. I'll see you in the morning." He studied his deputy's appearance, then asked, "Do you need a ride?"

Wayne waved his hand at Bradford, then walked away.

I said, "He's been drinking. You know that, don't you?"

My brother shrugged. "I can't babysit all my men, Jennifer. Wayne's working his way through some problems. He's been like this the last couple of days, but I'm hoping he snaps out of it on his own."

"So you're letting him drive around town drunk?"

"I doubt he's drunk, but what do you expect me to do, arrest one of my own officers for having a drink now and then? They're not Boy Scouts, Jennifer. I can't make them behave themselves when they're off duty."

"I know that, but you can keep them off the road when they're drunk."

He started down the stairs, and I called out, "Where are you going?"

"I'm going to follow him home to make sure he gets there all right. I'll be back in ten minutes. Don't start without me."

"What am I supposed to do in the meantime?" I asked.

"Guard the door until I get back. I need to finish up with the photographs. Then I have to collect the evidence."

Before I could protest, he was gone. Now what? I couldn't go inside, but I was tired of sitting on the stairs waiting. I had half a mind to go in anyway and take my chances, but I knew what would happen when Bradford got back, and I didn't want to have to tell my brother why I'd disregarded his orders.

He was back sooner than I expected, carrying a fishing tackle box in one hand. I asked, "Is something wrong?"

"No," he said, shaking his head as he put the box down and opened it up. "I was kind of hoping Wayne would drive home a little slower and straighter than he did. I'm going to have to have a talk with that boy first thing tomorrow morning. Whatever is eating him, he's going to have to just get over it. Now, let's get these pictures taken so we can eat."

Bradford shot a whole roll of film on the door in no time flat, and after he handed me the camera, he removed a large bag and a pair of pliers from his tackle box. I watched him as he pulled the nail, then caught the wig before it could fall. After both pieces of evidence were safely sealed and labeled, he took a swab and dabbed at the lettering. I watched in surprise as Bradford studied the end of the swab, then took a sniff of it.

He shook his head as he bagged that, too. I wasn't sure I really wanted to know, but I asked him anyway. "Is it blood?"

HANDCRAFTED CARD-MAKING TIP

For nature lovers, it can be great fun incorporating autumn leaves, bits of curled tree bark, even a flat stone with interesting markings on it, into the front of your card.

Chapter 12

Bradford rolled his eyes slightly as he answered, "No, somebody used ketchup to write with. If that wig hadn't been nailed to your door, I would swear this was just a bad prank. Why don't you get some detergent and we can clean this right up."

"I'll be right back," I said as I went inside. Sara Lynn was fussing as she peeked into my oven. The aromas coming from my kitchen were wonderful. Then my sister opened her mouth and spoiled it. "Jennifer, your thermostat is way off. You need a new one."

I'd never noticed a problem with it, but then again Sara Lynn was a fussier cook than I was. "I don't have any trouble with it."

I moved past her and grabbed a bottle of cleaner and a handful of paper towels. "What are you going to do with those?" she asked me.

"I'm going to clean up that threat before we get ants. It was written in ketchup, can you believe that?"

"Don't discount the message just because of the medium," she said. "We have a brother in law enforcement. Let him do his job."

"For your information, big sister, he asked me to clean it up himself."

Sara Lynn clucked at me. "Now don't get defensive with me, young lady. You know I only care about your safety."

"Sometimes I wish you didn't care quite so much," I said.

Sara Lynn's eyebrows elevated, but to her credit, she didn't reply.

I went back outside and tried to hand the cleaner to my brother. When he wouldn't take it, I said, "Hey, aren't you the one who's supposed to clean up a crime scene?"

"It's all been documented," he said. "Now it's just a mess on your door. Besides, if word got back to Cindy that a bottle of cleaner fit my hand, she'd never let me hear the end of it."

"You're such a sissy," I said as I sprayed the door and wiped it clean. The only evidence of what had been there before was a small nail hole in my door.

"So what do we do now?" I asked as I wadded up the dirty paper towels.

"Hopefully we're about ready to eat," Bradford said.

"I'm talking about this threat," I said. "And you know it."

"Jennifer, I'm doing all I can. Just watch your step, okay?"

I sighed. "That's all I seem to be doing lately. I just hate the idea that somebody's threatening me like this."

"I'm not too happy about it, either, but until we catch this woman, there's not much else we can do. Now, let's go inside and forget about this for a while. I'm starving, how about you?"

"I suppose I could eat something," I said. "Just as long as it doesn't involve ketchup."

"Come on, what's meat loaf without ketchup? You'll get over it pretty quick, I promise you."

We walked into the apartment as Sara Lynn was transferring the meat loaf from the pan to a fancy platter I didn't remember I owned. "You two are just in time," she said. "Dinner is ready. You've just got time to wash up."

Bradford asked me, "Where are your roommates?"

"They're probably asleep on my bed. Neither one of them cares much for company."

"What a shock, antisocial cats." Bradford hovered over the meat loaf for a second, wafting the smell to his nose. "Oh, man, that's what Heaven smells like to me. Is there any chance you . . . ? No, I'm sure you didn't—it's okay."

Instead of replying, Sara Lynn walked to the freezer and pulled out a large glass of milk, crystals already forming on the top of it. "Of course I froze some milk for you, Bradford. I would never forget that."

Bradford walked to her after she put the glass down, and picked Sara Lynn up in his arms. "You are the best."

"Put me down, you big oaf," she said, laughing as she swatted him with the dish towel thrown over one of her shoulders. He twirled her once in the air, then put her back down. "Now wash up before the food gets cold," Sara Lynn commanded.

After we were seated, Sara Lynn said, "Bradford, would you say Grace?"

"Grace," our brother said, a huge grin on his face. That had been his joke in the family, one he'd been swatted for on more than one occasion.

Sara Lynn said, "So you don't want any meat loaf after all."

Gravely, our brother said the blessing, and then the three of us set out to eat everything within reach. The sharp ache of knowing that someone wished me harm faded away in the warm love of my family. We'd always been close, and the next hour reinforced why. I found myself hesitating to eat at one point, just watching my brother and sister, loving the fact that they were both there with me now. Bradford noticed me watching them and asked, "Are you going to eat those potatoes?"

As his fork neared my plate, I swatted it away with

mine, something I'd grown adept at doing growing up. "You had your share. These are mine."

"Come on, I'm wasting away here."

"Oh, yes, I agree. I can barely see you; you're so thin."

After we were finished, I pushed my plate away. "I cannot believe all I ate. I'm stuffed."

Sara Lynn asked, "Does that mean you don't have room for dessert?"

"I'll have hers," Bradford volunteered.

"You don't even know what we're having," I said.

"Doesn't matter, if Sara Lynn made it, I want some."

She said, "Even if it's coconut pudding?"

Coconut was just about the only food in the world my brother wouldn't touch. He made a face, then said, "You wouldn't do that to me. Please tell me you're joking."

"I didn't realize you'd be joining us," Sara Lynn said. She watched his face pucker into a frown until she added, "I can't take it. I confess, I made banana pudding parfaits."

Bradford's eyes lit up like it was Christmas. "Bless your soul, Sis. Like I said, I'll eat Jennifer's."

"Hey, not so fast. I've got room for a parfait."

"Of course you do," Sara Lynn said as she got out our desserts. It was obvious my brother's portion was twice the size of mine. "That's not fair. Why does he get more than I do?"

Bradford smiled as he dug his spoon in. "That's because I'm just a growing boy."

"Growing wider, you mean. I'm telling your wife."

Sara Lynn said, "Enough. Must you two revert back to childhood? There's plenty for everyone."

I took a bite, then said, "We're not reverting. You and I used to be the ones who squabbled all the time. Bradford was the peacemaker of the group, remember?"

"All too well," Sara Lynn said as she ate some of her own dessert. "This has been wonderful."

"I agree," Bradford said. "We should do it once a week."

"You're just trying to get off your diet," I said.

He gave me his biggest puppy-dog-eyed look. "That hurts, Jennifer. You know all I want is to be with my sisters," he said solemnly before he couldn't hold it in any longer and cracked up.

"It has been great fun," I said.

Bradford looked at his watch. "I'll stay and help with the dishes, but after that, I have to get home."

Sara Lynn said, "Go on, you have our blessing. You need to spend some time with your family."

"You two are my family, too," he said as he stood and kissed our cheeks in turn. "Thanks for everything. I'm just sorry about the circumstances that brought me here. Lock up as soon as I leave, okay?"

"We will," I said as I walked my brother to the door. I thought about telling him about my earlier conversation with Wayne, but I didn't want to ruin the festive mood of our dinner party. Instead, I said, "If you get the chance tomorrow, why don't you come by the shop so we can chat?"

"Is there something on your mind?" he asked at the door.

"Nothing that can't wait," I said. I gave him a bear hug, and held on a little longer than I normally would. "Thanks for everything tonight. I can't tell you how much it meant having you here."

"Hey, I was glad to do it." He patted my shoulder, then added, "Don't worry, Jen. We'll catch her."

I just nodded, then dead bolted the door after he was gone. As Sara Lynn and I did the dishes, we had the chance to talk about anything in the world, but I was glad we spent the time reminiscing about our childhood rather than discussing what was going on in the present. Our conversation reminded me of everything right and good in my life, and for just a little while, I was able to lock my troubles away.

The next morning, I was ready to get started on the abhorrent wedding invitations when I was surprised to find Melinda Spencer—the mother of the groom—waiting for me as I approached Custom Card Creations.

"I hope I'm not too early," she said as I approached.

"No, by all means, come on in."

I unlocked the door, let her inside, then dead bolted it behind me. Having one customer inside was bad enough; I wasn't ready for any walk-ins thirty minutes before I was due to open.

"I was hoping we could have a quick lesson before you open for business this morning," Melinda said. "I need something to take my mind off these wedding plans."

"I didn't realize you were so involved in them," I said as I prepared to open.

"That's the problem. Poor Donna doesn't even have a say in most of the things being arranged. I've heard of bridezillas before, but it can't be anywhere near as bad as a mother of the bridezilla. You can't imagine the bridesmaids' dresses she's picked out. I can't even fathom what kind of invitation she's chosen."

"I've got a pretty good idea," I said.

"Oh, dear, she's commissioned you to do them, hasn't she? Jennifer, I'm sorry; I didn't mean to imply that your work is less than delightful."

I shook my head. "You will after you see them." I grabbed my choices—the fireworks theme and the brass fittings card—and showed them to her.

Melinda took the cards from me and said, "Why, they're perfectly lovely. I should have known you would come up with something nice, just seeing the examples in your shop."

I'd posted several different cards on the walls, including step-by-step instructions on how to make them, hoping they would inspire neophytes afraid to make that first card. "Don't get your hopes up. Mrs. Albright chose something a little less traditional."

"More modern than these? Do you have a sample?"

"I do, but I'm not sure I want to show it to you. To be honest with you, I was hoping to talk her out of it." The last thing I wanted to do was to face the groom's mother with the Bad Art Deco invitation.

"I'll see it sooner or later," she said. "It might as well be now."

I grabbed one of the mock-ups from the workroom, shuddering at the color choices and design. "Okay, but remember, I'm making these under protest."

I handed her the red, silver and black card, dreading her reaction. After a few moments of dead silence, she said, "They are certainly different, aren't they?"

"Listen, I'm so sorry. I was hoping she'd choose one of the other designs, I swear it."

Melinda shook her head resolutely. "I understand, Jennifer. Don't blame yourself. If I thought I had a prayer in the wind of changing her mind, I'd choose this as my battleground." Melinda thought about it a second, then said, "I've got an even better idea." She studied the two best cards, then handed me the one with the brass fittings serving as wedding rings, my original design. "How much trouble would it be to make a hundred of these?"

"I can do it," I said, "but Anne Albright is determined to use that version."

"And she shall, for all of the guests on her side of the family. My friends and loved ones will receive this one. Now, what are you charging her?"

"It's not fair to quote you that. Part of my fee is because she changed her mind after commissioning the job. I can't charge you that much."

"Of course you can." She whipped out her checkbook. "Give me the figure, and don't you dare shave a penny from it. Anne is parading her spending around as if it rivals the national budget, so I'll know if you try to charge me less."

I thought about fighting her, but Sara Lynn had taught me long ago that when somebody is trying to force money on you in your business, there are only two things you should do: keep your mouth shut and your hand out. Melinda didn't bat an eyelash when I quoted her the fee I was charging. She wrote the check with a flourish, and as she handed it to me, she said, "I wouldn't mention this to Anne if I were you. We'll just keep it our little secret."

"Believe me, I have no desire to tell her. Thanks," I said as I waved the check in the air before putting it in my cash register.

"No, I should be the one thanking you," Melinda said. "She may bollix up the entire wedding, but at least my side of the family will receive suitable invitations. Now that we have that settled, do you have time to teach me to make cards?"

"Absolutely." With the check she'd just written me, she'd more than paid for the privilege. I grabbed a few tools and supplies and met her at the desk in front. "Now there are lots of ways to do this. Why don't you choose a particular card and we'll start with that?" I'd laid out a sampling of some of the more basic cards, including ones with single folds, double folds, raised borders like I'd taught Lillian, and cards with an open window on the front.

"I always like to start off with the simplest and work my way up," she said.

I taught her how to fold a crisp edge; then we started discussing the possibilities. Melinda finally decided to make a card for her future daughter-in-law, something that I thought was a lovely gesture. As she chose ribbons, rubber stamps and paper flowers I'd made for sale, it was all I could do not to include a baby rattle. I swear, one of these days my sense of humor is going to be the death of me.

Once she had the outside of the card decorated, I

asked, "So what would you like to say inside the card?"

She didn't even hesitate. " 'Welcome to Our Family' sounds about right to me. Does that sound okay to you?"

"I think it's perfect," I said, knowing that Donna was getting the better bargain when it came to the mother-in-law derby. "We can use rub-on letters, or print something out on the computer. If you'd like, you can hand-letter it yourself. That's what makes it special, in my opinion."

She held up one of the samples of fancy lettering. "I've always wanted to learn how to do that. Would you mind doing it for me?"

"I'd be delighted," I said. I grabbed one of my best calligraphy pens and copied down her message inside the card. "That's lovely."

"I agree. I think you've done a great job."

I took an envelope I'd made of the same stock and slid her card into it. "There you go."

"What do I owe you?"

Now I'm as interested in making enough money to keep my business going as the next gal, but there was no way in the world I was going to take money for that lesson. I said, "Oh, didn't I tell you? I included that in the amount I quoted you earlier for the invitations."

"Jennifer," she said in a stern voice that I was sure had served her well as a mother, "I won't hear of it."

"Well, I suppose I could give you a refund if you insist," I said.

Her frown eased. "Very well, I give up. Let me ask you something. Do you happen to have any books on basic calligraphy? This will be the perfect time for me to learn."

I led her to the proper aisle. "I've got something even better. Here's a kit with paper, pens and tips, along with the best beginning book I've been able to find. It makes a perfect starter kit."

"I'll take it," she said.

"Is that all?" I asked as I moved to the register.

"Oh, no, I'd like to look around more, if that's all right with you."

There was no way I'd ever ask a customer with an open checkbook to leave my store. "Take your time. I'm just about ready to open."

I flipped the sign from CLOSED to OPEN and unlocked the door. Then I filled the cash register and started sorting through the mail. Lillian arrived a few minutes before we were officially due to open, and she looked startled to find Melinda there ahead of her. I just smiled and went back to my mail. There was a load of junk, a few bills and a card without a return address. My hands started to shake as I opened it, wondering if this was going to be another warning from the killer. Instead, to my delight I found a handmade card welcoming me to Oakmont from Hilda, my customer from a few days before who had expressed interest in joining the card club. She was really very good. I admired the card, then put it on the bulletin board behind the cash register.

Finally, Lillian couldn't contain herself any longer. "Did we change our opening hours? And if we did, why didn't you tell me?"

"We're on the same schedule as always," I said.

Lillian didn't like my answer, but I wasn't about to go into any more detail with Melinda standing right there.

"There, that should do it for now," she said as she put the basket on the checkout counter.

"Are you sure you got everything you'd like?" I asked, staring down at the collection of supplies, enough to keep a dozen card makers busy for a month.

Melinda laughed. "Whenever I start a new hobby, I tend to go a little overboard. Ring it up, Jennifer. I'm so excited about this."

As I started entering amounts into the register, I said, "Now remember, any time you have questions, I'm right here."

Lillian bagged each item as I handed it to her, and by the time we were finished, there was a substantial amount on the register display. As Melinda started to write the check, she tucked some of her luxurious silver hair behind one ear. It was all I could do not to scream.

The earring she wore was an exact duplicate of the one I'd found on the floor of the house where Tina Mast had been murdered.

Chapter 13

"That's quite an unusual earring," I said, fighting to keep my voice from becoming shrill.

"I suppose," she said. "They were a gift."

"Do you mind if I see both of them together? I might like to get some, but I can't tell if I like them or not until I see them balanced." That was complete and utter balderdash, but I didn't have a clue how else I could get Melinda to show me that she still had two earrings and hadn't left one behind at a crime scene.

Melinda looked a little puzzled, but she pulled the hair back behind her other ear as well, and I saw that she did indeed have two that matched perfectly. "What do you think? They're a little too gaudy for my taste."

"I don't know, I like them," I said. "Melinda, I hate to ask you this, but do you have any idea where they were purchased? I'd love to have a pair for myself."

Melinda said, "I'd give you these if I didn't have to wear them again. I can ask, though, if you're really interested."

"I am," I said.

Melinda finished writing the check; then as she handed it to me, she said, "You know, you could ask her yourself the next time you see her. I know she'd be flattered by the request coming from you. Anne bought them for the entire wedding party. Any woman even remotely associated with the wedding received a pair just like them earlier this week. It wouldn't surprise me if you end up getting a pair yourself."

I slid the check in the cash drawer, then handed Melinda her bags. It was all I could do to limit myself to, "Thanks again. I'll have those cards for you in a few days."

"Wonderful. That will give me a perfect excuse to come by and restock my supplies."

Before the door could even close, Lillian said, "Okay, Jennifer, what gives? Why the fuss about those gaudy earrings? They are completely not your style."

There was no way I couldn't tell her, though I would have preferred to discuss it with Bradford first. "Those earrings were identical to the one I found at the house where Tina Mast was murdered."

Lillian applauded. "Now aren't you clever? Call your brother and tell him."

"That was my plan," I said as I grabbed the phone.

He answered on the second ring. "Bradford, it's Jennifer."

"Hey, Jen. I had fun last night."

"So did I. Listen, I think I may have uncovered another clue."

He paused, then said, "Have you been digging around again, even after that warning you got last night?"

"If I'm going to be threatened at my own apartment, I might as well earn it," I said. Lillian's eyebrows lifted instantly, and I knew I'd have to recount what had happened the night before to her. "Besides, this clue walked straight into my shop."

"Okay, don't keep me hanging. What did you find out?"

Trying to keep a hint of triumph out of my voice, I said, "I found out where that earring came from we found at the house with Tina. Anne Albright gave every woman associated with the wedding party a pair. All you have to do is see who has just one."

Bradford let out a burst of breath. "That's all, huh?

So let me get this straight. You want me to go to this woman and demand she give me a list of who all she gave earrings to, then visit them one at a time to see who lost one? Let me ask you something, Sis. Is there any chance these earrings were a custom job, made just for the wedding?"

"I doubt it," I said.

"So they're for sale in probably two or three places on Oakmont Avenue alone. Should I get a list from them, too, just in case I get bored with all of the regular police work I have to do?"

I didn't appreciate his tone at all, especially since he was my brother. "I'm sorry. I thought you wanted to solve the murder."

"Of course I do," he snapped at me. "Give me something more concrete to go on and I'll follow up on it. As it is, I can't burn the manpower to track down a dozen women and check their earring trees."

"You might not be able to, but I can," I said.

"Jennifer, stay out of this."

"Sorry, you're breaking up," I said. "I'm going to—" and then I hung up. Lillian was shaking her head.

"What?" I said. "That's the way to kill a conversation believably. Hang up on yourself while you're talking, and nobody will ever believe it was deliberate."

"I seem to remember a few conversations with you that were terminated exactly like that."

"Hey, those were legitimate. You know cell phone reception is terrible in these mountains."

Lillian let that slide. Instead, she asked, "So what happened at your apartment last night?"

I wished I could avoid telling her, but I didn't see how. After I relayed the news of the wig and its accompanying warning, Lillian said, "So you've managed to poke the bear. Any idea who she might be?"

"Not a clue, but my list just narrowed. How would you like to run the shop by yourself today?"

"Let me guess. You're going to try to find the murderer. Do you honestly think that's wise?"

I grabbed my purse. "Do you think it's better if I wait for her to come after me?" I started for the door, then grabbed the invitation Mrs. Albright had commissioned.

"Where are you going with that?"

"It gives me a perfect excuse to butt into these people's lives. I'm going to ask their opinions about the invitation. Then I'm going to find out if they each have a complete set of earrings. When I find the one who's short, I'll tell Bradford."

"And what happens if she discovers what you are doing, and decides to stop you once and for all?"

I wasn't willing to admit that possibility. "Don't worry. I know how to be subtle about it."

"I need to go with you," Lillian said. "She won't try anything if there are two of us."

"And who's going to run the shop while we're running around all over Rebel Forge?" I asked.

"The shop can circle the drain, for all I care. We're talking about a dangerous situation here. Surely that's worth closing for the morning. Honestly, if you walk out that door alone, I'm going to make a call. You'll have a police escort before you can make it to the Gremlin, and no one's going to talk to you with your brother waiting outside in his squad car."

"You wouldn't," I said.

"Try me."

I thought about it ten seconds, then finally said, "Okay, I give up. You can come, but you have to promise me you'll let me do all the talking."

Lillian smiled brightly. "My dear, you won't even know I'm there."

"Hi, it's so nice to finally meet you," Donna Albright said as she extended her hand to me on the front porch of her home. "Mamma's told me what a great job you're doing on our invitations. We so appreciate you bumping us to the head of the line." Donna Albright was nothing like I'd expected her to be. And that was a very good thing, considering my impressions of her mother. Donna was a slightly pudgy blonde, and I wondered if it was from too many trips to the dessert bar or if her condition was already starting to show. I was willing to admit that I was being pretty harsh judging her at first, but in just a few seconds she won me over with her open warmth.

"This is my aunt Lillian," I said. "She's been helping me with your order."

"Then I should thank you, too, Ma'am," Donna said.

Lillian just smiled, so far abiding by her promise to keep her comments to herself. Goodness, I hadn't meant she couldn't speak, but perhaps that was a good thing.

"Mamma's not home right now," Donna said. "Is there something I could do for you?"

"I was hoping to steal a minute of your time," I said, angling to get in the door.

"Of course. Where are my manners? Would you-all like to come in? I just made a fresh pitcher of iced tea."

"That would be great," I said, following her inside. I could suddenly see where Anne Albright had gotten her taste for wedding invitations. The sitting room area where Donna led us was modern, full of chrome and shades of black with accents of red splashed everywhere. Unwittingly I'd designed a throwaway card that had somehow managed to meet the woman's odd tastes and preferences.

As Donna left us to get the tea, I told Lillian, "You could have at least said hello."

"Did you hear that? She called me ma'am," Lillian said through clenched teeth.

"She was just being respectful," I said, defending her.

"Of her elders," Lillian added. It was really a good thing I'd made her promise to keep quiet. Who knew where her line of questioning might lead?

When Donna came back with a tray holding a pitcher and three glasses, I said, "You have a lovely home," not meaning a word of it.

"Please, Ms. Shane, I know my mamma's flair for the dramatic better than anybody since my daddy died. Personally, I like simple lines and earth tones myself."

I reached into my purse and brought the invitations out. At the last second, without really knowing why, I'd included the other two I'd made. "Have you seen the one your mother picked?"

I handed her the modern one, then said, "I had a few other choices for her, but that was her favorite."

Donna barely glanced at the offerings. "I assure you, whatever you two decided is fine with me."

"You're certainly easy to get along with," I said.

"Don't mistake my agreeable disposition for weakness," she said with a sudden firmness in her voice that had been missing before. "Frankly, I don't care what the invitations look like, what kind of food we'll be serving, or which band plays at the reception. The only thing that matters to me is that I'm marrying Larry. We had a bit of a disagreement about the situation at first, but everything's right on track now."

I took a sip of tea and found it almost too sweet for me, though I was a big fan of the sugary drink. "It's funny, but most Southern women I know dream about their weddings from the time they're little girls."

"Well, I'm not most women. It's a formal ceremony I don't need, but Mamma is insisting, so Larry and I are going along with it."

"I met your prospective mother-in-law. She seems charming."

Donna's face lit up. "Isn't Melinda wonderful? She's already asked me to call her Mom."

"How does your mother feel about that?" I asked, despite the question's being offtrack from my intended line of questioning.

Donna took a sip of her tea, smiled, then said, "As long as she's my only 'mamma,' she doesn't care."

Okay, enough idle curiosity. It was time to get to the real purpose for our visit. "Melinda had the most darling earrings on when she came by the shop this morning. She said she got them from you."

"That was another one of Mamma's ideas. I thought it was sweet. How like Melinda to wear them in town."

"Have you worn yours yet?" I asked.

"Heavens, no. I hate earrings. No, I promised I'd wear them on my wedding day, but not until then, and certainly not after." I glanced at her ears and saw that they were unadorned. She had no jewelry on whatsoever, with the exception of a modest engagement ring. "That's lovely," I said.

"It's not much, but it was exactly what I wanted. Mamma wanted to upgrade it, if you can imagine that. I'm not marrying Larry for his money. I love him."

"About the wedding," I said. "I'm so sorry about you losing your friend."

The sun finally left Donna's face. "Poor Tina. We grew up together, and I felt kind of obligated to make her my maid of honor, but things were strained between us. I'd been hoping that the wedding would make us close again."

Donna started to tear up as the doorbell rang. I said, "Should I get that for you?"

She dabbed at the corner of one eye. "No, I'll answer it."

As she left the room, I whispered, "Is there anything else I should ask her?"

"See if she'll show you the earrings so you'll know she still has them both."

Of course. I didn't know how I could have missed such an obvious request. "Thanks."

Lillian patted my hand. "Don't worry. You're doing fine."

We heard Donna's squeals from the next room. "Larry, I'm so happy you're here."

She came in a minute later, a beaming smile on her face and a young man on her arm. Larry Spencer was a tall, gangly young man with the beginnings of a scruffy beard that matched his longish chestnut hair. He looked uncomfortable in the spotlight, and I wondered about how the poor guy would fare under the scrutiny due him on his wedding day.

"Larry, this is Jennifer and Lillian."

Larry offered us his hand as he said, "Do you run the card shop, by any chance?"

"I do," I said. "I'm pleased you've heard of it."

"Are you kidding? My mother is nuts about card making all of a sudden. She hasn't been this happy since she took up soapmaking."

"She's delightful," I said. "Donna, we need to get back to the shop, but I was wondering if you could do me a favor."

"Anything," she said, her gaze still on Larry.

"I'm thinking about getting a pair of earrings like Melinda had, but I'd love a closer look. Would you mind if I took a peek at yours?"

"Of course not. I'll be right back." She kissed Larry on the cheek and added, "Don't you go anywhere."

"I won't," he said as she left.

"So, are you excited about the upcoming nuptials?" Lillian asked, breaking her pledge at last.

"I guess," Larry said.

"It was too bad about Tina Mast, wasn't it?" I asked, trying to make conversation with him.

Larry looked at me as if I'd just shot him. The look of shock and raw grief hit his face in an instant. "Excuse me," he said as he bolted for the door Donna had left through.

"What did I say?" I whispered.

Lillian started to reply when Donna came back into the room. "Here they are. It took me forever to find them." She handed me a pair of earrings identical to

Melinda's and the single one I'd found at the crime scene. One edge of the cardboard they were mounted on was bent, and there was an odd crease in the top corner, but both earrings were there.

"Where did Larry go?" Donna asked. "He didn't leave, did he?"

"He had to go to the restroom," I said, guessing that was exactly where he'd headed. I handed the earrings back to her and said, "Donna, could you tell me who all is in your wedding party? I'm particularly interested in the girls involved."

"Now why on earth would you possibly want to know that?"

I hadn't expected her to ask me to justify my question, and frankly, I was stumped.

Lillian spoke up, saving me. "I'm thinking about writing an article for the *Rebel Forge Gazette,*" she said. "I thought your wedding might make a good story."

Donna said, "Mamma would love it. Hang on a second." She was gone for an instant, then came back with her purse. "Here's everybody involved with the ceremony. Mamma is so organized, sometimes I could just scream."

I took the list from her and said, "Thanks so much for your time. Congratulations again on your wedding. Tell Larry we wish him all the best, too."

"I'll do that," she said, looking over her shoulder, no doubt wondering what her fiancé was up to.

Once we were outside, I said, "Did you see how green his gills turned when I mentioned Tina Mast's name?"

"Perhaps he's just a sensitive young man," Lillian said. "At least I might think that if I hadn't spotted something else interesting about him. Did you see it, too?"

I racked my brain trying to figure out what she was talking about, but I didn't have any luck. "I give up. What was it?"

.

"He was sporting an earring himself, one just like his mother wore."

"But Tina kept saying 'she' on the phone with me. If it had been Larry, surely she would have said something different."

"You're probably right, but I do find it most interesting, don't you?"

"I don't know what to think yet," I admitted. "Right now I'd like to talk to the rest of the young women on this list."

Chapter 14

"So, should we tackle the bridesmaids, or should we go after the new maid of honor first?" Lillian asked.

I noticed that the bridesmaids were sisters living at the same address. "Let's take care of these two first. Maybe if we get lucky, they'll both be there."

As I drove to the address, Lillian said, "I can't help wondering if these two young ladies happen to be twins."

"Why do you say that?"

" 'Camellia' and 'Pamela' are a dead giveaway, don't you think?"

I risked glancing over at Lillian to see if she might be joking, but she was absolutely serious. She must have been able to sense my concern, but she left me hanging in the wind. She said, "Tell you what, why don't we bet on it? The loser has to buy lunch. You say they aren't twins, and I say they are."

I suddenly got suspicious. "Hey, you haven't met them before, have you?" Rebel Forge wasn't huge, but it was no small town, either. The place, especially on the outskirts of the downtown area, was large enough that I didn't automatically know everyone, though it was a rare place I could visit without running into at least one person I knew.

"I assure you, I'm going strictly by their names."

"Okay, then, it's a bet." I began to wonder if my aunt was just trying to buy my lunch and allow me to keep my self-respect when we pulled up to the house. I rang the bell, holding the wedding invitation in my hand as a way of introducing myself. A pretty young redhead barely out of her teens answered the door wearing a floral-print sundress and a pair of sandals that matched. "You must be Jennifer," the girl said. "Donna just called and said you might be coming by. Come on in. My sister's getting ready for work, but we can spare you a few minutes."

Lillian and I followed her inside as she said, "By the way, I'm Pam."

"It's nice to meet you, Pam," I said, scanning what I could see of the house for her sister.

"Now what is it you'd like to know?"

Lillian jumped right in. "As Donna told you, I'm thinking about doing a story for the newspaper. When I write, I like to focus on one particular item to use so my readers can relate to the mood I'm trying to convey."

"You mean like a metaphor?"

"Certainly," Lillian said, obviously glad for any excuse that made her story a little less flimsy.

"So what are you focusing on?"

"I found it fascinating that each of the women in the wedding received pierced earrings," Lillian said. "May I see yours?"

"If you've seen one pair, you've seen them all. They're identical."

Lillian didn't accept that for an answer. "That's part of the reason I'd like to see them, to examine them closely enough to see if they differ in any way."

Pam said skeptically, "You writers are something else. Hang on a second."

"Could you ask your sister to bring her earrings, too?" I said before she could disappear.

"Sure, I'd be glad to." Pam was gone a few minutes, then returned without her sibling, but with two identical sets of earrings. "She's still not dressed yet, but she told me it was okay if you wanted to look at hers, too."

There were four earrings in the collection, and I knew we'd hit another dead end. "And everyone in the wedding party got the same earrings?" I asked.

"Absolutely. Well, everyone except Tina. She didn't have pierced ears. Can you believe it?"

"So she didn't get any at all?"

Pam frowned. "No, she got some, but they were clip-ons. That poor thing."

"Were you two close?" I asked.

"Back in school we were, but she went off to college, and my sister and I stayed in town. It doesn't take long to drift apart."

"Do you have any idea who would want to kill her?" I asked.

"The sheriff asked me the exact same thing the other day. Tina was a fun girl, you know what I mean? The only thing that might have gotten her into trouble was poaching another girl's boyfriend. She loved a challenge, at least she did in high school. Who knows, though? Maybe she changed. Goodness knows, enough of our other friends did when they went off to college."

Another girl joined us, identical to the one sitting with us. "It's about time," Pam told her sister. "We're going to be late."

"You can't hurry perfection," the girl said.

"No, but you're not it," Pam said. She turned to me and added, "Sorry to rush off like this, but we've got to get to work."

"We understand completely," I said as I stood. "It was nice meeting you, Pam." I turned to the other sister and said, "And you, too, Camellia."

"Oh, please, everybody calls me Cam," she said. "Sorry I couldn't help, but Pam knows almost everything I do."

"More, I'd say," her sister protested as they got into a compact car and drove away.

I turned to Lillian. "That's not fair. I missed it completely. Pam and Cam. Can you believe that?"

"Dear, I'd believe anything. I was tutoring at the grade school before you were born, and there was a set of twins in attendance. You're not going to believe me, but their legal names were Snook and Rook. Since then, nothing has surprised me." She glanced at her watch, then said, "Should we tackle that last name on our list before lunch or after?"

My stomach rumbled. "Why don't we grab something quick so we can get back to the shop?" I added, "I'm not reneging on the bet. You choose the place and I'll pick up the check."

She pretended to think about it a moment, then said, "Since Darby's is closed for lunch and The Chateau is on the other side of town, why don't we go to The Lunch Box?" Darby's and The Chateau were the two fanciest places in all of Rebel Forge, while The Lunch Box was a local hangout where construction workers and doctors ate side by side.

"I think I can afford that," I said as I drove to the diner. The parking lot was nearly full, but I managed to squeeze my Gremlin in between two SUVs.

The Lunch Box was hopping, but I spotted two stools together on the continuous roping bar. There were no conventional tables inside, just a serpentine ribbon of counter and stools with a single break for Savannah Jones to whisk in and out from the kitchen with trays of food. Her daughter Charlie helped out, and Savannah's husband Pete worked the grill in back. In all the years I'd been going there, I hadn't heard Pete say more than a dozen words altogether, but Savannah and Charlie more than made up for it.

As we walked to our seats, Savannah said, "Look at that, the Shane ladies are playing hooky. Jennifer, I thought you had a new business to run."

"We still have to eat, Savannah. Everybody knows your hot dogs are the best in this corner of the state."

Savannah laughed as only she could, loud enough to shake the rafters and even interrupt some of the conversations going on around the pit. "You folks need to listen to her. She speaks the truth."

As we slid onto our stools, Savannah put two sweet teas in front of us, mine with lemon and Lillian's without. "What if I've changed my mind and want lemon today?" my aunt asked her.

"Did you?" Savannah asked simply.

Lillian smiled. "No, of course not. I was just wondering what you'd do."

"I'd say you're sour enough as it is." The two had been friends since grade school, and they loved nothing more in the world than to tease each other about anything they could find.

Lillian said, "Yes, you'd probably be right."

Savannah stepped closer. "Lillian, are you all right?"

"I'm fine, why?"

"Woman, in all the years I've known you, you've never let me get away with a zinger like that."

Lillian just smiled, then said, "I believe I'll have my usual house salad, and Jennifer would like a hot dog all the way."

Savannah walked back to Pete to give him the order instead of shouting it like she usually did. I whispered, "What was that all about?"

"I just wanted to see what Savannah would do if I went limp on her. You have to admit, it's got her rattled, doesn't it?"

"Now Lillian, play nice with your friends."

My aunt frowned at me, then said, "If I must."

In a few minutes, a subdued Savannah brought us our food. "There you go."

Lillian stared down at her plate and pointed to the salad. "This isn't right."

"It's just like you always have it," Savannah said. "What's wrong with it?"

"It's missing something. I believe I'll have a hot dog

with my salad today," she said. "Why don't you throw a couple of lemons on the side while you're at it, and be sure to get one for yourself, too."

Savannah whooped with laughter, though I didn't think my aunt was all that funny. There were so many inside jokes between the two of them that I rarely understood the humor in their exchanges.

"You serious about that dog?" Savannah asked.

"What do you think?" Lillian said as she had her first bite of salad.

"I think that last shred of sanity you were hanging on to just broke."

Lillian grinned. "You may be right."

As we ate, I saw that Charlie looked just as bewildered as I was by the conversation.

We were just about finished when Grady Farrar walked in. As he took the stool beside me, I asked, "When did you start leaving the hardware for lunch?"

"Shh," he said with a smile, "I don't want Martha to know I'm goofing off. I had to make a delivery to Betty Olmsted's place, and this was right on my way."

I took a sip of tea, then said, "Betty Olmsted's house is on the other side of town. Grady, you had to pass your hardware store to get over here."

"Well, I was out making the delivery in the truck anyway," he said.

Charlie approached him and asked, "What would you like, Mr. Farrar?"

"I'd like you to start calling me Grady," he said.

"I wish I could, but it's awfully hard."

"Let me tell you what's hard, young lady. I may look like an old man, but inside I'm still in my twenties. Can you imagine what it does to my spirit to have a pretty young lady like you call me mister?"

Charlie smiled brightly, and I could swear I saw the hint of a blush on her cheeks. "Okay, if it will make you feel better. What would you like to eat, Grady?"

Savannah was walking past and swatted her daughter with the bar towel in her hand. "Girl, I raised you better than that. You speak to Mr. Farrar with respect."

Grady said, "Now Savannah, I asked her to call me Grady. Demanded it, in fact. Shoo, woman, we're having a conversation here."

I felt a chilled hush fall over the place. Nobody, not even her husband Pete, challenged Savannah in her restaurant. I stopped in midbite, waiting to see what would happen. Savannah's eyes narrowed for a second, then she started laughing. "You quit flirting with my little baby, you hear me?"

Grady looked shocked by the accusation. "Why, she's young enough to be my granddaughter. I was just being friendly."

"I'm pulling your leg, you old coot. Now quit jabbering and tell Charlie what you want to eat."

After he ordered, I said, "You're taking a real chance sniping at Savannah that way."

"Not as much as you'd think. I used to chase that girl out of my orchard every weekend for stealing apples."

I couldn't imagine Charlie being that bold. "I can't believe Charlie would ever do that."

"I'm not talking about Charlie; I mean Savannah." He looked at me a second, then said, "It looks like I'm not the only one playing hooky. Why aren't you at your shop?"

"I'm running an errand for business, too," I said. I had the invitations in my purse, and I had asked Donna about them, so it wasn't a complete lie.

"And who's running things while you're gone?"

"I shut the place down," I admitted.

Grady took a sip of coffee, then said, "I'm not trying to tell you how to run your business, Jennifer, but you can't sell anything if you're not there."

How could I tell him that there was something more important at the moment than selling handmade cards? My life was on the line, and the threats were getting more direct. I was afraid if I didn't unmask the killer soon, there wouldn't be anyone around to run my shop ever again.

I patted his hand. "Thanks, I appreciate your advice."

"But you're saying, 'Mind your own business, old man'? Is that it?"

I swiveled slightly on my stool. "I wouldn't have used those exact words."

"But the sentiment is the same. I understand, and of course you're right." He leaned forward so he could make eye contact with Lillian. "You're pretty quiet down there," he said.

"I'm sorry, were you talking to me? I was lost in thought."

Grady grinned. "Good for you."

Lillian said, "They might think you're amusing, but I don't."

He shrugged. "Hey, every rose needs a thorn."

We were nearly ready to leave when Grady asked, "Is something going on with you, Jennifer?"

"What do you mean?" I asked, hoping that the grapevine around town hadn't gotten hold of my connection with the murder. I knew tongues had started wagging as soon as Tina's body had been discovered, but I'd hoped to avoid any connection to it, at least until Bradford found the killer.

"Well, I don't mean to be nosy, but I was walking past your place this morning on my daily routine and I saw a deputy sitting in his truck watching your apartment. At least I had to figure it was you he was keeping an eye on."

"Did you happen to see which deputy it was?"

"It was Wayne Davidson."

"Are you sure?"

He looked at me a second before answering. "There's no mistaking his vehicle, or his profile. What's going on, kiddo?"

I thought about telling him the truth, but even whispering anything in The Lunch Box was a guarantee

that before I got back to my shop, all of Rebel Forge
would know about it. Blast it all, if my brother was
going to have his men watch me, they were going to
have to be more discreet about it. "I think he's sweet
on me," I said, that being the first thing that popped
into my head.

"Well now, who could blame him? Do you have a
young man at the moment?"

That was absolutely a conversation I was going to
avoid. "Well, I had my heart set on an older man, but
he's married."

Grady looked serious. "Jennifer, I'm not your father, but I must say, it's bad news whenever you get
involved with a married man."

I couldn't take his somber demeanor. I wrapped my
arm in his and said, "Then I'd better move before
people notice us."

"Us? What?" He started to stammer when he
caught my grin. "Jennifer Shane, you are incorrigible."

"Gosh, I sure hope so," I said.

Lillian said, "If we're through here, we really should
be going." She grabbed her purse, and I put a hand
on it. "This is my treat, remember?"

"I won't fight you for the check, dear. I just planned
to get the tip."

"You can plan all you want, but if a single penny
leaves that purse, you're in trouble. Do you understand?"

Lillian shrugged. "I offered; you refused. The case is
closed as far as I'm concerned. Thank you for lunch."

"You're most welcome," I said. As I left a tip and
grabbed the bill, I said, "Have a nice lunch, Grady."

"Thanks, it was good seeing you."

"And you."

I paid Savannah, then Lillian and I left the restaurant. "So what should we do now?" I asked.

"Well, what are our options?"

"We could go back to the shop, or we could tackle
Beth Anderson. She's the last-minute substitute maid

of honor." I was torn between my desire to talk to Beth and my need to be at my card shop. I wouldn't have felt nearly as guilty if Lillian had stayed behind, but that wasn't fair to my aunt, either. I knew she wanted to be out tracking down clues just as much as I did.

"It's your decision, Jennifer," she said. "I'll do whatever you'd like."

"Including going back to the shop and reopening while I talk to Beth Anderson?"

Lillian shook her head. "Anything but that," she said. "Whither thou goest and all that."

"I'm getting awfully tired of having people watch me day and night," I said.

"Then you're just going to have to learn to deal with it," Lillian said in a stern voice. "As long as this murderer is loose, someone needs to be with you at all times."

"Then let's go talk to Beth," I said. "The sooner we resolve this, the better."

Chapter 15

As we drove to Beth Anderson's house, Lillian asked, "Do you really believe she killed Tina just so she could be the maid of honor?"

"I don't know what to believe," I said. "But I do know I'd like to talk to her."

When we got to the address, I parked in front. "Is there any chance I could get you to wait here?"

"Not a single one," she said. "Let's go see what Beth has to say for herself."

I knocked on the outside door of the apartment and rang the bell, but there was no answer. I was about to give up when the door next to hers opened and an older woman reached out for her newspaper. I wondered how late she'd been up the night before if she was still in her bathrobe after lunch.

"You looking for Bethie?" she asked us.

"We are. Is she home?"

"Did she come to the door when you pounded on it, Einstein?"

Lillian said, "There's no reason to be rude. We were just asking."

The woman appeared to be contrite. "Listen, I'm sorry I snapped at you. I've got the monkey's own hangover, and I feel like I'm going to die."

"I'm sorry," I said, not meaning a word of it. "Do you know where we might find her?"

She scratched her left ear, then said, "I bet she's at work."

We waited for her to supply the name of Beth's employer, but she started to close the door, so I had to shout to catch her attention. "Where does she work?"

"Easy," the woman said, holding her head in both hands with the paper tucked under one arm. "She works at Hurley's over on King Street."

"Thanks," I said, and we started to go.

The woman called out, "Hang on a second. Do you happen to know how to cure a hangover?"

Lillian said, "I have the perfect cure."

"Come on, give it to me. I'm dying here."

"Don't drink so much the next time you go out," Lillian said.

"Thanks for nothing," the woman said, and slammed her door. This was immediately followed by a string of profanities from the other side.

As we got into the car, I said, "That was cruel. I know you take a nip now and then yourself."

"I admit that I don't have a problem with the occasional tipple," she said. "But she asked, didn't she?"

"You're one tough broad, aren't you?" I said with a smile.

"It's so sweet of you to notice. I assume we're going to Hurley's."

"I need to talk to Beth before she talks to anybody else we've interviewed. It's a shame she wasn't home."

Lillian nodded. "I know. How are we going to make sure she has a complete set of earrings?"

"I'm sure we'll think of something," I said as I drove back toward my shop. King Street is close to Oakmont Avenue, so I decided to park in my usual spot so we could walk over, then back to Custom Card Creations. Maybe I'd be able to finish my interviews and fit in a sale or two at the shop before the day was a complete wash. Then I remembered the two sets of invitations I'd committed myself to making. It looked like I was going to have to put in some heavy-duty overtime if I was going to meet my commitments in the next few days. Well, I'd hoped I'd be busy. I just hadn't planned on helping my brother solve a murder while I was starting a brand-new business. On the plus side, I didn't have any romantic entanglements to slow me down. On the downside, I didn't have any romantic entanglements to slow me down. I was fine without a boyfriend, but I had to admit that it usually made the sky a little bluer and the air a little crisper when there was a new love in my life.

Wayne was not an option. Not only had Corrine's story creeped me out, but the man himself was starting to bother me. As Lillian and I walked over to Hurley's, I grabbed my cell phone and called Bradford. I'd forgotten to turn it on that morning, and there were messages waiting, but they'd have to stay there until I was ready for them.

"Where have you been?" my brother shouted the second he heard my voice.

"I've been working," I said.

"Not at your shop. I've been by twice. We've been worried sick about you."

"Don't tell me who the 'we' is. You've talked to Sara Lynn?"

Bradford let out a puff of air. "You're kidding, right? She came by your shop to talk to you and found it locked up. I had to go search your apartment and I've got my guys looking for that Gremlin of yours."

"Well, you can call off the dogs. They must not be very good. I haven't exactly been hiding."

He snapped, "Then where have you been?"

"I'm not sure I want to answer that. I don't like your tone of voice."

Lillian kept tugging on my arm so I'd move the phone enough for her to listen, but I had enough to worry about without letting my aunt eavesdrop on the conversation.

In a calmer voice, he said, "Listen, I'm glad you're okay, but you can't blame us for being worried, not with what happened last night."

I started to waver in my resolve. After all, as frustrating as their behavior was at that moment, my brother and sister loved me. "I've been talking to members of the wedding party."

"About what?" he asked suspiciously.

"About the wedding invitations, if you must know." Okay, again it was a half-truth, but at the moment, half the truth was better than none of it. At least that was the position I was taking.

"That's fine, but from here on out, keep your cell phone turned on, would you? And call Sara Lynn; she's going nuts."

I hung up, and before I could dial my sister's number, Lillian asked, "Do I even need to ask what that was about?"

"I'm guessing you got enough of the gist of it from my end."

Lillian shrugged. "They have a right to be worried. You never got around to telling him why you were calling him in the first place."

"Well, he was so upset, I didn't want to bring it up."

Lillian wouldn't let it go at that. "So what were you going to talk to him about?"

"I was going to ask him to assign someone else to guard me if he's bound and determined to have me followed."

"You don't trust Wayne Davidson," she said as we waited to cross King Street to Hurley's.

"There's something about him that really makes me uncomfortable," I admitted.

"Surely you can't think he's the murderer. Jennifer, Tina told you it was a woman there with her."

"That's true," I said, "but he still gives me the creeps."

Lillian said, "Then that's reason enough. I learned long ago to trust my instincts, especially when it comes to men. Talk to Bradford about it."

"I will, but first I have to tackle Sara Lynn."

Lillian bit her lip, then said, "You're on your own there. I believe I'd rather face the murderer."

Sara Lynn answered on the first ring. I said, "Hey, Sis. I heard you were looking for me."

I held the phone out away from my ear for two reasons: one, she was shouting, and two, I wanted to let Lillian hear, as well. After Sara Lynn started to wind down, I said, "I was working, even though my shop wasn't open. Sara Lynn, I appreciate your concern, I really do, but I just got it from Bradford, and my patience to listen to both of you lecturing me is gone. I'll keep my phone on from now on, but I'm fine. Lillian's with me."

"I'm sorry, Jennifer. I may have overreacted. We can talk more tonight."

I took a deep breath, then said, "We can talk, but I won't stand still for another sermon. Is that understood, or are you ready to move back home with your husband?"

She paused a few moments, then said, "I agree. I'll see you tonight."

When I hung up, Lillian was looking at me with a new respect in her gaze. "What's up with that look?" I asked her.

"I never thought I would see Sara Lynn cave in to anyone like that. You're tougher than you look, Jennifer."

"I can be when I have to be," I said. "Now, let's go talk to Beth Anderson."

"I'm not about to try to stop you," Lillian said, falling in step behind me. I hated to use that tone of voice with one of my siblings, but with everything going on in my life at the moment, I was really stressing out.

I just hoped Beth Anderson could give us more than we'd gotten from everyone else we'd interviewed so far.

*   *   *

Hurley's was a place that catered to tourists, a faux Irish pub that served hamburgers and deli sandwiches at exorbitant prices. No locals ate there as far as I knew, but they did a bang-up job with the tourist trade.

Jack Hurley was behind the bar, wiping it down with a rag and polishing it until it gleamed. Jack had gone to school with Sara Lynn, and once upon a time they'd dated. Though I was now old enough to know better, every time I saw Jack I reverted back to a twelve-year-old girl. I'd had a huge crush on him and had been so jealous of Sara Lynn for getting to go out with him. He was happily married now, with a wife pregnant with their fifth child.

"How's the family?" I asked as Lillian and I approached the bar. My aunt pretended to study a menu, but I knew she was listening to every word.

"Growing day by day, Shortcake," he said.

I fought the blush creeping onto my cheeks. He'd called me that as a kid, and I'd never been able to convince him that I was all-grown-up now.

"Listen, I hate to bother you, but I need to talk to one of your employees."

Jack said, "What are you going to do, make a card for her?"

"Jack Hurley, I run a business just like you do, and I'd appreciate it if you'd show me a little more respect."

My outburst probably surprised us both. He said, "Easy, Jennifer, I didn't mean anything by it. In fact, two ladies were in here talking about your shop earlier. They said how disappointed they were that you were already closed. Sorry about that crack. I should have known better."

"I was closed for the morning, not for good," I said. I promised myself that the next time I took one of these little field trips, Lillian was going to have to stay behind and run the shop whether she liked it or not. What could she do, quit?

"I'll be sure to pass that along," he said. "Now, who would you like to see?"

"Beth Anderson," I said.

He shrugged. "She's working in the kitchen and waiting on tables. You can talk to her, but Miss Lillian needs to stay out here. Don't get in Beth's way or slow her down, Jennifer. I need her working."

"I understand." I looked at Lillian to see if she'd agree to being excluded, but she wasn't putting up any fight at all. I'd have to ask Jack what his secret was.

I walked back into the kitchen and found a young woman preparing two salads. Though it was pretty obvious she was battling a lot more pounds than I was, her attire was skintight. I couldn't imagine Jack allowing it, but then again, he was short on staff, so maybe he didn't have any choice. Her hair appeared to have gone through several wildly different color incarnations, and I wondered if Mrs. Albright was going to make her wear a wig to the wedding. "Do you have a second?"

"Nobody's supposed to be back here," she said without looking up. Then she glanced at me and said, "If you're the new waitress, I don't have time to show you anything right now."

"I'm not here for a job," I said. "I'm a friend of Donna Albright's." That was as close to a lie as I'd come to yet, but she had been friendly and we'd gotten along all right.

Beth dropped one of the salad bowls she'd just filled. "What's happened now?"

"Nothing," I said as I helped her clean up the mess. I kept expecting Jack to poke his head into the kitchen and evict me, but there was no sign of him. "I'm here to talk about the wedding, and the invitations."

The look of relief on the poor girl's face was obvious. "I was so afraid she was going to call the whole thing off after what happened to Tina."

"Did you know her well?"

Beth snorted. "I guess. She waitressed here last

summer. She wasn't very good, in my opinion, but the customers seemed to like her well enough."

"Whatever happened to not speaking ill of the dead?" I asked before I realized that probably wasn't the best way to pump her for information. I had a few things to learn if I was going to do any good at all looking into the murder.

"I'm sorry," Beth said defensively, "but I think it's hypocritical to talk nice about someone just because they're dead. We didn't get along when she was alive, and I won't sugarcoat it now."

"It must have crushed you when Donna picked her for her maid of honor, the way you felt about her."

Beth's nostrils flared. "It was a mistake, but it's been corrected, as far as I'm concerned. Donna and I grew up together. She didn't meet Tina until kindergarten." As she spoke, Beth waved the knife she'd been using to cut fresh carrots in the air around me. This was one woman I wanted to stay on the good side of. She looked suspiciously at me, then asked, "So if the wedding's not off, then why are you here? You're not going to be in the wedding party, too, are you?"

"Gracious, no," I said before she could get the wrong idea. "My aunt and I are doing an article for the paper about the wedding festivities, and we're asking everyone to show us the earrings the bride gave them."

"That's silly. Each pair is identical to every other one."

"Let's just say it's our hook to involve the reader more," I said, stealing a line from my aunt.

"Well, I can't show you mine," she said resolutely.

"Beth, I didn't expect you to have them on you. We can drop by after work if that's convenient."

She hesitated, chopped a few more carrots, then said, "I suppose I'll have to confess to someone sooner or later. I don't have mine."

"What happened to them?" I asked, suddenly very aware of that knife in her hand.

"I lost them, okay? I've torn my whole room up, but I can't find them. I swear they were on the dresser in my bedroom, and the next thing I knew, they were gone."

"When did you first notice they were gone?" I asked, hoping she'd say the day of the murder.

"Yesterday," she admitted. "I had a bridal shower at my place and invited every woman in the wedding party for a little get-together. I was going to wear them to the party, but I forgot to put them on before everyone got there. When I realized I'd forgotten to wear them halfway through, I slipped back into my bedroom and they were gone."

"Do you mean that someone took them?"

Beth looked exasperated. "Of course not, I don't mean that at all. Why would someone steal something they already had? After all, we each got a pair. I must have mislaid them somewhere and then forgot about them. I'm afraid I do it all the time. I don't know what I'm going to tell Donna. I've been looking all over town for a pair to replace them, but she must not have bought them in Rebel Forge."

"Don't worry; I'm sure they'll turn up," I said.

Jack poked his head in the door. "Beth, your customers are waiting for their salads. Jennifer, you need to scoot."

"Thanks, we were just finishing up."

Beth grabbed my hand. "You won't tell anyone about the earrings, will you?"

"Donna won't hear it from me," I said. There was no way I was going to keep that to myself, but I would keep my pledge not to tell the bride.

"Thanks."

I followed her out of the kitchen, said good-bye to Jack, then collected Lillian and left. As we walked toward Custom Card Creations, Lillian said, "Now, tell me everything she said."

"I don't know what to think about her story. Maybe you can help me figure it out." I relayed Beth's tale as we walked, finishing up as we neared the card shop. "So what do you make of it?"

"There are several possibilities."

"Enlighten me," I said as I unbolted the door.

HANDCRAFTED CARD-MAKING TIP

Use foam tape on your adornments to make them jump off the front of the card! It's amazing what a little added dimension will do to enhance your card's visual appeal.

Chapter 16

There was a pile of mail on the floor by the slot, as well as a few handwritten notes. They would have to wait, though. It sounded as if my aunt was on to something.

She said, "First, we need to consider the fact that Beth just mislaid them as she claimed. But we can't disregard the more ominous possibilities. She could have lost one earring at the murder scene while she was killing Tina. There was no love lost between them, according to your conversation with the girl."

"You actually think she killed her so she could be the maid of honor instead?" I couldn't believe that.

"I'm not saying it was the only reason, but it could have been the final indignity for her. After all, if that was her motive, she was rather successful at achieving what she wanted, wasn't she?"

"What else have you got?" I said as I sorted the mail from the handwritten notes.

"The other possibility is that someone from that party is the murderer, and she saw an opportunity to steal a complete set of earrings without throwing suspicion on herself. If a single earring shows up somewhere, it could be a plant in order to frame someone else, especially since you can't just buy these earrings in town without special ordering them."

"You have a devious mind; you know that, don't you?" I said as I smiled at my aunt.

"My dear child, no one could survive the marriages

I've had without one. So I'm afraid we're back where we started."

"At least we can be pretty sure we talked to the killer today," I said. "We covered everyone in the wedding party."

"And that means that you showed the murderer you weren't taking her warning seriously enough," Lillian said. "I don't like that."

"There's nothing I can do about that," I said.

"Do you mean the added menace, or my disapproval?"

"Either one," I said. "I can't let anything stop me from doing this."

"So where does that leave us?" Lillian asked.

"We take care of business, make some wedding invitations and wait to see what happens."

"Being passive doesn't sound like you," Lillian said.

"I don't know what else to do at this point, and those cards are due in a few days. Don't worry; I'm not giving up yet."

"Then by all means, let's make cards."

I held up a hand, going through the notes in the pile. There were three from Sara Lynn, one demanding that I get an answering machine for the shop. I'd written that on my opening-day wish list, and then had promptly forgotten to buy one. One note was from Bradford, scolding me for vanishing without telling him first, one was from Anne Albright wondering when she could pick up her Art Deco invitations, and another was from Greg Langston asking me to call him at my earliest convenience. When pigs fly, I thought as I crumpled up that particular note. The last thing I needed in my life was another round with him.

"Is there anything urgent in there?" Lillian asked.

"No, it's about what I expected. How would you like to make some wedding invitations?"

"I thought you'd never ask," Lillian said.

*   *   *

I never thought I'd say it, but thankfully, we had a slow day at the card shop. By closing time, Lillian and I had managed to put a real dent in our orders. She'd cut the jagged patterns out of red stock for Mrs. Albright's cards while I'd worked on Melinda's. I'd run the stock through the printer earlier, something I'd sworn I'd never do, but there was no way I could handle a big order on such short notice and still manage to ink them all myself. It was a little tricky attaching the rings to the wire on the cards, but I'd come up with a system that made it possible, though I'd burned my fingertips a dozen times with my glue gun and managed to stab my thumbs three or four times with the sharp wire ends. My gun was supposed to be a cool one, but the glue still got hot enough to sting my fingers when I accidentally touched some of the melted glue.

"That was certainly an interesting day," Lillian said as she put her scissors down.

"It had its moments, didn't it?" I said as I kept working.

"Aren't you going to go home?"

I looked at the pile of cards still to do. "I wish I could, but there's too much to do if I'm going to make my deadline."

"Sara Lynn won't approve, and neither will Bradford," Lillian said.

"So what else is new?" I said as I rubbed my fingertips.

"You still have to eat. Let me run out and get us something. Then we can jump right back on it."

"You don't have to stay," I said. "You're just a volunteer, remember? I'm sure your social calendar is full."

"Posh, let him wait. It will do him good."

"You never did tell me the name of the new man you were dating," I said.

"Imagine that," Lillian replied. "So what would you like for dinner?"

"If you're hungry, be my guest, but I'm going to keep working. I'd better call Sara Lynn and tell her I won't be home in time to eat."

I dialed my apartment and my sister picked up on the first ring. She said, "Are you on your way home? My chicken potpie will be out of the oven in three minutes."

"I can't do it," I said. "I've got a deadline I'm up against, and if I don't put in some extra time, I won't make it." To give my sister credit, she didn't mention my AWOL performance that morning. "Why don't you take that home and feed your husband?"

"We had lunch together," Sara Lynn said. "I don't want to spoil him."

"Whatever," I said. "I'd appreciate it if you'd feed the cats. Oggie gets kind of cranky when his meals are late."

"And how could you possibly tell?" she said. It looked like the two of them were having a bit of a power struggle, but I wasn't about to get involved. I said good-bye, then told Lillian, "You're free to go if you'd like, but you're welcome to stay, too."

"I'll stay."

"Then at least go get something to eat. I don't want your hunger pains on my conscience."

Lillian snorted. "It wouldn't hurt me to miss a meal now and again. Let's get back to work."

We closed the shop, then continued our invitation-making party. Twenty minutes later there was a knock on the door. I peeked outside and saw Sara Lynn standing there with an enormous picnic basket latched on one arm.

"It looks like we're going to eat after all," I said as I unlocked the door.

As Sara Lynn stepped inside, I said, "This is above and beyond the call of duty, Sis."

"Nonsense, I had no desire to sit in your apartment alone and eat with your roommates watching me." She put the basket down on the counter. "So where should we eat?"

I glanced at the table in the window where we'd been working, and realized what a pain it would be to move everything, then put it back after the meal. "Why don't we eat in back?"

"That suits me," she said. "Lillian, would you mind setting the table?"

She took the basket from Sara Lynn and said, "I'd be delighted. You are a special woman; you know that, don't you?"

"I've suspected it on occasion," Sara Lynn said with a smile. She moved to our worktable and examined the cards.

"They're still works in progress," I explained as I pulled the prototypes out of my purse. "Here's what the finished products will look like."

She studied the cards, and despite myself, I found I was holding my breath waiting for her response. My sister's professional opinion meant a great deal to me, more than I was willing to admit to anyone, most of all myself.

"They're certainly different, aren't they?" she said. "But why are you making so many of each design?"

I explained the double order, expecting her to disapprove. Instead, she started laughing. "How wonderful. Everyone gets what they want and you get paid twice for the same job."

"For the same wedding," I gently corrected her. "I'm still doing two jobs for two fees."

"Of course you are," she said. "And you designed these yourself?"

I admitted as much, though I didn't tell her one had been done as a bad example that had gone horribly wrong.

"They're wonderful," she said as she handed the cards back to me. "I was wrong not to listen to you."

Were those angels singing in the background? It was all I could do not to whoop with delight. "Hey, Forever Memories is your shop. You have a right to stock what you want."

"Yes, and let's look on the bright side. If I hadn't

told you no, you wouldn't have this wondrous shop of your very own, would you?''

Lillian poked her head out of the storeroom. "Are you two ready to eat?''

"Suddenly I'm starving," I said as I grabbed my sister's arm. "Let's go.''

Our chitchat at dinner was confined to ordinary topics of conversation, and I fought the temptation to tell Sara Lynn what we'd been up to in our investigation. I knew she wouldn't approve of Lillian and me interviewing suspects, and I didn't want to ruin the party atmosphere we were enjoying.

After dinner, Lillian said, "Sara Lynn, that chicken potpie would have done your mother proud.''

My sister actually blushed. "Go on," she said as she cleaned up the clutter.

"I'm serious," Lillian said. "You might even have surpassed her as a cook.''

"Now I know you're just teasing," she said, though she looked remarkably pleased by the comment.

"So how can I help you with your orders?" Sara Lynn asked after the dishes were all stowed safely back in the basket.

"You've done enough," I said. "That was heavenly.''

"Nonsense. I'm here, I'm able, willing and ready, so put me to work.''

"I don't feel right about asking you," I said. "After all, you put in a full day at your own shop.''

"So pay me whatever you're paying Lillian, if you can afford it," she said.

I reluctantly admitted, "She's volunteering, at least until I can afford to give her a salary.''

Sara Lynn put her arm around me. "Don't you think I know that? If our aunt can volunteer, you certainly can't say no to your sister.''

I was too tired to fight her on it. "That would be great," I said. "Grab a glue gun and I'll show you what to do.''

Sara Lynn said, "I can handle this myself.''

I shook my head. "Not if you don't follow my directions to the letter. Sara Lynn, you're wonderful at what you do, and there's nobody in Virginia who can make a better scrapbook than you, but I'm the professional card maker here."

Sara Lynn looked taken aback by my statement, and for a second I thought she might leave. Then she looked at Lillian, who responded, "Don't ask me for help. She read me my rights on my first day, too. Jennifer is in charge here."

Sara Lynn smiled. "If you can take it, then so can I. Okay, baby sister, tell me what you want me to do."

I didn't even resent the "baby sister" crack. I'd put my foot down, and it had stayed there. The rest of that night, we made wedding invitations, told stories from the old days and solved all the world's problems. The one subject we avoided was the murder.

The next morning at Custom Card Creations, I felt relieved that we'd been able to complete the invitations ahead of schedule, though it had taken all three of us working until past midnight. I wasn't all that much of a night owl, but having Sara Lynn and Lillian with me made the time sail right by.

I was feeling it the next morning as I opened the shop, though. I'd been straightening up for five minutes when there was a knock on the front door. Assuming it was Lillian wanting in, I dropped what I was doing and opened the door.

Anne Albright was there instead. She swept in past me before I had the chance to tell her we weren't open for business yet. I was going to have to stop answering the door or learn to put body blocks on intrusive people.

"Where are they?" she asked, as if I were hiding her family's crown jewels.

"Good morning," I said as pleasantly as I could manage. "If you're talking about the wedding invitations, they aren't due until tomorrow."

"You mean you haven't finished them? How hard could it be to do a hundred invitations?" She eyed me closely, then added, "Unless you've been derelict in your duties. Have you given my order your full attention?"

"I am running a shop here, too," I said. From the tone in Mrs. Albright's voice, I could tell she'd heard about my impromptu investigation. It would have been a miracle if she hadn't, given the range of people I'd talked to who all had ties to her.

"Among other things," she said. "How's that article coming?"

"It's a work in progress. Honestly, I didn't think you'd mind."

She looked startled by my statement. "Mind? Why on earth would I mind? I think it's absolutely brilliant. Will there be photographs, as well?"

Considering the fact that there was never going to be an article, I couldn't exactly promise pictures. "I'm sorry if we didn't make it clear, but Lillian and I are doing this on spec. Once we have the article written, we'll pitch it to the editor." Lillian had actually done a few articles for the paper that way in the past. She hadn't bothered with writing about perfect cream puffs or how to grow the rosiest tomatoes; my aunt had written about Las Vegas in one piece and Cancún in another, always managing to barely skirt the censors.

"Oh," she said, the disappointment in her voice obvious. "Well, we will cooperate in any way we can. Now, about those invitations . . ."

Her words trailed off as she spotted them on the worktable up front, and the second I followed her gaze, I realized that I'd made a horrible mistake. Stacked neatly right beside hers were the ones we'd made for Melinda. Mrs. Albright walked to the table and instead of selecting one of hers, she grabbed one of the brass-ringed ones like it was a snake.

"What is the meaning of this?" she asked, the thunder booming in her voice. "Did you think you'd get away with this?"

I honestly didn't know how to respond. Before I could think of some way to tell her about Melinda's order, she continued. "You didn't trust my judgment, did you? What did you do, go behind my back and recruit my daughter in this abomination? Well, you made these for nothing. I won't pay for them, do you understand?"

That was about all I could take. I'd apologize to Melinda later, but I wasn't about to stand there and allow anyone to use that tone of voice with me in my own shop. Besides, I'd already cashed her check. What was she going to do, demand a refund? If she so much as whispered the word, I'd coldly inform her that Custom Card Creations did not give refunds or even store credit on special orders, and she could sing in the wind, for all I cared.

"Those aren't yours," I said as I snatched the invitation from her hand.

"Please, I saw the announcement, Jennifer. These invitations are for my daughter's wedding."

"But she's not the only one getting married, is she?"

It slowly dawned on her what I was talking about. "So you pitched the mother of the groom on making her own invitations? That's not very ethical, is it?"

"Mrs. Albright, Melinda Spencer was here about something else entirely, and she happened to see the alternate invitations. She liked yours well enough, but she felt she wanted something different for her own guests. You should be happy she cared enough to go to the effort and expense. After all, you both want to see the same thing happen, and that is for your children to get married."

She seemed to think about that for some time before she finally spoke. "You are right, of course. Why, it's only natural she'd choose something a little more traditional." Mrs. Albright smiled at me as she added,

"After all, not everyone gets our cutting-edge taste, do they?"

So now I was a coconspirator? Whatever it took to avoid the storm. I readily agreed. "Honestly, this way everyone gets what they want."

I was putting her invitations in a sturdy box when there was another knock at the front door. I was seriously considering changing my hours when I saw Lillian waiting impatiently for me.

When I opened the door, she said, "There's a young man who'd like to come in, too."

"We don't open for another five minutes," I said, hoping to get Mrs. Albright out of there before I started getting regular customers.

"He's the prospective groom," Lillian said, a twinkle in her eyes.

"By all means, the more the merrier, then." I stepped aside and motioned for Larry to come in. The second I saw him, I realized why Lillian had been so urgent in her request to allow him inside. "I like your earring, Larry."

He thumbed his ear nervously. "Yeah, everybody in the wedding party got them."

Lillian asked sweetly, "I've always been curious. What do men do with the other earring in the pair?" True to form, Lillian wanted to find out what had happened to his spare.

"I've got a drawer full of them," he said. "They come in handy when I lose one."

"Enough chitchat, Larry, there's the box." Mrs. Albright pointed to it like a queen instructing one of her handmaidens. He glumly retrieved the box of invitations, and I wondered if "sullen" was his normal disposition, or the prospect of the upcoming wedding was enough to steal the spark from his spirit.

"Sorry," he mumbled as he retrieved the box of invitations.

"Don't dawdle, Son," she said as she produced a list that must have had thirty entries on it. "Larry has kindly volunteered to help me today. He's going to make a perfect son-in-law, isn't he?"

"I'm sure he will," I said, sure of nothing of the sort.

After they were gone, I said, "I messed up. I should have put Melinda's invitations in the back until Mrs. Albright got hers. Things almost got ugly."

"And how did you diffuse it?" Lillian asked.

"I'm not sure, but somehow it ended up that Melinda's tastes were too pedestrian for our visionary stand."

Lillian laughed. "I can't imagine how in the world you kept a straight face coming up with that one."

"Oh, she supplied the theory. I just didn't refute it. It was a lot of fun last night, wasn't it?"

"Yes, I had a good time working with you both. In a way I'm sorry to see both orders completed."

As I finished putting Melinda's invitations in another box, I said, "Hopefully we'll get more custom jobs soon."

"Dear girl, does that mean you're going to be actively courting the wedding invitation trade?"

"Hardly, though I don't mind cashing the checks. No, I'm afraid that once Mrs. Albright's go out in the mail I won't be doing many more of those. But there are lots of cards, and we've got everything here to make them special." I was in a good mood, too, having delivered half my special orders already. "So, are you ready to make more cards today?"

Lillian nodded. "Whatever you'd like to do is fine with me. I didn't realize we had anything else to mass-produce."

"I was talking about another private lesson in making individual cards. That's really what this shop is about, after all."

Lillian's smile brightened. "In that case I'd love to."

Chapter 17

"I'll be right back," she said as she dashed into the storeroom. Thirty seconds later she'd retrieved a shopping bag and rejoined me up front.

"What have you got there?"

Lillian started pulling things from the bag. "This is from our last lesson. I thought we could actually do something with them, since I've learned the proper way to fold paper now." The last was said with a smile, and I knew Lillian was getting back into the spirit of card making.

I chose a few of her samples, one with a half fold and the other with a dual fold. "Okay, which one would you like to start with?"

Lillian said, "Can we use one of these instead?" She pulled out the two she'd already embellished. One had an open framed front, while the other sported a raised edge.

"Whatever you want to do," I said.

She selected the simple fold with the raised border. "Let's do one of these. After all, this is the type of card I'm used to seeing."

I laid the other aside for later. "Okay, but the window cards are fun to do, too. Now, do you have a particular occasion in mind?" I asked.

"I'd like to do a thank-you card," she said.

"Good enough. If you'd like a calligraphy message inside, I'd be happy to do it for you."

"Thanks, but I want to make this one all by myself."

I'd planned on going into greater detail with her about the different ways to embellish a card, but I didn't want to kill her enthusiasm with too much instruction. "Give me five minutes to teach you some of the basics. Then you've got the run of the shop."

"Okay, but I took a few books home last night and I have a good idea what I want to do. I'll need some foam tape, some hot glue and lots of extras."

I couldn't keep myself from laughing. "You know what? Have fun. The shop is yours."

She started walking the aisles, carefully considering nearly everything I had in stock until she found exactly what she was looking for. I pretended to be busy going through the mail for the third time that morning, but she was so fascinating I couldn't bear not watching her.

Lillian took some lacy gold ribbon and tied a beautiful tight bow, then snipped its edges and mounted it on the front of the card with foam tape. I hadn't even needed to tell her that the foam tape gave cards more of a three-dimensional look; she must have picked that up from one of the books she'd read. But when had she had the time? I'd been beat last night, barely managing to undress before I'd crawled into bed, and Lillian had found time to study basic card making after our late-night session at the shop.

I nearly missed her next step when she attached a string of small beads intertwined with ribbon. It was a little formal for my taste, but that was one of the great things about making your own cards. You could choose whatever style pleased you most, or create your own as you went. Lillian embellished the raised border with a series of small red rhinestones, then turned her attention to the inside of the card. She carefully penned her message, studied the entire card again, then handed it to me.

It was lovely, in a uniquely elegant way that shouted Lillian's name as its creator.

I said, "I'm impressed" as I handed it back to her. "Look inside," she said.

I flipped the card open and read the message printed there in her careful hand. "Thank you for giving me a bright new reason to be."

"How lovely," I said. "Is it for your new beau?"

"Jennifer, I made it especially for you. I mean it, too. Life was getting much too predictable for my tastes before you called."

I hugged her, happy that the circumstances—though bad enough—had led to such a perfect fit of having my aunt work with me at my card shop. "I'm glad you're here, too," I said.

We were still hugging when the front door opened. As Lillian and I pulled away, I saw Greg Langston standing there, a puzzled expression on his face.

Lillian must have seen it, too. "I'll put all of this away," she said as she quickly gathered her materials together and returned them to the storeroom.

"What can I do for you?" I asked Greg.

"You can stop taking so many chances with your life," he said, and I knew we were in for another row. Suddenly I was in no mood for my ex-fiancé's meddling.

"Outside. Now," I barked.

He followed me out to the sidewalk in front of my shop, and I noticed Deputy Wayne leaning against a tree nearby watching me. The second we made eye contact he scurried away, and I wondered if he was watching over me on Bradford's orders or if he'd taken to stalking me. I'd have to deal with that soon, but at the moment I had another stubborn man to set straight. Before he could say a word, I lit into him. "Greg Langston, when are you going to get it through that thick skull of yours that you no longer have a say in how I live my life? If I want to twirl fire batons wearing a skirt made of tissue paper, it's none of your business. Do you hear me?"

He started to say something, but I cut him off before he could answer. "And another thing. I'd appreciate it if you'd stop sticking your nose where it doesn't belong. Who's feeding you all of your information, anyway?" I knew the answer the split second I asked the question. My brother had always been one of Greg's biggest fans, so it wasn't much of a stretch figuring out who his source was. "Stop listening to my brother, too."

I started back into my shop when he said meekly, "Don't I even get to say anything in my defense?"

I whirled around and stared at him. "Do you really want to risk it?"

"I'll take my chances." He stared intently at me with those big brown eyes, and despite my anger, I felt my heart start to soften. The next time I had a confrontation with Greg, I was going to make him wear sunglasses. "Jennifer, I'm not trying to pry. I just want to be part of your life again."

"Then stop butting into it unannounced. Be my friend; don't try to be my protector."

He grinned. "That's a tough promise to make."

"The choice is yours, Greg. I'm serious about this."

He held up both hands. "Okay, I'll do it. From now on, I won't watch out for you." He added softly, "I can still care about you, can't I?"

"As long as you don't let it show," I said with a slight smile of my own.

I left him on the sidewalk and went back into my shop. Lillian was standing right by the door, and I figured she'd probably heard every word of our exchange. I had to give her credit; she didn't say a word, though she did keep staring out the window.

"Don't tell me he's still there," I said.

She hesitated, then said, "No, he's just leaving. You really put that man through the fire, don't you? You must care for him still. Don't try to deny it."

"I might," I admitted, "but I'm fighting it. Why, does it show?"

"Not from the way you act, but you did agree to

marry him twice. I know you've loved him in the past."

I sighed. "But this is the present, isn't it?" I looked around the shop for something to do, but everything appeared to be in perfect order. "So what would you like to do now? We could have another lesson, or are you beyond that?"

"Don't fool yourself, Jennifer. I spent last night going through those books searching for the perfect card to make for you. I'm far from being competent at it."

I admired my card again. "I wouldn't say that." I took it and mounted it behind my cash register. "You don't mind if I display it, do you? I honestly don't have anything like it. It's lovely."

"I'd be honored," she said as the front door opened. I was ready for Greg, just in case he was back for another tongue-lashing, but instead I saw my brother come in.

It was perfect timing. I had a dozen things I needed to talk to him about, and he wasn't going to like a single one of them.

"I need to talk to you," I said.

"Can we take a walk and do it, Jennifer?" He looked at Lillian with a mixture of fear and dislike.

"What is it with you two?" I asked. "Why can't you get along?"

Lillian said, "Ask him. I'm sure I wouldn't know."

"Come on, Aunt Lillian, you know full well why there's so much bad blood between us."

She blew out a puff of air. "Don't tell me you're still upset about the banana pudding incident. Bradford Shane, that was thirty years ago."

Bradford shook his head. "Doesn't matter. Mom made it especially for me, and you stole it."

"I was hungry, you nitwit," Lillian said. "Christine never told me it was for you, and by the time she realized what I was eating, it was too late. I made you another bowl myself the next day."

"It wasn't as good as Mom's."

I couldn't help myself; I busted out laughing. They both looked at me as if I were insane. Once I got my breath back, I said, "That's it? You've been battling all these years over a bowl of banana pudding? You both are unbelievable."

For the first time in thirty years, it appeared that my brother and my aunt were in perfect agreement that I was the only crazy one in the room. I grabbed Bradford's arm and said, "Let's go. I can't take the two of you at the same time."

He huffed slightly as we walked outside. I said, "Here all these years I thought you were the great peacemaker, and now my illusions are shattered."

"There's more to it than that," he protested.

"I certainly hope so, but you two can deal with it yourselves. I have enough to worry about without your squabble. There are some things I need to talk to you about."

"Yeah, well there's something I need to tell you, too."

"Me first," I said, steamrolling over him. "You need to tell your deputy to stop watching me. He's giving me the creeps."

"Which deputy are you talking about?" he asked.

"Wayne Davidson. He's been stalking me the past few days, and I don't like it, whether it's been on your orders or he's doing it on his own."

Bradford looked puzzled by my statement. "Sis, I haven't had him on you since he blew it the other night. That's the honest truth."

"Then he's developing a new obsession."

I relayed my conversation with Corrine in the bank line, and Bradford whistled softly. "That's it. I'm pulling him in. Let me know if you spot him again, okay?"

"What are you going to do?"

Bradford said, "I'm going to have one last talk with him, and if that doesn't work, he's gone. We're here to make folks feel safer, not add to their worries.

What else is on your mind? Let's get it all on the table."

"Okay, here's something else that's been bugging me. Have you been keeping Greg Langston up-to-date on what's been going on in my life? He seems to know what's happening with me the second I do."

Bradford actually reddened slightly. "Sis, he's a good guy. You two belong together. At least you would if you weren't so stubborn."

"Stop matchmaking, Bradford. We're through."

He looked shocked by my statement. "Come on, Jennifer, I didn't mean anything by it. You can't cut me out of your life."

"I'm not talking about you, you big oaf. I won't deny that Greg and I had a good thing going, but it's dead. You can trust me on that, okay? So would you stop telling him everything that's happening in my life?"

"You may not love him anymore, but I've got a feeling it's not mutual."

"That's his problem," I said. "Just kill the pipeline, okay?"

"Okay. Anything else you want to chew me out about while you're in the mood?" I glanced over and saw a couple of tourists approaching us warily. When I thought about how it must look to them to see a civilian upbraiding the sheriff in his full uniform, I had to laugh.

"What's so funny?" Bradford asked.

"We must look comical to everyone else," I said. "I knew we should have had this conversation in my shop."

"No thank you," Bradford said.

"So I know you didn't come by for an earful of grief from me," I said. "Was there something you wanted to tell me?"

"I don't know if I should," Bradford said. "It's police business, but I thought you had a right to know."

"You know you can trust me to keep my mouth shut," I said. "Besides, I'm on your payroll, remember?"

"Well, it concerns—"

At that moment, Bradford's radio went off. "Boss, I need you over on Hastings Avenue. We've got a hit-and-run, and it looks pretty bad."

"I'll be right there," Bradford said as he started running back to his patrol car.

"Bradford, what were you going to tell me?"

"It'll have to keep until later," he said as he got into his car and sped away.

My brother couldn't have devised a better way to drive me crazy if he'd tried.

There wasn't much I could do about it, though, so I walked back to my shop. At least I'd gotten a lot off my chest. It felt good standing up to Bradford and Greg. Though I knew they both meant well, it wasn't enough. I was a grown woman, perfectly capable of handling my problems in my own way. If I needed some furniture moved, I'd call one of them, but as far as the rest of my life was concerned, it was off-limits to their meddling from now on.

When I walked back into the card shop, Lillian was waiting by the door. "What did your brother want?"

"I have no idea," I admitted. "He never got a chance to tell me."

Lillian said, "You were gone an awfully long time. Have you just been walking up and down Oakmont by yourself?"

"I had some things I had to get off my chest first," I said as I straightened a stack of envelopes that didn't need it.

"Jennifer, what did your mother used to say about that?"

I was in no mood to have my mom's pearls of wisdom dropped back in my lap. "I don't want to talk about it."

Ignoring me completely, she said, "Her favorite saying was that you never learn a thing by talking."

"I didn't run him off for good; Bradford will be back. There was a hit-and-run he had to take care of first. Have you just been hovering by the door all this time waiting for me to show up?" I asked the last part with a slight smile, trying to get things back on a light footing. I loved my aunt dearly, but when she started quoting my own mother to me, it was time to put a stop to the conversation. Though she was Mom's sister, I still thought I knew my mother better than Lillian did, whether that was true or not.

Lillian accepted the jab. "Of course I haven't been idle. Actually, I've been studying your card offerings, and I have a suggestion."

"Okay, I'm willing to listen to just about anything."

Lillian chose one of my cards. "No offense, my dear, but these are just too sweet. If you're going to compete with the giants, you need an edge."

Fascinating. My aunt had been in the card business less than a week and she was already telling me how to compete with Hallmark. "Go on."

"Here's what I suggest." She handed me a card, obviously one she'd just made while I'd been gone. "It's a sympathy card. Well, kind of."

I took it from her and saw a graveyard sketched on the front of the card. Lillian had always had a knack for drawing; I had to say that for her, even if I didn't approve of her subject matter. "It lacks something, wouldn't you say?" Something like taste, I thought to myself.

"Open it," she suggested.

As I did, I saw that my aunt had made the card a pop-up. She had been doing her homework, at any rate. A tombstone lifted out of the ground, and on it was printed, "My sympathies for your upcoming nuptials."

Despite my initial reaction, I had to laugh. "Did you have anyone in particular in mind for this?"

"Myrtle Entwistle is getting married to the most dreadful man in a few weeks. Believe me, I have nothing but sympathy for the poor woman."

"Okay," I said, "so you want to do this tongue in cheek. I get your humor, but will Myrtle?"

"Oh please, we've been friends for ten years. How else do you think we've lasted that long?"

"And you're suggesting a new line of these? Why not? Come up with five or six prototypes and I'll give you a corner." I knew what it felt like to have my ideas crushed by a family member, and I wasn't about to stomp on Lillian's enthusiasm. We might even manage to sell a few. I wasn't cynical enough to write them, but Lillian wouldn't have any problem with that.

She looked delighted by my commission. "This is going to be fun. Listen, lunch today is on me."

"You're going to lose money working here; you know that, don't you?"

"Money I've got plenty of," she said. "This is fun."

"Fine, I'm too tired to argue about it," I said. "Get us whatever you'd like."

She grabbed her purse and bolted out the door, no doubt fleeing before I could change my mind. Twenty minutes later Lillian was back. Blast it all, I knew I shouldn't have let her choose. She'd picked up two salads for us from Sassy's. It was Lillian's idea of a feast, not mine.

"I've been thinking about something we need to discuss," she said as she set them up on our worktable in the window.

"We're eating here?" It would feel like living in a zoo, eating my lunch in front of the world.

"Why not? We're finished with our orders, and there's nothing pressing."

"Don't remind me," I said. I couldn't count on getting two orders for wedding invitations every month, and the walk-in traffic was much less than I'd hoped.

"Don't worry, dear. You'll succeed if it kills us both."

" 'Kill' isn't exactly a word I'm fond of these days."

Lillian said, "That's what I want to talk to you about."

Chapter 18

"I'm not in the mood for one of your jokes, Lillian." I looked at the salad, but I couldn't bring myself to try it. I enjoy a simple mixed green salad on occasion, maybe with a few carrots and peppers thrown into the mix, but there was something dripping off this one that I couldn't identify if my life depended on it.

"This is no joke," Lillian said after taking a bite of hers. Whatever it was didn't kill her, so I tried mine. It was a little salty, but I didn't want any more information than that, and there was no way on earth I was going to ask her what I was eating.

Lillian continued. "We're going about this all wrong."

That was enough. "Listen, I know you mean well, but I've been planning this card shop in my mind for months, and I think I've done a pretty good job. Maybe you should work here longer than a week before you start remodeling."

Instead of the scowl I'd been expecting, Lillian started laughing. "Jennifer, I'm not talking about your shop. I think you've done an admirable job."

"Then what are you talking about?"

"Our murder investigation," she said, then took another bite.

"What else can we do?" I asked. "We've talked to everyone we can think of, and nobody broke down and confessed."

"This isn't bad television, dear; this is real. We need to make a list and quantify our findings."

"What did you do, check a book out from the library on crime solving?"

Lillian's scowl came on full blast then. "Don't be a nit. It doesn't become you." She took a bite, then said, "Herbert, my second husband, was a crime fiction nut, and he got me hooked on the classics. A lot of famous literary detectives made lists."

I got up, grabbed a white marker board from the back and handed her a pen. "Write away."

If Lillian had any idea I'd just been teasing her, she didn't let on. She drew four columns on the board, and for the head of each one, she wrote *"NAME," "MEANS," "OPPORTUNITY"* and *"MOTIVE."* Under the name heading, she wrote *"Donna," "Beth," "Pam," "Cam," "Melinda," "Anne"* and *"Larry."*

"Have you lost your mind completely?" I asked.

"I know Larry's a stretch, but he had an earring, too, and I'm certain that's a telling clue."

I shook my fork at her, getting into the debate without meaning to. "Tina kept referring to a 'she' on the phone with me. Larry couldn't have done it."

Lillian frowned, then erased his name with the back of her hand. "I just hated seeing all those women's names without having a man there, too."

"Lillian, our reasoning could be faulty. What if the murderer wasn't tied into the wedding at all?"

"That I refuse to believe," my aunt said. "Tina was back in town to meet with Donna about her wedding. We mustn't forget that you found that earring in the bathroom, one that Beth couldn't find anywhere in town. No, it has to be one of these women."

"And you think Melinda or Anne Albright could have done it?"

Lillian frowned, then said, "Melinda seems sweet, but what if she didn't want her son to marry Donna so badly that she was willing to kill to stop it?"

"Then why didn't she just murder the bride instead?"

"And kill her own grandchild in the process? No, if I were determined to stop this wedding, killing Tina would be the perfect choice."

I pushed my salad away, more interested in working on the list than eating. "If that's the motive, you can strike Anne Albright's name off, then. Nobody wants to see those two get married more than that woman, and that includes the bride and groom."

Lillian started to erase her name, then hesitated. "Let's leave her up there for now, shall we?"

I shrugged. After all, it was her list. "What about the others? Do you think any of them had motive?"

"I admit, that's the difficult part. The weapon was from the house, so anyone could have killed her with that. As to opportunity, none of them have to give us alibis, do they? The only thing we can play with is motive."

I studied that part of the list again, then said, "Beth has one. At least she might believe she does. Who's the one person that we know profited from Tina's murder?"

It was Lillian's turn to look shocked. "Are we really willing to consider the possibility that she killed Tina to get her job as maid of honor? It's a little extreme, wouldn't you say?"

"You didn't hear her in the kitchen," I said. "Beth made it sound like she and Tina had been battling for years."

Lillian circled Beth's name. "So there's our killer."

"Not so fast," I said. "We still need to talk about the other three women."

"Do you think we can find motives for them, too?"

"Lillian, if we're going to do this right, we can't just jump on the first likely suspect."

"I suppose that's true," she said as she removed the circle with her thumb. "How about the others?"

"That's the problem. We don't know Cam and Pam well enough to guess their motives."

"So let's leave them for now," Lillian said. "Donna is the only one left on our list."

"Again, I can't think of a motive for her."

"I didn't say this method was foolproof, but I would like to talk to Beth myself. Why don't we go grab some lunch?"

I pointed to my half-eaten salad. "I thought we just ate."

"Nonsense. I know how much you love red meat. I'm going to treat you to a hamburger."

"At Hurley's, right? We're going to go talk to Beth again."

"If we happen to sit at her table, we'll naturally chat with her a little."

There were a great many reasons I probably should have said no, and shutting my card shop down again was just one of them, but that salad had done little to satisfy my appetite, and I did want to talk to Beth. "Let's go."

"That's the spirit," Lillian said as the front door opened. So much for our plans to investigate the murder.

The man who walked in looked bewildered by the array of cards up front. "May I help you?" I asked.

"I'm sorry, but could I see a menu?"

"Excuse me?"

He rubbed his forehead. "I'm not sure I want to eat here," he said as he looked around. "But I saw you eating salads in the window, and they looked good to me."

I shot Lillian a dirty look, then directed him to Sassy's. After he was gone, I said, "That's the last time we eat up front."

Lillian shrugged off my stern language. "Let's go. You can berate me along the way."

"Hang on one second." I took the time to make a sign up that said CLOSED FOR LUNCH. BACK SOON. I stuck it in the window; then we walked to Hurley's to interview one of our suspects, and get me a little protein in the process.

Hurley's had a nice crowd, so Jack frowned when he saw us. "Back again so soon? Now's not a good time."

"For lunch?" I asked as innocently as I could.

"Don't be smart, Jennifer. Would you two really like a table?"

Lillian said, "If we can have one in Beth Anderson's area."

"She doesn't have time to answer your questions, Ma'am," Jack said.

Lillian didn't reply; she merely kept looking at him intently until he broke. "Fine, I'll seat you in her section, but you're here for lunch, understand?"

"Of course we do, dear boy." I didn't know how Lillian managed it, but she could get her way without saying a word more often than I could by using every argument I could think of. I was beginning to realize that my aunt could teach me a thing or two about dealing with people, if I just paid attention.

Beth greeted us at our table without making eye contact. "Welcome to Hurley's," she said automatically. "What can I get you to drink?"

"Hi, Beth," I said, putting as much warmth into my voice as I could. "We'd love a couple of iced teas."

"Oh, hi, Jennifer," she said. "I'll go grab them."

While she was gone, Lillian said, "Dear, I know this is your investigation, but would you mind terribly if I interrogated her myself?"

"Be my guest," I said. "But you know Jack's going to get mad if we upset Beth."

"Trust me, my child," Lillian said as Beth returned with our drinks.

As she slid them in front of us, she asked, "Are you ready to order, or would you like a few minutes?"

"What would you recommend?" Lillian asked.

"The soup's good today. It's cream of broccoli. That's what I had for lunch."

"Then I'm sure you're right. It sounds delicious."

Beth nodded her agreement, looking pleased with Lillian's affirmation. "How about you?"

I was willing to appease our waitress, but there was no way I was eating at Hurley's and just getting soup. "I'll have a Jack Stack Burger," I said, not even looking at the menu. Jack had created his own hamburger by throwing everything in the kitchen on it, and being Jack, he had named it after himself.

Beth nodded and left to place our orders with the kitchen.

"I thought you were going to interrogate her," I asked after I took a sip of sweet tea.

"In due time," Lillian said. We spent our time waiting chatting about some of Lillian's other card ideas. They were witty and dry, and some of them were just a little mean. In other words, we would probably manage to sell quite a few of them. I'd have to be careful how we displayed them, and I certainly didn't want Lillian's humor to be on the first cards to greet our customers. Maybe I'd tuck them into one of the back corners and direct any folks with a wicked twinkle in their eyes to them.

We were still chatting when Beth returned with our food. Lillian again stroked her ego, but Beth was gone before she'd asked a single question about her alibi.

"You're not much of an investigator, are you?"

"I'm getting around to it," Lillian said as she tasted the soup. "She's right, you know. This is excellent."

I looked at my burger with a smile. "I'm sure this is, too." I considered picking it up to eat it, but there was no way I could manage it without walking out of there with half the thing on my shirt. Taking the knife, I cut it into sections, making it much easier to handle. Even if Lillian didn't get a single answer out of our waitress, it had been worth the trip.

Beth came by to check on us a little later, and Lillian asked for the bill. As Beth handed it to her, Lillian said, "You know, you look awfully familiar to me."

"I've been here forever," Beth said as she waited for the money.

"No, this wasn't where I saw you. Let me think. I've got it. Last Tuesday night I saw you at the video store arguing with the manager. You were complaining that he was charging you for a late fee you didn't deserve."

"No, it wasn't me," Beth said.

"My dear, I'm positive. I thought you were fully justified in complaining. They've done the same thing to me. What movie was it, by the way?"

"I'm telling you, you're mistaken. I was here working a double shift from noon to midnight."

"Surely they give you time for a break," Lillian said. "At least enough to dash out and return a tape."

"Are you kidding me? Two other waitresses called in sick. I had to handle everything myself. Jack even had to back me up. I didn't have time to go to the bathroom, let alone take a tape back."

"My mistake, then. I'm sorry I said anything."

"It's no problem, really. Those video guys are relentless, aren't they?"

"They can be," Lillian said as she paid the bill. "Keep the change. It was delightful."

When Beth saw the size of her tip, she brightened immediately. "Come back any time."

"We will, I assure you," Lillian replied.

On our way out, Lillian hesitated at Jack's station up front. "Can I help you?" he asked.

"We tried to come by on Tuesday afternoon, but someone met us outside and told us the service was horrid."

Jack frowned. "Yeah, I'm sorry about that. We were jammed with customers, and Beth was my only waitress. I thought she was going to quit on me, I worked her so hard."

"Well, today's fare was delicious," Lillian said.

"Thanks," Jack said. "I appreciate that."

I waited until we were out on the sidewalk before

I applauded. "Neither one of them even knew what hit them. I'm the first to admit it; I was wrong. Not only did you get an alibi from Beth, but you confirmed it right on the spot. I'm impressed."

"Please, it wasn't all that difficult," Lillian said, despite the slight smile. I could tell she was pleased with the praise, but she deserved it. I was definitely going to school on my aunt's techniques for dealing with people.

"At least we can cross one name off our list," I said.

"Yes, but I hate losing our best suspect."

The rest of the day was uneventful, and we were thirty minutes away from locking up for the night when I saw my brother's squad car drive up.

"What's wrong?" I asked the second I saw his face.

"We still have something to talk about," he said.

I turned to Lillian as I blocked Bradford's view of the inside. "Can you handle things here for a little bit?" There was no way I wanted my brother to see that marker board with our musings scribbled all over it. He would probably lock us both up if he did.

"I'd be happy to," she said.

"I shouldn't be long," I said as I steered my brother outside. As Bradford and I started walking, he said, "Listen, I'm sorry I ran off like that before, but I had to go."

"I know that. I'm not completely unreasonable," I said, though I had to admit that at times I could be the slightest bit difficult to deal with.

If he had a response, he kept it to himself, a sure sign that something was troubling my big brother. I grabbed his arm and stopped him in front of The Apothecary, a drugstore that carried a little of everything a tourist could want. "What is it?"

"I shouldn't tell you this, but I don't want you finding out from somebody else, either. Jennifer, if I tell you something that's confidential, do you swear not to breathe a word of it to anyone, at least not until it is common knowledge?"

I didn't even have to think about it. "No, I can't swear that to you."

He looked surprised. "You're kidding, right?"

"I'm not. Bradford, if it involves Tina Mast's murder, and I'm pretty sure it does, I'm not promising anything I can't keep. I'm sorry, but I won't lie to you."

He thought about it a few seconds, then said, "You drive me nuts; you know that, don't you?"

"Hey, everybody's good at something."

"Okay, I'm going to tell you anyway. It's going to be all around town in a day or two, so I'm not sure how much damage you can do. One thing, though. If you tell anyone where you heard this, I'll deny it. Do we understand each other?"

"I can live with that," I said, dying to hear what he had to say.

"I've known about this since last night. They finished the autopsy on Tina Mast."

"You mean she wasn't killed the way we thought she was?" I didn't even want to think about what that might mean.

"No, her death was directly due to the blunt trauma she suffered, all right. That wasn't the interesting part, though.

"Tina Mast was pregnant when she was murdered."

Chapter 19

"Do you have any idea who the father was?" I blurted out. This put an entirely different spin on her murder. I just wasn't sure how yet.

"We don't know, and none of her friends are talking. Listen, that's all I know at the moment. I just thought you'd like to hear it from me before everybody else in town finds out."

He started to walk off when I thought of another question. "How far along was she?"

Bradford hurried back to me. "Keep your voice down, Jennifer."

"I'm sorry. Did the report say?"

"She was just four weeks," he said. "She might not have even known she was pregnant herself. Sometimes I think I should have gone into some other line of work."

"You're doing exactly what you should be doing," I said, gently touching my brother's shoulder. "There's no one else in the world I'd rather have as sheriff of Rebel Forge."

"It didn't do Tina Mast or her baby much good, did it?"

"Bradford, you can't save everybody."

He sighed. "No, but that doesn't mean I don't wish I could."

My brother walked me back to the shop, then left. I found Lillian working at the table, no doubt coming up with another acerbic card for her new collection. "Get out your board," I said. "I just learned something that could change everything."

"What did he say?" Lillian asked.

"Tina Mast was pregnant."

My aunt's face went white. "How horrible."

"It's pretty tragic, isn't it? I wonder if the murderer knew."

Lillian swept her cards aside and put the whiteboard on top of the desk. "It's something that finally makes sense. Somebody wanted to get rid of that baby."

I studied the list. "Do you honestly think it's relevant? Why would a woman kill her because she was pregnant?"

"Why does anyone commit murder?" Lillian asked. "If it's not for love or greed, it could be that the killer was trying to protect something."

"Like her upcoming marriage," I said, remembering how detached Donna had seemed when she'd talked about the wedding.

It was Lillian's turn to look surprised, but it only lasted for an instant. "You're saying that Larry got both of them pregnant at nearly the same time?"

"It makes sense," I said, tapping her name on the board. "Remember what Donna said? They had an argument a while back, but they managed to patch things up."

"So you think he found some solace in Tina's arms. It's an interesting theory, but how do we prove any of it?"

I thought about it a few seconds. "We need to talk to Donna again. I want to see if she's got an alibi that stands up."

"And if she doesn't?" Lillian asked.

"Then we tell Bradford what we know and let him start digging into it himself. I'm not arrogant enough to think that I can do this alone, but I think my brother needs a nudge in the right direction. What do you think?"

"Let's go find Donna," she said.

I remembered my pledge to keep the shop open. "Lillian, I need to ask you a huge favor. You don't have to do it, but it would mean a great deal to me."

"Let me guess," she said dryly. "You want me to stay here."

I touched her hand. "I'm trusting you to run my shop while I'm gone. It's the most important thing in my life besides my family. Will you do it for me?"

She bit her lower lip, then said, "When you put it that way, I don't see how I can refuse you. Just be careful, Jennifer. If we're right, she's already killed once to protect her wedding. I doubt hurting you would even faze her."

"I'll watch my step," I said. "You can close up in twenty minutes."

"Don't worry; I've got things under control here."

I left Lillian and went off in search of a woman who just might turn out to be the ultimate bridezilla of all time.

Anne Albright answered the door when I rang the bell.

"Jennifer, whatever in the world are you doing here?"

"I was hoping to speak with your daughter for a few minutes," I said. I should have come up with a reason for the visit on my drive over, but I'd been too nervous about the pending interview to create anything that even bordered on a rational excuse for the questions I had.

"May I ask what it is regarding?"

"It's about the wedding," I said.

"What about the wedding?"

This woman was not about to let me in the house, let alone talk to her daughter, unless I could come up with something good.

"I'm thinking about getting married myself, and I hoped I could discuss it with her."

Mrs. Albright looked pleased by the news. "How delightful. I didn't even realize you had a young man in your life."

"We've kept it quiet up until now," I said, burying myself deeper and deeper in the lie. "Please, could I speak with her?"

Mrs. Albright said, "I'm afraid she's not here."

Why hadn't she said something in the first place before forcing me to come up with a very bad lie? "Would you mind telling me where she is?"

"She and Larry have been at the church for their last counseling session, and then she was going to pick her wedding dress up at A Clean Well-Lit Shop. Her dress is the same one I wore on my wedding day, you know."

"How delightful for you," I said as I backed away. "I'll catch up with her later, then."

"Congratulations, my dear. I recommend marriage for everyone."

"Thanks," I said. I couldn't wait to get out of there. At least I hadn't let her bully me into giving the name of my fictitious fiancé. I'd been about to blurt Greg's name when she'd asked, and that had shocked me. I thought my feelings for him were long over, but his name had popped into my head like the answer to a question on *Jeopardy!* What in the world did that mean?

I thought about bracing the couple at the church, but then I realized I might have better luck if I ambushed them at the dry cleaner's. That way I could pretend to be out on an errand of my own. The story wouldn't hold when Donna spoke to her mother, but it might help me to catch her off guard. All I had to do was find a way to cut Larry away from her so I could grill her without interruption.

I drove to A Clean Well-Lit Shop and waited across the street. Hopefully they hadn't gotten there yet, but I was willing to give it some time. As I waited, I thought about the puzzle pieces of the crime, and considered them with Donna as the murderer. She certainly fit the description as a woman, and she'd had earrings along with everyone else. I wondered about the earrings she'd produced, but she could have easily had a spare pair, or she could have just stolen her fiancé's single one left over. Who would have better access to it than the bride-to-be? Was she capable of murder, though? I thought about the strength of will it would take to kill another human being and I doubted I could ever bring myself to it, but not everyone was wired the way I was. I knew the urge to protect was strong in many women. So could Donna kill to protect her upcoming marriage? I didn't have much doubt, if Larry was indeed the father of Tina's baby. I was still thinking about the possibilities when I saw Donna get out of a car. Larry waved to her, then drove off, no doubt taking care of an errand of his own. I raced across the street and walked in just as Donna was collecting her dress.

"What a coincidence, running into you here," I said.

"Hi, Jennifer." She held the dress up. "Isn't it lovely?"

"It's beautiful," I admitted. There were pearl beads on the bodice, and the silk of the dress had an old-world sheen to it. "Could I talk to you a second?"

"Certainly," she said. Donna told the woman behind the counter, "Just put it on our bill, Angela."

"No charge, Donna. Think of it as an early wedding present."

Donna hugged her, then said, "Thanks so much. You did a great job."

"You're very welcome," the clerk said. "It will look even lovelier on you than it did on your mother. Tell her I said hello."

"I will."

As we walked outside, I asked, "That was your mother's wedding dress?"

She admitted as much. "Angela and Mamma go way back. When Mamma suggested I use her dress for my wedding, I thought it was a wonderful idea. Unfortunately, I had to have it altered; I'm not nearly as top-heavy as Mamma is. But Angela did a great job. It looks magnificent."

"Donna, could I ask you something?"

"Anything," she said, admiring the dress in the sunlight.

All of a sudden I didn't know how to ask her for an alibi. She looked so pleased holding that dress up, as if it were her ultimate good-luck charm.

So I chickened out. "How long did it take to have it altered?"

"Let's see. Angela worked on the fitting all Tuesday afternoon. It took her four hours to get it just right, and I have the pinpricks on my chest to prove it. She had to make sure it was perfect."

"When did you get started?" I held my breath as I waited for her answer.

"She closed early, a little before three o'clock. I remember how hungry I was when we finished." Donna added softly, "I'm watching what I eat before the ceremony. I want to look good for Larry."

"I think you look great just the way you are," I said, suddenly deflated. If Donna was getting the dress altered when she said she was, that knocked another suspect off my list. "Your mother must have been so proud to see you wearing her dress."

Donna frowned for an instant. "She would have been if she were here with me."

"She didn't come with you for the fitting?"

Donna shrugged. "She had to interview caterers. It's unbelievable how much work goes into a wedding. I'm just glad I'm only getting married once."

I wasn't about to dispute that claim while the woman was holding her own wedding dress. There was a toot of a car horn behind us and I saw Larry blocking traffic. "Let's go, Donna," he said impatiently.

I wouldn't have minded a few words with him alone, but I didn't see how I could talk to him without Donna hovering nearby, and that wouldn't be a good time to ask him if he'd gotten another girl pregnant lately.

If she was perturbed by his abrupt summons, she didn't show it. "Thanks, Jennifer. It was good seeing you." Before I could reply, she said to Larry, "Now don't look at my dress. It's bad luck for you to see it."

"The superstition is that I can't see you wearing it on our wedding day," he said.

"Well, I still don't want to take any chances," she said.

Since Mrs. Albright couldn't back up her daughter's story, I decided to go inside and talk to Angela.

"May I help you?" she asked.

"I was just in here with Donna Albright. She's thrilled with the beautiful job you did on her wedding dress."

Angela beamed. "It took forever, but I finally got it just right."

"Donna said it took most of Wednesday afternoon," I said.

"No, it was on Tuesday. My kids threw a fit because dinner was so late. I told them if they were hungry, they should fix it themselves without waiting for me. Do you have kids?"

"No, Ma'am, I don't."

"I love them, but they drive me nuts sometimes."

A man came in with four suits thrown over his arm. "How long will these take?"

She glanced at me, then said to him, "Let's see what you've got."

I left the dry cleaner's with my proof. I'd purposely named the wrong day, and Angela had corrected me on the spot. So it looked like Donna had an airtight alibi after all.

I drove back to Custom Card Creations, but there were no parking spots nearby. That's when I remembered the barbeque festival in the square at the other end of Oakmont near Sara Lynn's shop. I finally found a place to tuck the Gremlin into, then I walked to my card shop. Lillian was gone, the lights were off, and the sign was flipped to CLOSED. I thought about grabbing a bite and going home, but I was too restless to do that. Sara Lynn was having dinner with her husband; Bailey had been so lonesome for his wife that he'd even offered to take her out to eat, so I was on my own.

I walked down the avenue to the nearest vendor, bought a sandwich and a Coke, then returned to my shop. After I ate what was some pretty decent pork barbeque, I got Lillian's whiteboard out and ran a red line through Donna's name. That left Melinda, Anne, Pam and Cam. I still couldn't believe the sisters had had anything to do with the murder, unless one of them was pregnant, too. If that was the case, I was sure Larry would have been the murder victim and not Tina. That just left the two mothers. Melinda seemed to accept the upcoming nuptials, trying to put a good spin on them, but Anne Albright had been driven from the beginning. I thought about her first visit to the shop, and the phone call I'd gotten. Did the timing work out? It would have meant that Mrs. Albright had killed Tina soon after leaving my shop. Maybe she'd run into her outside on the street, gotten her into the car on some pretext, then murdered her daughter's competition. There were a lot of ifs involved, and I didn't have a shred of evidence I could take to my brother.

But maybe I could set a trap that would give me something other than conjecture that I could take to Bradford. I wished Gail were in town. It always helped talking things out with my best friend, and the habit had saved me from doing some colossally stupid things over the years. But I didn't have her there to be my sounding board, so I was just going to have to go ahead with my plans. If my suspicions turned out to be correct, it was going to end up being the worst wedding party in the history of Rebel Forge, and that was saying something.

I was still considering the best way to trap Anne Albright when there was a tap on the glass by my table. It was the woman herself! What could I do? I considered ignoring her summons and calling Bradford, but what could I say to him? Even if he believed me, I'd look pretty foolish if it turned out I was wrong. It would have been nice to have Lillian in the shop as my backup, but that wasn't happening, either.

The keys tapped on the glass again. I was going to have to do something; that was certain. Then I remembered the festival outside. It was dark out there, but at least there were people milling about, and that had to be safer than being alone in my shop with the woman if she was indeed a murderer.

I held one finger up to her, then shut the lights off and walked outside.

"Jennifer, I was hoping we could talk inside," she said.

"Sorry, but I'm really late."

"This won't take a moment," she said. "It really is quite important."

"You can tell me as we walk to my car," I said, searching for a familiar face somewhere around I could call over to join us. All I saw were tourists, though. Unfortunately, I was parked on the other end of the avenue, away from the direction the crowd was heading. Should I go there anyway and forget about my car for now? Yes, that was my best hope. If Bradford wasn't there himself, at least one of his deputies would be, and at that point, I'd even take Wayne.

Mrs. Albright caught my arm before I could get two steps away from my door.

"Your car is that way," she said, pointing toward my Gremlin and away from the crowd.

"What makes you think that?"

"I'm parked right in front of you. There are entirely too many people walking around tonight."

Not enough for me. I had no choice now. Taking a deep breath, I started walking quickly toward my car, with Anne Albright right on my heels.

Chapter 20

"Would you slow down, Jennifer? I can't talk to you at this pace."

That was my plan. "Sorry, but I'm meeting someone for dinner. It's my brother. He's the sheriff, you know." Okay, it wasn't the smoothest lie I'd ever told in my life, or even in the past couple of days, but it was the best I could do on the fly.

"He won't mind. This is important."

Finally, I was at my car. I had my key in my hand, ready to jump in, when Mrs. Albright stepped in front of me and cut off my access. "You'll talk to me right now," she said with a growl.

"What do you want?" I asked, trying to keep the fear out of my voice.

"I want to know why you've continually refused to ignore my warnings," Mrs. Albright said as she brought a long kitchen knife out from under her coat.

"Are you insane?" I screeched at her.

"Don't say that to me! I wouldn't allow the doctors to say it, and I certainly won't stand for it coming from you. You had to keep digging, didn't you?"

"I don't know what you're talking about," I said as I saw a movement in the bushes nearby. Was Wayne still stalking me? If he was, I didn't know that I would have a problem with it at the moment. I had to keep Mrs. Albright talking until he could make his move.

"Don't toy with me. What I want to know is, who

else have you told?" She hesitated, then added, "I think I know one person."

"You answer some of my questions. Then I'll answer yours," I said, fighting for time.

"Please, I already know what you're going to ask. I knew you'd finally gotten it when you asked my daughter for my alibi. You were so transparent. Did you honestly think she wouldn't tell me about your little conversation?"

"I was asking her about her alibi," I said. What was Wayne waiting for, a handwritten invitation?

Mrs. Albright laughed. "You honestly think my sweet child could do anything so vile?"

"If she's so sweet, why are you letting her marry Larry? You know what he did, don't you?"

I saw the knife tighten in her hand from the glow of the street lamp. "He made a mistake. That tramp Tina seduced him in a moment of weakness. She was demanding that Larry marry her instead of Donna. Can you imagine that? At least he had the good sense to come to me with it. There was no way I was going to stand by and watch Tina Mast wreck everything. I needed to take action, and I did what had to be done to preserve the sanctity of the wedding. Larry was going to meet her at the abandoned house to discuss it, only I showed up instead. Now that Tina's out of the way, I believe Larry's going to work out just fine."

"And you trust him to stay quiet about all this?"

She shook her head. "Jennifer, you don't understand. We're going to be family soon, and I explained to him carefully how a family protects one another." Mrs. Albright paused, then added almost wistfully, "It's a shame you're going to miss the ceremony. It's going to be a lovely wedding."

"Even if it means your daughter is marrying a man who is unfaithful? Is that really what you want for her?"

Mrs. Albright said, "He was just sowing his last few

wild oats. As soon as he's married, I know he'll come around. Larry comes from fine stock."

That was more than I could say for Donna. I was about ready to shout at Wayne to do something when the person lurking in the bushes shifted his weight. It was only for an instant, but I caught his face clearly. It wasn't Wayne in the bushes after all.

It was Frank, the homeless man I'd run into earlier. It looked as though if I was going to be rescued, I was going to have to do it myself.

"So the earring I found at the house was yours," I said, trying to figure out how I was going to battle that knife with just my purse and a lunatic.

"Honestly, for what they cost me, the backs should have held better than they did. I knew you'd found it the second you walked out of that house."

"I was in disguise," I said. "How did you know it was me?"

"Please, you can play dress up all you want; you couldn't hide that loping gait of yours if you tried. Your walk gave you away. Now enough of this talk. I can't trust you to keep this to yourself, and I'm not about to let you ruin everything I've so carefully planned."

"I won't tell anyone. I promise."

Mrs. Albright didn't believe it any more than I did. There was only one more thing I could do. "Frank," I called out, "she's holding a knife on me. Are you going to let somebody threaten your wife like that?"

Mrs. Albright said, "How stupid do you think I am? That's insulting." She started to raise the knife over her head, and I prayed my idea would work. Frank came out of the bushes moving so fast I couldn't believe his speed, but I still didn't think he could get to her in time. I thought about trying to dodge out of her reach, but Mrs. Albright had me thoroughly pinned against my car. The blade was six inches from my chest when Mrs. Albright was jerked violently to one side. I heard the snap of her wrist as Frank broke it, and then all she did was sob.

He stood and stroked my hair. "Are you all right, Honey?"

"I'm going to be," I said as I collapsed against him.

Then a floodlight hit me full in the face. "Step away from her or I'll shoot!"

"Bradford, stop!" I shouted. "You don't understand. He just saved me."

My brother took in the scene, glancing at Mrs. Albright, who was still on the ground, moaning and cradling her ruined wrist in her other hand. "He attacked her. I saw it."

My brother's gun didn't waver.

I did the only thing I could do. I stepped between Frank and that revolver and said, "If you're going to shoot him, you have to kill me first. Anne Albright is the one you want."

That got his attention, and my brother's gun lowered, just as Frank's hands went around my throat. "You're not my wife," he snarled. "You tricked me, just like she used to."

He looked at Bradford. "If that gun comes up, I'll break her neck like a dry stick."

My brother dropped his gun on the pavement. As calmly as I could, I said, "Frank, I'm not your wife, but I know where she is. If you let me go, I'll take you to her."

"Suzanne's dead," he said in a voice devoid of all emotion.

"No, she's not. She's just been away, but now she's back, and she's asking for you. Let's go get her."

"Suzanne?" he said in a pitiful voice. "I love her so much." His hands dropped from my neck, and I could feel the sting from his grip on my flesh.

"She's not far," I said as I took his hand in mine and led him toward my brother. "Bradford will take you to her."

After we had him cuffed and in the car, my brother said, "That was too close for my taste."

"I know. One second he was saving me, and the next he was trying to kill me."

"What is that all about?" Bradford asked. "Did Anne Albright really try to kill you?"

"She did," I said as I looked back at her.

There was only one problem. During the commotion, Anne Albright had slipped away. There was a killer on the loose in Rebel Forge, and though I finally knew who she was, my family and I were in more danger than we'd ever been before.

"Get in the car, Jennifer."

"I can't," I said. "Lillian's in trouble."

"How do you know that?" Bradford snapped.

"It's something Mrs. Albright said. I've got to save her."

"Get in. I can get there faster than you can."

I did as I was told, and Bradford hit the sirens and the lights of his patrol car as he raced to Lillian's house. We'd have to get there in time. If something happened to my aunt because of my snooping, I would regret it with every breath I ever took again.

Bradford barely had time to slow down in front of her house before I jumped out and raced to the door.

Lillian answered, looking a little startled. "Jennifer, whatever is wrong with you?"

"Are you alone?"

Lillian glanced back inside, then admitted, "No, I've got company."

"If it's Anne Albright, get out of there. She's the murderer."

Lillian looked surprised. "It wasn't the daughter? I was sure it was Donna."

At that moment, Anne Albright came tearing out of the bushes, the knife clutched in her good hand. She was screaming as she neared us, and I could see the murderous intent on her face. I threw myself in

front of Lillian as I pushed my aunt back. I might not
be able to save myself, but I was going to at least give
her a chance. Then I steeled myself for the attack. If
I could grab Anne Albright's arm before she stabbed
me, and somehow manage to hold her off, I knew
Bradford was half a step behind.

Actually, he was closer than that. I could almost
feel the heat from Anne Albright's hatred when she
was suddenly hurled sideways, the knife ripped from
her grasp. Bradford had made a running tackle that
would have made a professional football player
proud, and before I could even react, my brother had
her face pinned in the grass, his knee planted solidly
in her back. He slapped the cuffs on her and said, a
little out of breath, "That should hold you."

"Where are you going to put her?" I asked, mo-
tioning to Frank sitting in back of the squad car. My
knees were shaking, but I was going to hold it together, at least until Anne Albright was safely
locked up.

"I'll call for backup," he said. "She's not getting
away from me again."

"You saved me," Lillian said to me.

"Bradford did that," I protested.

"Yes, but you pointed him in the right direction."

Bradford said, "Yeah, we're all heroes. Now let me
get my prisoners locked up before anyone else gets
hurt."

The next morning Lillian and I were back at the
card shop, both of us happy to have some normal
routine to return to. Melinda walked in and said, "I
can't believe Anne Albright is a murderer. You never
can tell about some people, can you?"

I thought about how much I liked Melinda, and how
little I thought of her son. It was true; you never could
tell. "I suppose that changes things, doesn't it?" I had
her invitations ready. The money had already been deposited, but I couldn't see the wedding going on now.

I was wrestling with my temptation to give her a refund when she said, "Believe it or not, the kids want to get married in spite of what happened. Donna told me this morning nothing has changed. She still loves Larry, and he wants to marry her, as well."

I handed her the box of invitations as Melinda added, "You won't believe Donna's reasoning."

"Try me," I said. "Right now I'll believe anything."

Melinda said, "She told me she and her mother had already mailed the invitations out you made for them, and she didn't want to disappoint anybody. I wonder how Anne is going to feel about that."

"Triumphant" was the first word that came to mind, but I wasn't about to say that out loud. "I think she'll be happy she won after all."

"What do you mean?"

"Think about it. She claimed everything she did was to make sure the wedding actually happened. She's getting exactly what she wished for."

That obviously troubled Melinda, but she didn't comment on it and I decided I'd already said enough. After she was gone, Lillian asked, "So what's next for us?"

"I'd love to make a few new cards for display."

Lillian rubbed her hands together and said, "Oh, good. You wouldn't believe what I came up with this morning."

From my aunt, the only thing I expected was the unexpected. As she led me back to her latest creation, I looked around my shop and was glad, despite everything that had happened, that I had taken the risk and opened a place of my very own.

I was going to turn down all offers to do any more wedding invitations for a while, though.

I just didn't think I could bear dealing with another mother of the bride.

MAKING YOUR OWN WEDDING INVITATION
or
ANY CARD THAT ANNOUNCES A FORMAL OCCASION

There are many ways to make your own handcrafted greeting cards, from the simplest fold and cutout like Jennifer uses in this book, to the most elaborate card imaginable, chock-full of embellishments and adornments. You can even create your own envelopes, but for most cards, I like to buy the basic card stock and envelopes right off the shelf. They are available in an amazing array of colors and hues, and many have the added advantage of already sporting a crease.

Following the card-making theme of this book, I'd like to show you a quick and easy way to make your own formal handcrafted card using premade adornments available in just about any craft store. Since scrapbooking and card making have many similarities, I like to browse the sections filled with stickers, small collages, stamps and ornate lettering when I need to make a formal card. For a wedding, there are even small sewn outfits signifying the bride and groom that look just as good on the front of your card as they do on your scrapbook pages. Though it might get expensive buying such detailed adornments for a great many invitations, they're perfect for a small and intimate ceremony. Simply peel the self-adhesive stickers off the back of the collages and place them on the front of your card. Sometimes the collage itself is enough for the front, but if you'd like to add your own lettering, there are sheets of adhesive letters

cont'd.

available so you can send your very own message. I like to scan the sticker aisle, because many times I can find the perfect message already made for me.

To begin, I like to coordinate my embellishments with my card stock. For example, a white wedding dress will disappear on plain card stock, but a pastel green or pink background makes it jump off the card. After I've got my components, it's simply a matter of laying out the card first before I peel a single adhesive strip or drop that first touch of glue. Now is the best time to play with your design. Don't be afraid to try something unorthodox. At this point, nothing is permanent. After I'm satisfied with my layout, I do a rough sketch of the card's front, especially if it's a complex design. This way I know exactly where everything goes! I like to place my lettering first, since the paper is still flat at this point and nothing gets in my way. When that's done, I add my embellishments and the front is complete. Inside, I add whatever message I'd like. If it's an invitation, I like to print these out on my computer before I do anything else, but they can be hand-lettered, as well.

It's a true delight giving these cards that you've crafted yourself, and I'm willing to wager that soon you'll be looking for excuses to make your next card!

Turn the page for an exciting peek at the first chapter of the next card-making mystery by Elizabeth Bright

DEADLY GREETINGS

Coming in June 2006

I never really believed in ghosts until Francis Coolridge tried to kill me two months *after* she died. I've made a ton of handcrafted greeting cards for hundreds of occasions, but never anything remotely like the one I wished I could create for her. I might head it WISH YOU WERE (STILL) DEAD, or maybe even YOU'RE INVITED TO YOUR VERY OWN EXORCISM, but I doubted either one would do much good. It was pretty apparent that Francis didn't want me living in her apartment, and just as obvious I wasn't about to move out. We were at a stalemate, and while it was true that I was going to have to get used to Francis's presence, it also meant that she was going to have to get used to mine. I loved my new quarters at Whispering Oak, and it was going to take more than a scatterbrained poltergeist to make me pack up my stuff and leave.

My name's Jennifer Shane, and I own Custom Card Creations, a small handcrafted-card shop in Rebel Forge, Virginia. My business is on one end of Oakmont Avenue—a road that runs through the heart of downtown—and my sister Sara Lynn's scrapbooking store is on the other. I'd worked for her at Forever Memories before opening my card shop, but I loved being on my own, even if I was just a sale or two away from the brink of bankruptcy. Our brother, Bradford, is the sheriff for all of Rebel Forge, and my aunt Lillian helps me out at the card shop. Sometimes the pluses and minuses of living in a small town are one and the same. My family is close, both in proximity and in our hearts, but it can be stifling at times. As the youngest of our clan, I often find myself chafing against their desire to protect me, even though I know they are motivated out of love.

"What do you call that ghastly hue?" my aunt Lillian asked as she came into the card shop one morning. I was displaying a new shade of paper I'd made in my small workshop in back, and I was proud of it.

Without glancing in her direction, I said, "Don't you like it? It's called 'Lillian's Dream.'"

"It's more like a nightmare," my aunt muttered under her breath; then she waved a hand in the air to dismiss the topic. "But never mind that. You've got to close the shop and come with me at once."

"Lillian, I'm barely making enough to feed Oggie and Nash, let alone myself. I can't afford to shut the place down." My cats, though not fancy eaters, were finicky in their preference of national brands over generic fare. Hoping to squeeze another nickel out of my budget, I'd tried them on Stylin' Stew and Jumpy Cats, but they'd refused to eat either one.

Lillian flicked a strand of dyed henna hair out of her face as she said, "You still hate your apartment, don't you?"

"You know I do," I said, remembering what had happened there the month before that had completely robbed me of my sense of security. Someone had made a rather concerted effort to scare me, and they'd done a pretty good job of it. The memory of the threat at my door lingered every night as I tried to sleep.

Lillian nodded. "Well, I've got just the place for you. We have to go now, though, before someone else grabs it." My aunt was a woman of action, proved by a string of seven ex-husbands; she was only partially teasing when she said that she was always on the look-out for number eight.

"Do they allow cats?" I asked as I slid the rest of the paper onto the display.

"My dear, they embrace them. Now let's go."

After grabbing my coat, I flipped the sign on the door to BACK IN FIFTEEN MINUTES and locked up. Honestly, I had no idea how long we'd be gone, but I was hoping whoever saw it would hang around, since I couldn't afford to alienate the few customers I had.

"So where are we headed?" I asked as we hustled toward her car, a classic candy-apple-red Mustang in mint condition.

"Have you ever heard of Whispering Oak?"

I thought about it a second before answering her. "Wasn't he an Indian guide around here two hundred years ago?"

Lillian shot me one of those looks that spoke volumes about her thoughts on my sanity, but I was being serious.

She explained, "Whispering Oak is a fine old house on the outskirts of town. There's even a path from your doorstep to the lake. It's wonderful."

"If it's so wonderful, why is it vacant?"

Lillian took a curve sharp enough to fling the paint off her car, and by the time I caught my breath she had shot down a side road at the edge of town that I'd never noticed before. I've lived in Rebel Forge nearly all my life, and I'd always assumed the graveled path was a driveway to the house facing the road. Instead of taking us to the Jackson place, though, it led on through the woods until we came to an ancient Victorian home, replete with fancy shingle siding, gingerbread trim adorning the porch and a pastel palette that belonged on a greeting card.

"This place is for rent?" I asked, knowing full well I couldn't afford to live there on my modest income.

"Not the entire house, Jennifer," she said. "However, there is a free room upstairs that would be perfect for you."

"If it's free, then I guess I'm willing to look at it," I said. "That's about all I can afford."

"You know perfectly well I meant it was available, not without cost." She bit her lower lip, then said, "It is reasonable, though—less than you're paying now, I'll wager."

"I'll take that bet," I said. One of the few advantages of my current apartment was that the rent was within my means, though just barely.

Lillian parked; then I followed her as she walked to the front door with a purposeful stride. I was expecting her to knock, but she strolled right in like she owned the papers to the place. There wasn't much for me to do but follow. The foyer had been divided into a vestibule with two doors that were obviously later additions. "Which one are we going to look at?"

"Neither one of these," Lillian said as she shook her head. Then she pointed to a narrow staircase in back that I'd missed at first. "We're going up."

I eyed the tight passage suspiciously. "I'm not sure I'll fit, let alone the cat carriers."

"Jennifer, can you really choose to be that particular on your budget?"

"Okay, fine, I'll look at it," I said, doubtful it would suit even my meager needs.

The stairs went on and on, but we finally made it to the top. There was a narrow door there, perched on a landing barely big enough for both of us to stand on at the same time.

I was getting claustrophobic without even going inside. "What is it, the attic?"

"Certainly it was at one time, but it's a perfectly delightful space now." Lillian reached under the rug and pulled out a key.

As she slid it in the lock, I said, "I just love these modern security features, don't you?"

Lillian ignored my comment, unlocked the door and

flung it open. As she stepped inside, I moved past her, finally having enough room to stand without her imprinting her elbow into my side.

I thought I'd hate it. In fact, I was already planning a few choice words that involved chasing wild geese and hunting snipes.

Then I looked around. It was nothing short of charming. While it had been an ordinary attic in another incarnation, it was now the perfect studio apartment. The bead board walls enchanted me, painted a pastel green that reminded me of springtime. Light bounced around the room, filtering in from large windows on either end while two dormers also served to illuminate the place, making it bright and airy, nothing like what I'd expected the second I'd realized it was a converted attic space. It was fully furnished with antiques built in the Shaker style, and while some folks found the clean design rather plain, I adored it. A handcrafted quilt covered the queen-sized bed, and a faded Oriental rug adorned much of the open floor, leaving just enough of the honey-toned heartwood pine beneath it to make me want to roll back the rug.

"I don't have to share a bathroom with anyone else, do I?" I asked, searching for any flaw I could find in its charm.

"No, the north dormer has been outfitted as one. It's not all that large, but you live alone. There should be plenty of room for you and your cats here."

I shrugged, not willing to commit to it yet. "So what's the catch?"

Instead of answering my question, Lillian said, "Look out that window."

I walked to the window she'd pointed to, and looked out. A small deck beckoned just outside the window, replete with an iron chair and side table. For a finale, Lillian pointed through the canopy of leaves beyond. "The lake is just a few steps away. Autumn is nearly here, and you'll soon have a glorious view. Isn't it delightful?"

I thought it was, but I realized Lillian must have misunderstood the price. "I can't imagine how I can come anywhere near to affording this place."

When she told me the rent, I didn't need to know anything else. "Where do we go to sign the lease?"

Lillian smiled in approval. "I took the liberty of acquiring one from Hester Taylor." Hester was one of Lillian's best friends, operating a combination copy store–apartment rental agency–ice cream shop in town ever since her husband had disappeared one day ten years ago. The rumor was that he'd taken their cash, their savings and their dog with him when he vanished. Hester claimed besides the cash, the only thing she really missed was the dog.

"So where do I sign?" I asked.

Lillian gestured to the places Hester had marked, then took the document from me. "Don't worry about the deposit or the first and last months' rents. I've got those covered."

When I started to protest, Lillian said, "Think of them as housewarming gifts."

"I'd rather think of them as paid by me," I said. I'm not letting you do this."

"It's too late," Lillian said. "You already signed the lease."

"Then I'll default," I said. "Or you will. I mean it." I'd learned early on that if I didn't stand my ground with her, I'd be stampeded.

She huffed out, "Blast it all, child, do you always have to get your way?"

"Think of it as a character defect I inherited from my favorite aunt," I said.

Lillian thought about it a few moments, then said, "Let's compromise. You can pay me back, but only after your shop makes a profit two months in a row."

"Are you sure you can wait that long?"

She scolded, "Have faith in your store, Jennifer. I do."

I knew better than to push her any more than I had. There was only one thing left I could do. "Okay, thanks, I can live with that."

"You're most welcome," she said as she hugged me. We were downstairs, ready to go back to the card shop, when one of the tenants on the main floor came out into the foyer. "Who are you?" an elderly man with a black cane asked us fiercely.

"I just rented the apartment upstairs," I said. "I'm Jennifer Shane," I added as I offered my hand.

He refused it, then took a step back from us. "You can't be serious."

"Why? What's wrong with it?" I was beginning to think that there might be something I'd failed to ask.

The man shook his head. "You really don't know?" He lifted his cane and shook it in Lillian's direction. "You should be ashamed of yourself, madam."

Lillian laughed. "I often have reason to, but I rarely am. Now go away."

With a grunt, the man retreated back into his apartment, slamming the door in our faces.

"Gee, thanks, Lillian, it's sweet of you to make such an effort to get me accepted by my neighbors."

"Pooh, he'll come around. Give him time."

An odd-looking tiny woman with blue hair and a nose like an ice pick was standing outside when we walked onto the porch.

Lillian said, "Hester, what are you doing here? I told you I'd take care of this."

The woman fluttered her fingers in the air like a hummingbird's wings. "I just thought . . . I was nearby. . . . Did she sign it?"

"I'm standing right here. Ask me yourself," I said.

Hester continued to ignore me. "Do you have the lease agreement?" she asked Lillian.

"It's right here, Hester. Now calm down before you have a heart attack or, worse yet, give me one."

Hester grabbed the lease Lillian held out and without another word she bolted for her parked car, a Cadillac that was tinted the most unpleasant shade of green.

I turned to Lillian and asked, "What in the world was that all about?"

"Hester always was a tad high-strung."

I touched my aunt's arm. "Lillian, stop dodging. There's something you're not telling me, isn't there?"

"Jennifer, I knew if I said anything, you'd miss out on a wonderful opportunity. It's all nonsense anyway."

"I wish I'd had a choice, but I'm already committed. So what is it you haven't been telling me?"

She frowned a moment, then admitted, "There's just one thing I neglected to mention. Honestly, it shouldn't matter one bit."

"Come on, Lillian, out with it."

My aunt scowled at the ground, then finally said, "Very well, if you must know, some folks think the place is haunted."

"What, the entire place?" Great, that was just what I needed, moving into Amityville.

Lillian shook her head. "No, the rest of the house is fine. It's just your apartment that's said to house a ghost."

And that was the first time I'd ever heard of Francis Coolridge's demise.

"So now I'm living in a haunted house?" I tried to keep my voice from shrieking, but it was tough to do.

"It's all nonsense, Jennifer. Honestly, I expected you to be more levelheaded about the whole thing."

"Well, I expected my aunt to look after my best interests. The world's just full of disappointments today, isn't it?"

Lillian took a deep breath. "Let's discuss this as we walk by the lake. The air has such a soothing quality to it."

I stood my ground. "I'm not taking another step until you tell me what this is all about."

Lillian frowned, then said, "I know you; you won't quit until I tell you, so you might as well hear it all at once."

I planned to stand right there until she told me, but Lillian had other ideas. If I wanted to hear why my new apartment was haunted, I was going to have to follow her as she walked down the path toward the lake.

"Jennifer, first of all, you must know that I would never put you in harm's way. Will you at least give me that much credit?"

I wasn't ready to give her anything, but I knew until I threw her some kind of bone, I was going to be doing laps around the lake until my shoes wore out. "I realize you wouldn't do it knowingly," I said grudgingly.

She paused, glanced at me for a second, then nodded. "Fine." Lillian's step faltered a moment. Then she said, "Francis Coolridge was a friend of mine in another lifetime."

"Oh, please don't tell me you're going to say you two shared a past life. Who were you, Cleopatra?" Some folks around town thought my aunt was eccentric, but I'd always stood up for her. It was starting to look like I'd been a tad hasty in my support.

"Don't be ridiculous," she said. "Do you want to hear this or not?"

I was beginning to wonder that myself. Maybe I should trot over to the library and look it up on the microfiche. Then again, the newspaper would report just the facts, and I knew I could count on Lillian to supply the backstory, and that was often more telling than what found its way into print. "Sorry, I'll try not to interrupt, but I'm not making any promises."

"As I was saying," Lillian continued, "Francis and I knew each other a lifetime ago. We were locker mates in high school, and the very best of friends."

"Then how come I never heard of her until today?" I asked. "You'd think I would have, if the two of you were so close." Okay, I didn't mean to interrupt, but I couldn't help myself.

"We had a falling-out at our graduation party. I should have apologized to her, but I kept delaying it until the issue became bigger than it really was; all the while a wall built with every minute our conflict continued."

This was getting good. "What did you do? It must have been something huge."

"Jennifer, the details aren't important. All you need to know is that we became estranged that night."

"Aunt Lillian, there's not a chance in the world I'm letting you off that easy. Tell me what you did."

She stopped and looked at me long and hard. "I told you, it doesn't matter."

"Then I don't want to hear the story," I said as I turned around and started back to her car. She was stubborn, but I'd gotten my mulish streak from her, so I knew I could outlast her. Sometimes it was hard to get Lillian to talk about herself, but I knew once she got started, she'd have a tough time stopping until she finished.

I was twenty steps back up the path before she said, "I danced with her boyfriend that night."

"When you say 'dance,' what exactly do you mean?"

"Jennifer, don't be vulgar. It was one dance, no more and no less. Francis was in the powder room, and Herman asked me. I still don't know why I said yes."

I couldn't hide my smile. "You had the hots for a guy named Herman?"

"He was rather dashing, as I remember him," Lillian said frostily. "Now, do you want to hear the rest of this or not?"

"You've got my undivided attention," I said.

At least Lillian dropped her plan to circle the lake. She stood there and continued. "Francis never spoke to me again, a difficult thing to do in a town this small.

She moved away soon after high school, but came back here to live after her parents died. They were quite wealthy. The family fortune started with a gold mine in North Carolina, but they quickly branched out into acquiring properties all over the South. Then they started buying up newspapers here and there as a hobby. But the rumors around town were that they barely left anything to Francis, choosing a charity in Richmond to receive the bulk of their wealth instead. The only things Francis inherited was a doorstop and some other equally worthless things, or so the story goes."

"So why is she haunting my room? How did she die? And why didn't I ever hear about this?" It was hard to believe that someone could die in Rebel Forge without the entire town knowing about it.

"Francis's husband was related to the Dunbars, and the owners of the newspaper weren't about to let one whisper of the scandal out. For once, something happened here that no one else knew about. As for the rest of it, you'll have to get the details from your brother."

Great. Grilling Bradford was the last thing I wanted to do. "Lillian, you started this story; now finish it."

"Bradford really should be the one to tell you. After all, he was the one who cut her down from the rafters. You see, she hanged herself."

A feeling of dread swept over me. "Please tell me she didn't do it in my beautiful living room."

"Of course not," Lillian said, and I felt instantly better.

Then she added, "There wasn't anyplace to attach the rope there. She used your bathroom."

So there it was. I was going to be taking a shower in the middle of a crime scene. How in the world did Lillian think that would be better than my old apartment? "I never should have signed the lease," I said. "At least no one ever died in my apartment."

"Not that you know of," Lillian said.

"Why, what have you heard?"

She shook her head. "Jennifer, I assure you, there's no such thing as ghosts. You'll be fine, I promise."

"If you're so sure, then why don't you move in with me?"

Lillian looked shocked by the suggestion. "I have my own place, my dear girl. Besides, there's no room for both of us there."

"Okay, then, I'll move into your place and you relocate here. The cats will love romping around in your big old house."

Lillian said, "Jennifer, you're delusional. I'll tell you what I will do, though. Spend one week here. If you absolutely hate it, you have my blessing to move out and I won't hold it against you."

"Do you honestly expect me to stay here for a full week?" I looked up at my room and saw the curtain fluttering in the breeze. There were just two problems with that: there wasn't the slightest whisper of wind in the air, and that window had been closed when I'd left it.

She said, "Oh, pooh, don't be so dramatic. Now let's get back to the card shop. You really shouldn't leave it unattended this long."

I didn't even know how to respond to that. While it was true I was eager to leave my apartment, I hadn't expected to go someplace worse. Still, Lillian had paid for two months there; if I could stand it for a week, maybe I could get used to rooming with a ghost.

Honestly, how bad could it be?

About the Author

Elizabeth Bright is the pseudonym for a nationally best-selling mystery author. Though never credited with solving a murder in real life, Elizabeth's alter ego has created scores of handcrafted greeting cards over the years.

A **Crime of Fashion** Mystery
by Ellen Byerrum

Hostile Makeover

As makeover madness sweeps the nation's capital,
reporter Lacey Smithsonian interviews TV show
makeover success story Amanda Manville. But with
Amanda's beauty comes a beast in the form of a
stalker with killer intentions—and Lacey may
be the only who can stop him.

0-451-21616-4

Also in the **Crime of Fashion** series:
Killer Hair
0-451-20948-6

Designer Knockoff
0-451-21268-1

**Available wherever books are sold or at
penguin.com**